"I WANT THIS HANDLED BY STONY MAN."

"If we do have someone passing information to the enemy, I can't hand this over to our security departments. Sensitive information could be intercepted and used against us. Stony Man is a separate entity. No allegiance to any other departments here or abroad."

The President leaned forward, fixing Brognola with an unflinching stare.

"The main reason I want you in on this, Hal, is information I received from a genuine source." The President didn't elaborate on his source, so Brognola raised an eyebrow but remained silent.

"I understand your curiosity about that, but I can't say anything right now," the President said. "Just take my word it's on the level. The asset has warned that the threat of the strikes is real. There will be an attempted strike on Pakistan and the U.S. mainland. Hal, it's going to be nuclear. And we have a name. Colonel Jabir Rahman. Is that a good enough reason to bring in Stony Man?"

"Good enough, Mr. President," the big Fed said grimly.

Other titles in this series:

#51 DOOMSDAY DIRECTIVE
#52 TACTICAL RESPONSE
#53 COUNTDOWN TO TERROR
#54 VECTOR THREE
#55 EXTREME MEASURES
#56 STATE OF AGGRESSION
#57 SKY KILLERS
#58 CONDITION HOSTILE
#59 PRELUDE TO WAR
#60 DEFENSIVE ACTION
#61 ROGUE STATE
#62 DEEP RAMPAGE
#63 FREEDOM WATCH
#64 ROOTS OF TERROR
#65 THE THIRD PROTOCOL
#66 AXIS OF CONFLICT
#67 ECHOES OF WAR
#68 OUTBREAK
#69 DAY OF DECISION
#70 RAMROD INTERCEPT
#71 TERMS OF CONTROL
#72 ROLLING THUNDER
#73 COLD OBJECTIVE
#74 THE CHAMELEON FACTOR
#75 SILENT ARSENAL
#76 GATHERING STORM
#77 FULL BLAST
#78 MAELSTROM
#79 PROMISE TO DEFEND
#80 DOOMSDAY CONQUEST
#81 SKY HAMMER
#82 VANISHING POINT
#83 DOOM PROPHECY
#84 SENSOR SWEEP
#85 HELL DAWN
#86 OCEANS OF FIRE
#87 EXTREME ARSENAL
#88 STARFIRE
#89 NEUTRON FORCE
#90 RED FROST
#91 CHINA CRISIS
#92 CAPITAL OFFENSIVE
#93 DEADLY PAYLOAD
#94 ACT OF WAR
#95 CRITICAL EFFECT
#96 DARK STAR
#97 SPLINTERED SKY
#98 PRIMARY DIRECTIVE
#99 SHADOW WAR
#100 HOSTILE DAWN
#101 DRAWPOINT
#102 TERROR DESCENDING
#103 SKY SENTINELS
#104 EXTINCTION CRISIS
#105 SEASON OF HARM
#106 HIGH ASSAULT
#107 WAR TIDES
#108 EXTREME INSTINCT
#109 TARGET ACQUISITION
#110 UNIFIED ACTION
#111 CRITICAL INTELLIGENCE
#112 ORBITAL VELOCITY
#113 POWER GRAB
#114 UNCONVENTIONAL WARFARE
#115 EXTERMINATION

DON PENDLETON'S

STONY

AMERICA'S ULTRA-COVERT INTELLIGENCE AGENCY

MAN®

TERMINAL GUIDANCE

A GOLD EAGLE BOOK FROM
WORLDWIDE®

TORONTO • NEW YORK • LONDON
AMSTERDAM • PARIS • SYDNEY • HAMBURG
STOCKHOLM • ATHENS • TOKYO • MILAN
MADRID • WARSAW • BUDAPEST • AUCKLAND

First edition December 2011

ISBN-13: 978-0-373-62000-5

TERMINAL GUIDANCE

Special thanks and acknowledgment to Mike Linaker for his contribution to this work.

Printed in U.S.A.

TERMINAL GUIDANCE

PROLOGUE

Peshawar, Pakistan

Jay Crawford stepped aside as the rickety bus pushed through the crowded market. The interior was crammed with passengers as usual. More were perched on the roof and others clung to the exterior of the wheezing, smoke-billowing vehicle. Crawford had been in the country for almost twelve months and he still couldn't get used to the constant congestion.

He glanced around the market area. The place teemed with people. Hundreds of them. They moved and jostled around the stalls in a colorful swirl, all seeming to be talking at once. Add to that the music coming from different locations, the cooking smells from the market traders… He never tired of it.

He turned in at the entrance of the crowded, open-fronted store that sold English-language newspapers and magazines. Crawford visited once a week to buy *Newsweek* and *Time* magazines. The man who ran the store nodded at him and produced the periodicals. He was stooped, bony, his face creased with a beaming smile as Crawford paid for his magazines.

"Good day, Mr. Crawford," he said. "Are you well?"

"Yes, and you, Mr. Pradesh?"

"Yes. Yes."

It was the same each time Crawford called in. Conversation seldom went beyond the polite exchange.

When Crawford stepped back outside the store's cool interior, the solid wall of heat struck him. He checked his watch. An hour yet before he needed to make his daily report to his CIA section head in Washington. It would take him just over thirty minutes to walk back to his apartment. No rush. Crawford took out a pack of Marlborough cigarettes and lit one, enjoying the nicotine rush. He merged with the crowd and went with the flow. He had learned to go with the crush rather than try to fight against it.

He reached the edge of the market, where the street ahead was quieter by comparison with the hectic trading area.

He heard the hiss of tires on the dusty street, sensing the vehicle before he saw it. A battered old British Humber Hawk. A relic of a long-gone era. The car swayed on soft springs as it drew level with him. Crawford glanced around. He saw the passenger side rear window roll down, and had an impression of a figure inside the car a second before the ugly muzzle of an SMG appeared.

Crawford stiffened with shock as he stared into the black barrel. There was no time for anything else. The SMG crackled with autofire no more than three feet away. The long burst of gunfire delivered a half magazine of bullets that cleaved their way into his chest. The impact stunned him, his body reacting to the massive onslaught. A number of slugs tore all the way through him, bursting out through his back in ragged spurts of blood and flesh.

Crawford stepped back, briefly remaining upright before his severe injuries overwhelmed him. He crashed to the street, jerking in spasms. The muzzle of the SMG was lowered and a second burst was directed at his face and skull, tearing open his cheeks and jawline. Crawford's head bounced back against the street, its skull cracked and bloody.

As the street crowd scattered in panic the Humber moved off, tires squealing as it disappeared around the corner, leaving a cloud of gritty dust in its wake.

Onlookers, realizing the vehicle had gone, began to move back onto the street, attracted by the sight of Crawford sprawled in a pool of his own blood, the front of his once white shirt now a sodden mess. Beside him his magazines soaked up some of the blood spreading out from his body.

AN HOUR LATER an explosion rocked the offices of New Relief, a U.S. charity set up in the city. Later examination revealed that a package delivered to the offices shortly before the blast had contained a large amount of Semtex. The explosion wrecked the building, blowing out the front wall and upper and lower floors. The detonation extended out into the crowded street, killing ten pedestrians and wounding thirty more. The thirteen workers inside the building all died. Structures on either side were badly damaged, with people inside suffering minor injuries and shock. Fires were started. By the time emergency services arrived, having to force their way through the mass of spectators, the damage was done.

News reached the American Consulate. Officials were sent to check on the victims. It soon became apparent that U.S. casualties were high. Over half the staff at New Relief were American citizens. The information was relayed back to Washington and soon reached the security community. Agency interest was generated in record time.

Jay Crawford, it turned out, was a CIA operative working covertly in Pakistan. And two of the people killed in the New Relief bombing also had CIA status.

Over the next few days three more people with Agency connections were killed. One was an American of Pakistani descent who had been working up country gathering information. Riding to work on his bicycle one morning he was targeted by a sniper, who hit him in the head with a single shot. The following day another sniper killed an American woman employed by a tourist agency. Her job was to gather information and pass it on to her handler, who also worked for the tourist company. He died the day after, when the offices were bombed. Both were also in the employ of the U.S. agency.

THERE WAS SOMETHING close to panic the day after all the details emerged—mainly because internet chatter picked up by the surveillance agencies was dropping hints that more was in the wind. Even Echelon, the information-gathering system that allowed various security agencies within the intelligence circle to collate their findings, had been picking up scraps of conversation that started to make sense when it was all brought together.

A substantial threat emerged, basic but with enough detail to raise the level of concern.

The unknown group voiced discontent over U.S. influence within Pakistan. The group declared a need to destabilize the elected regime and show that American interference would no longer be tolerated. Nuclear devices were to be detonated within Pakistan and on the American continent. Locations not specified. Date not specified. The operation was already in motion—thus the assassination of U.S. security agents working inside Pakistan.

It gave logic to the killings. Not that knowing why provided any comfort to the families of the dead. Nor did it justify the wanton slaughter of Pakistani civilians. That was par for the course. Indiscriminate death would be described as collateral damage by the perpetrators. They always cleared themselves of blame by disregarding the rights of anyone who happened to become involved by the simple fact they were in the wrong place at the wrong time. It cleared the conscience.

TWO DAYS ON and a CIA section head was gunned down on a street in Georgetown. The agent had just returned to Washington after a meeting in London with his U.K. counterpart. Said London-based agent was also snatched off the U.K. city street as he walked from his car, heading for his apartment. His mutilated body was found on the shoulder of a highway twelve hours later, after being dumped from a van.

Two weeks earlier

COLONEL JABIR RAHMAN WAS addressing his men.

"The detonation of a dirty bomb will have two major effects. First, the release of radioactive elements that will cause contamination," he said. "The spread will not be as great as a conventional nuclear explosion, but it will kill people and contaminate the area. The second effect may have the greater potential. How is the American public going to react when this device explodes and all efforts of the U.S. administration to halt it prove useless? I will tell you, my brothers. There will be hysteria. Panic. Americans are still recovering from 9/11. Confidence will be shattered. The public trust will be lost. Wall Street will slump."

Rahman smiled. "People will be withdrawing their savings and heading for the Midwest. Searching for safety. If Boston is not safe, what about New York? Los Angeles? Washington? And in reality there is no Jack Bauer to save them from the evil Islamic terror."

"Psychological terror?" one man interjected.

"Terror in the mind can often be more lethal than a bullet."

"And what about our own territory?" someone else asked. "The detonation in Pakistan? "

"In essence the same. We explode the device near the secret American base the Pakistani president has allowed on our soil. He has been coerced into letting the Infidels bring their rancid presence to our land. This destruction of their base will make them realize they cannot be allowed to bring their poison here. A painful, sacrificial lesson, but it will show that Pakistan must shake off the chains that bind it to the U.S. That our own government is so weak because it allowed itself to be seduced by the Americans' false promises. They cajoled our president into believing that if he allied himself to the Infidels he would make Pakistan stronger. Able to stand against the so-called evil trying to subjugate us. In truth it has been America wanting to enslave us. Flaunting its power. Demanding we bend our will to it. The bombs will show the inherent weakness that exists. That both America and Pakistan are vulnerable."

"But many of our own people may die. There will be contamination...."

"To a far lesser degree. The device we detonate here will be a third the power of the bomb in America. Not as many of the rods will be used, just enough to destroy the American military here. Civilian deaths will be less, and the lingering radiation will fade at a far quicker rate. An area will be isolated after the blast, true, but the memory of the day will stay with the people, and once the president has been exposed as weak and ineffectual, our control and strength will grow rapidly. This one act will propel us into a favorable position with the public."

"Colonel, do you believe we can achieve all this?" a man asked.

"If I was not one hundred percent certain, then I would abandon everything. But I know we can do it. And achieve greatness for our beliefs. Our cause. By inflicting harm on America this way we will take a great step forward. My friends, brothers, a victory against the Great Satan must be worth the risk."

Umer Qazi watched the faces and listened to the murmurs of the assembly. He allowed himself a thin smile. He moved closer to Rahman.

"I believe you have them on your side, Colonel. Completely."

"Did you doubt me, Umer?"

"Never for a moment. I was simply waiting for them to realize the truth in your words."

"Words are *your* great skill," Rahman said. "You use them well."

"Are you telling me something?"

Rahman nodded in acknowledgment, at the same time raising a hand in salute to the assembly.

"I believe it is timely for you to make a trip to London. So you can use your honeyed words to bring young Anwar Fazeel fully into the circle." Rahman glanced at his companion. "You have told me he is ready."

"Assuredly so. Should I make travel arrangements?"

"Already taken care of," Rahman said. "You leave tonight."

London

BORN IN THE U.K. of Pakistani parents, Anwar Fazeel felt his religion was important to him. Very important. Although legally British, he did not enjoy his life in the U.K. He considered himself an outsider.

The highly intelligent twenty-four-year-old was a computer programmer at a local company. Known to be a hard worker, with an innovative mind and impressive IT skills, he had few friends outside work and not many within his place of employment. He shunned contact with those he considered the tainted inhabitants of the country, and immersed himself in radical groups that were forming in and around his hometown.

His parents and two brothers lost touch with the young man as he edged away from them, preferring to be in the company of true believers. Fazeel felt his family had become too Westernized in their thinking and their daily lives. His father was a successful businessman who owned two restaurants and a number of shops. He belonged to a golf club and had many non-Pakistani friends. All this pushed Fazeel closer to the dissatisfied crowd, who met regularly at the local mosque for political and religious discussions, berating the country and condemning the culture that surrounded them.

One of the regulars at the gatherings was Umer Qazi, a quiet, studious man who looked like a university professor with his conservative dress and manner. Sometimes he was simply there, watching and listening, his presence unobtrusive. But he did more than just observe. He took note of those young men who stood out from the crowd. The ones who exhibited more than simple group fervor. It was his task to pick out the men with real passion. With fire in their bellies.

The ones who were sincere in their beliefs.

Who would stand up to be counted when the time came.

One of those was Anwar Fazeel.

Qazi saw the potential. Realized that Fazeel, with his background in IT, was someone worth cultivating.

Umer Qazi was a recruiter, strategically placed among the dissenters to seek out ones who might prove useful. Qazi represented the cause masterminded by Colonel Jabir Rahman. He had been sent to the U.K., where many young men had been drawn into the fold. They were the easiest to recruit, with their impressionable minds, and the isolation many of them felt meant persuasion was often relatively simple. Promises of a welcome by brothers in arms, the glories of martyrdom and the delights of the afterlife were often all that was needed to draw them in. Qazi was a master of his craft. His subdued manner, his educated personality and his gentle coaxing were powerful weapons at his disposal.

When he employed them all on Anwar Fazeel, he hooked the young man quickly. He began to see him one-on-one, choosing quiet cafés where they could sit and talk for long periods. Later, as Fazeel allowed himself to be seduced by radical thinking, Qazi introduced him to other individuals who, working to plan, made Fazeel believe he was special. That his way forward was with the group. With Rahman, who wanted to steer Pakistan onto a better path, away from the influence of those who were allowing the country to become little more than an American pawn.

An arranged meeting where Fazeel was brought face-to-face, via video link, with Colonel Rahman himself was the final push that propelled the young man to the forefront of the upcoming campaign. The encounter took place in the home of a close friend of the colonel. Once the connection was made, Rahman and Fazeel were left alone. Slightly overawed by being in the great one's presence, albeit via satellite, Fazeel felt awkward as he sat in his chair. Rahman, noticing his nervousness, spoke to him with encouragement.

"Anwar Fazeel, this is a great day for me. I am honored to be meeting you, a young man who will be instrumental in orchestrating the great crusade against our enemies. Without your skill and knowledge our plan would not come together, but with your help we will achieve our victory."

Fazeel stared into the benevolent face of the man he worshipped.

Jabir Rahman.

The leader of the cause.

"No, sir, it is I who consider myself honored. Through you I will be able to contribute my part. Whatever you need from me, just ask."

"Soon you will start on a journey that will bring you to Pakistan," Rahman replied. "Have you ever been here?"

"Once, to visit with my father's family."

"Then you have stepped on our soil and breathed in the air of our spiritual home. This time, Anwar Fazeel, you will go on a special journey. You must prepare yourself for this. Pray for guidance. For strength. There may be a need for sacrifice. You will have to sever all contact with your family, here and there. Can you do that?"

"My relatives have given themselves over to the nonbelievers. They have abandoned Islam for the ways of the West, so are no longer my family."

"Good," Rahman said. "Now, listen to me, Anwar. Tomorrow is the start of the weekend. Qazi will take you to see what you will be working with. You must familiarize yourself with all the data. Learn everything about it. But there must be no talking about it outside of the group. You understand?"

"Of course, sir."

"If anything leaks out, then our plan will be compromised. I cannot stress how important it is that nothing—*nothing*—gets out."

"When will I leave for Pakistan?"

"Very soon—a pleasant flight that will allow you study time. When you arrive, I want you to fully understand the equipment, so that when we deploy there will be no hesitation."

"It will be done, sir."

"Qazi chose well. You are to be an important part of our plan. I have every faith in you, Anwar Fazeel. We may not see each other again until you reach Pakistan. Until then, may Allah smile upon you."

When the conversation ended, Fazeel was joined by Qazi again.

"He is well pleased with you." Qazi handed over a folded paper. "Can you be here at eight in the morning?"

"Of course."

"Tell no one where you are going. No one."

QAZI PICKED FAZEEL UP at the rendezvous spot, then pulled the silver SUV into the traffic and drove on. Fazeel knew nothing about this part of the city, but Qazi negotiated the streets with ease. Eventually they arrived at an area signposted Tilbury, which Fazeel vaguely knew was a seaport and container base. He spotted cranes and warehouses edging the river, truck depots and sprawling storage yards.

Qazi eventually stopped at a pair of manned gates, leaning out to speak to a security guard and show him a pass. The gates opened and Qazi drove to the dock, which had a number of seagoing freighters moored alongside. Being a weekend, there were few people about.

Again Qazi seemed to know exactly where he was going. He rolled along the line of warehouses and stopped outside one that bore the name Saeeda Hussein Import-Export.

The warehouse was large. The main doors were closed, but Qazi took Fazeel to a side door, tapped in a code at the small panel and led him inside. The interior was full of crates, and racks holding smaller items. Their footsteps echoed on the concrete floor as they approached a row of offices along the far wall.

"Good to see you, brothers," Qazi said to the two men occupying the first office.

They returned the greeting, then turned their attention to Fazeel. "Is this the one chosen?"

"Indeed. This is Anwar Fazeel. Anwar, this is Ahmad and Shiran. They will guard and protect you. When you leave for Pakistan, they will go with you."

Fazeel inclined his head. "I am happy to meet you, brothers."

Ahmad laughed as he noticed the way Fazeel was looking around the office. "He is so eager to see his new toy. Come, Anwar, let us introduce you."

He was ushered through a connecting door into a larger office, where only the soft hum of an air conditioner broke the silence. In the center of the floor stood a large piece of equipment partly covered by a dust sheet. When Shiran slid off the sheet, Fazeel's electronic unit was revealed.

The other three stood back, smiling, as he examined it, first walking around it, then focusing his attention on the detail of the control console. He was familiar with the keyboards and monitors. Though some of the other components were new to him, his keen intellect absorbed the layout, quickly assimilating the schematics.

"Can you understand it all?" Qazi asked.

"I will learn. It will not be difficult."

"I think he's fallen in love," Shiran said.

"Will it do what we require?" Qazi pressed.

"I would be able to give you a better answer if I knew exactly what it was for."

"A mystery to be revealed," Qazi said. "Come."

They took him to the far end of the warehouse, where a plastic-sheeted section had been constructed. The closest panel was pulled aside and they all stepped through.

Fazeel got his first look at the Barracuda.

It had a sleek aerodynamic configuration. A slim fuselage, with a generous wingspan. The engine was mounted at the rear, encased in a smooth pod of metal. Fazeel noticed immediately there was no facility for a pilot. No cockpit. A number of antennae and probes extruded from the smooth, silver-gray finish. It stood on a fixed, slender undercarriage and wheels.

"A UAV," Qazi explained. "An unmanned aerial vehicle. Also called drones."

"A robotic aircraft," Fazeel said. "They can be programmed via a control center."

"Like the one you have just seen," Ahmad said.

"And with this machine we will bring about the colonel's plan?"

"I believe the colonel prefers to call it his *operation,*" Qazi said. "He is very precise about these things."

"Where did you get this thing?" Fazeel asked.

"We acquired it," Qazi said. "For now that is all you need to know. What you must do is study all the manuals that came with the machine. Learn to master the complexities of the control module, because, brother, one day you will sit at that console and make the drone do what we want."

Fazeel was presented with thick printed manuals and a set of DVD discs.

"Tomorrow the drone will be disassembled and packed

into protective crates for the journey to Pakistan," Qazi said. "The control module will also be packed. You will not see it again until you arrive in the country yourself. Between now and the end of your journey you will have learned everything needed to make the drone fly to the targets we designate. Fazeel, you have been chosen because your computer skills are excellent. You understand, and you have the intellect to make the Barracuda do whatever you want."

"I won't let you down, brother," he said. "Or the colonel."

"We will find you a quiet, safe place where you can concentrate on your studies. Ahmad and Shiran will stay with you and see you are provided for. Now, is there anything you need to help with your studies?"

"Writing pads and pens. Most importantly a top-of-the-range laptop computer. It must have a large-capacity hard drive. USB connections. And a number of flash drives, again with large storage capacities."

Qazi nodded. "All these things will be provided. Anything you require. The colonel has ordered that you must have the best."

Fazeel found it hard to conceal his rising excitement. He stared at the UAV, understanding that he alone would control this machine. Make it carry out the tasks asked of him. It was a great responsibility. Only for a second did he feel inadequate to the task. The feeling quickly vanished. The colonel had entrusted him with the operation. It was a great honor. He would not let Rahman down. He would prove his worth. To the cause and to himself.

Gwadar Port, Balochistan, Southwest Pakistan

"THE CARGO HAS ARRIVED, Colonel," the caller said. "The freighter docked last night. The goods are being unloaded even as we speak."

"All in good order?"

"Yes, Colonel. The voyage was without incident."

"And the freight aircraft?"

"Ready at the airfield. It will take off once the cargo is on board."

"Good news indeed. Once it arrives we can step up the operation."

CHAPTER ONE

The White House, Washington, D.C.

The President of the United States waited in uneasy silence while Hal Brognola read through the assembled data. The two men were alone in the Oval Office. The President had made it known he was not to be disturbed for any reason less than the imminent outbreak of total war.

Hal Brognola, director of the Stony Man SOG organization, was aware of the other man's close scrutiny. He did not allow it to intimidate him. He read the file, absorbing much of the detailed information as he went through it. Later he would reread and assimilate the data so he could assign his people to the operations that would follow. Now he needed talking points he could discuss with the President.

Brognola laid the file back on the desk.

"And you want Stony Man to take this on board why?"

The President kept a straight face. Brognola's response might have been judged a little out of order, but the President understood the big Fed's question. He knew how Brognola worked—always direct, respectful to his commander in chief, but wanting specifics when it came to committing his teams to the field.

"The U.S. is on a high wire where Pakistan is concerned. Trying to keep the administration on our side as an ally and at the same time keeping a watchful eye on elements in the country who would like nothing better than to see us kicked out. The extremists see the U.S. as opportunists with an eye on the main chance. Plenty of people over there simply don't like us. Don't like what we stand for, and see America as an imperialistic nation that wants Pakistan as just another stepping stone in a long-term plan to subjugate their corner of the world.

"That's not the way we see things, Hal. Yes, we have an interest in the country and the area. I don't see our involvement as anything but prudent, given how the extremists want al Qaeda and the Taliban to gain a greater foothold in the region. I see our obligation to the Pakistani president clearly. He's doing what he can to hold things down, but he has people in his administration who are sympathetic to the extremists. And we know only too well how dedicated these extremists are."

The President tapped the file on the desk. "These assassinations are an undeclared act of aggression against the U.S.A. There has been an internet posting stating that the killings are just to show us we can be hurt wherever we are. That the U.S. and its rabid allies have no protection from the followers of Allah. The details they put in the postings reveal they had in-depth information on the people murdered. They claim this is only a beginning and suggest what might follow when the curtain goes up. This group is taunting us, letting us know they can hit us when and where they like. They warn of a larger terrorist strike both here and in Pakistan. That's worrying, Hal. We need to act. Our people have been killed because they were, according to their reports, starting to get information on the extremists. It saddens me to admit that we might have a traitor in the ranks.

"The U.S. has allies in the war against terrorism. We're not on our own. There are deep ties to other security agencies across the globe. Europe. The U.K. Information passes back and forth. Links are formed between departments. There are multiagency teams. I don't need to tell you how it works, Hal, but the fact that delicate information reached the assassination team suggests they were fed by a source inside our combined agencies. If there is a mole somewhere in our ranks it's going to make any decisions we make hard to isolate. I want this handled by Stony Man, Hal, in case we do have someone passing information to the enemy. I can't hand this over to our security departments knowing sensitive information could be intercepted and used against us. Stony Man is a separate entity, with no allegiance to any other departments here or abroad."

The President leaned forward, fixing Brognola with an unflinching stare. "The main reason I want you in on this, Hal, is information I received from a *genuine* source." He didn't elaborate, so Brognola passed, and the President said, "I understand your curiosity about that, but I can't say anything right now. Just take my word it's on the level. The asset has warned that the threat of the strikes is real. There will be an attempted strike in Pakistan *and* on the U.S. mainland. Hal, it's going to be nuclear. And we have a name. Colonel Jabir Rahman."

The President sat upright, fixing his gaze on Brognola. "That a good enough reason for you to bring Stony Man in?"

"Good enough, Mr. President."

War room
Stony Man Farm

AROUND THE CONFERENCE room table sat the members of Phoenix Force and Able Team, along with the cyber group under the leadership of Aaron Kurtzman. Hal Brognola and

Barbara Price sat at the head of the table. Once the general banter had been exhausted, everyone settled down for the mission agenda. First up was the youngest member of Aaron Kurtzman's team, Akira Tokaido.

"We didn't have a great deal to work with," he said. "The information Hal handed us was based on existing data from various agency reports, so we used that to feed our own files and search for links."

He used a handheld remote to pull images onto the plasma monitors ranged around the War Room walls.

"This is Colonel Jabir Rahman, the guy whose name keeps cropping up when we dig. A Pakistani military guy with diplomatic credentials. The man does not like the U.S. Outspoken in his criticism of American policy and our involvement in the region, he is also not much of a fan of the Pakistani administration. He's been in any number of confrontations with the Pakistani president. Rahman has a lot of influence with extremist groups, sections of the military and sympathizers among the general public."

The image on the monitor showed a man in his late thirties, uniformed and with an erect military bearing. Rahman would have been called handsome by women. His features were strong, his eyes dark and penetrating. His black mustache was neatly trimmed, his thick, oiled hair just starting to show streaks of gray. Overall, he displayed an arrogant image. A confident man who would command respect and not be shy to correct anyone who failed to give it.

"So why is he in the frame?" Carl Lyons asked. The broad, powerfully built ex-cop was the leader of Able Team. "He a bad guy?"

"Rahman has been on numerous agency lists for a number of years," Brognola said. "He comes and goes without challenge because he has diplomatic immunity. He knows he's on watch lists, and enjoys playing the game. The Brits, U.S., French and Spanish have all had him in their sights. Rahman is a slippery guy.

"There's a source in Pakistan who points the finger at Rahman. Apparently, he's close to the man's group and picked up on conversations about the upcoming operation, passed it on, then dropped out of sight. The guy is working undercover, so there's no way to get in touch with him. Right now there's no knowing if he's alive or dead."

"So do we accept his information as genuine?" McCarter asked. The fox-faced Briton was the leader of Phoenix Force.

"This came via the President, who told me the guy can be trusted and so can his word."

"Piecing together every hit we've found suggests there's definitely something going on," Price said. "Rahman and the names linked to him, the recent visits between these people, their allegiances and a pretty strong hint anything Western goes against their thinking all add up to something big," the mission controller explained.

"Doesn't stop them making money from us," James said.

"Yeah? Well, what they make goes toward the latest atrocity," Lyons said testily.

"Freedom of speech and beliefs," Rafael Encizo said. "And before you jump in and bite my head off, Carl, it's what this country is all about. We start discriminating against religious and political diversity, we end up just like them."

Lyons took a deep breath. It seemed he was about to challenge Encizo's comments, but then he shook his head. "Rafe, you've got too many smart answers for me."

The truth was Carl Lyons knew exactly what Encizo was saying. It was one of life's ironies. Individuals who had nothing but contempt for America were able to live and work within its borders, their freedom and right to free expression protected by law. Until they actually went ahead and committed some crime, without definite proof there was nothing that could be done except put them on a watch list. *Watch* being the operative word.

"Rahman has a number of dubious friends." Carmen Delahunt, a valued member of Kurtzman's cyber team, the vivacious redheaded former FBI agent spoke decisively. She raised a hand to Tokaido, and more images appeared on the plasma screens. "Take your pick. The skinny guy is Umer Qazi. He is under suspicion of being an arranger for various flaky organizations within the Islamic world. He has ties to al Qaeda, so the story goes. In Afghanistan he was spotted in the company of Taliban members. On the surface he's polite, urbane. Don't underestimate him. The man is smart. Apparently he coaches young Muslims into becoming hard-liners. Likes to visit London a lot."

"And while he's there," Tokaido said, "he spends time with this guy, Samman Prem. Prem owns an export-import company based in the city, with a warehouse facility on Tilbury docks—you know the place, David?"

McCarter nodded. "Large port area. Used to be a lot bigger years ago. Still a busy place."

"Prem ships mainly to Pakistan and India. Some in the Middle East. He uses freighters belonging to Saeeda Hussein. He's another suspect, wealthy and not a lover of Western ideology. They're both on a watch list because of their affiliations, but that's as far as it goes. Prem especially has been known to express his anti-Western views privately."

"I traced Prem's cell phone calls," Kurtzman said. "Discounting nonimportant stuff, that left a lot of contacts. I broke them down into blocks." He worked his own remote, and lists appeared on a plasma screen. "Most calls were to this number. I ran it, and it came up as belonging to Khalil

Amir. Originally from Pakistan. Had an import business over there until he relocated to the U.S.—Boston to be exact. Still works the import business, but now also deals in real estate."

Akira Tokaido brought up images of the named men.

"Interesting points are that both these guys have a history of being involved with our friend Colonel Jabir Rahman. We picked this up from a sweep of friendly agencies. British intelligence have been running a dossier on Rahman for a couple of years. He's suspected of having links with radical sympathizers based in Europe, as well as Pakistan and the U.K."

"This *sweep* of friendly agencies?" Brognola queried. "How should I interpret that?"

Kurtzman cleared his throat. "Better you don't," he said.

Aaron "the Bear" Kurtzman and his cyber team were undisputed experts when it came to infiltration. Kurtzman had developed programs of such sophistication that they allowed covert entry into the most dedicated systems without the agencies ever having knowledge that they were being scrutinized. The details of Kurtzman's invasive programs were known only to himself. He kept them in his head, running them only when Stony Man needed instant access to information vital to missions.

Like the one they were into right now.

Brognola nodded. "Okay. So, you checked databases and picked up what you wanted?"

"MI5 and MI6 have information on Rahman that ties in with the proposed Phoenix Force and Able missions," Akira said. "It confirms the guy is deep into this radical culture. He basically just doesn't like the U.S. He's especially ticked off about our close ties with the Pakistani administration. I pulled up these." More images appeared on the big screens. "A U.K. operative took this a few weeks ago. Rahman and Khalil Amir. They were in Lyon, France, at some antiques junket. Rahman affects an interest in antiques. They stayed at a swish hotel along with other import-export players. The U.K. agent tailing Rahman reported he returned to Pakistan after his meet with Amir."

"The Brits kept a watch on them all," Carmen Delahunt said as she overlaid photos of Amir arriving at London's Heathrow Airport. "This was Khalil Amir arriving. He stayed in London for three days before returning to Boston. While he was in the U.K. he visited Prem."

"Any significance in this U.K. visit?" David McCarter asked. The Phoenix Force commander was sipping from a frosted bottle of Classic Coke. "I'll bet they weren't taking in the sights."

"Like Akira said, Amir did make contact with Prem, who's on the U.K. watch list as a possible radical," Delahunt stated. "Under surveillance, but he can't be tagged with anything vital."

"All these meetings can't just be bloody coincidences," McCarter said. "Too many in a short space of time."

"I'm guessing none of the agencies can do anything in case they scare these people and drive them underground," Calvin James said. The black Phoenix Force member had been watching and listening in silence, taking everything in and filing it away. "If they scare these guys off we could lose valuable leads."

Brognola nodded. "Exactly. Keep all this in mind once you get into the field. If we're right about a possible upcoming threat, we need to stay well back until we have solid evidence these people are involved."

"Easier said than done," Rosario "the Politician" Blancanales, of Able Team, pointed out. "We start probing, it could easily generate contact. If that happens what are we supposed to do?"

"Look, Pol," Brognola said, "I'm not saying you have to put yourselves at risk if the situation changes. If it comes down to the wire I want you guys walking away alive. All I'm saying is try to keep things low-key until you have something we can use."

"With the chance these idiots are serious about setting off nuclear devices, are we supposed to walk around on bloody tiptoe?" McCarter retorted. "Step back from doing anything to upset them? Hal, you presented us with this threat. Why all the pussyfooting? We should go with whatever we have, and nail these bastards. Squash them into the ground and put a stop to their harebrained scheme."

"Son of a bitch," Carl Lyons said. "That's exactly what I was going to say."

"He stole the boss's line," Hermann Schwarz, the third member of Able Team, whispered.

Blancanales gave a melodramatic gasp. "I'm shocked."

"Should we duck and cover?"

"Nah, I want to see the fight."

For once Lyons failed to bite. He sat back, a thin smirk on his face because he had beaten Blancanales and Schwarz at their own game.

"Now that isn't fair," Blancanales said. "No reaction means no fun."

Schwarz nodded. "He's doing it on purpose. Let's not talk to him for the rest of the briefing."

"Now the children have put their toys back in the box," Brognola said, wiping the grin off his own face, "we can get down to business."

The short break had given them all a breather from the tension of the moment. Hal Brognola knew his people well. Horseplay was to be expected from the teams. It was part of who they were. They were consummate professionals, and the missions they undertook for the special operations group were life threatening. They stepped into the thick of combat, taking on savage opposition without a flicker of regret. Brognola sent them out on missions that stretched the limits of their skills, pitting them against truly dangerous enemies. He understood that, shouldered the responsibility, knowing his people—and he considered them to be *his* people—would give their utmost.

"In the field, guys, you make your own decisions. I'll back whatever you do. However you achieve it. What the hell, you're the experts. If eggs need to be broken, that's it. Look, I'm just the administrator here. Let's get it right."

Barbara Price stood up and began to circle the table, dropping thick mission folders in front of each man.

"Everything we have is in these files. Backgrounds on participants. Photographs. Contacts. Locations. Let me know if there's anything else required. Once you've studied the files we can discuss individual needs."

"I don't see my luncheon vouchers," McCarter said. "You're always expecting us to do it on the cheap."

"Okay," Price said sternly, "listen up. We can arrange transport to get you to wherever you want. Paperwork, too, as per usual. Depending on location there might be problems with weapons, so we'll have to find local suppliers. With the current tensions, some regimes are very hot on loose weapons, so be careful. You'll have to use any local contacts you have yourselves. I'll let you have anything we might find on file."

"Work out your dispersal plans as fast as you can," Brognola said. "We want you fully organized, but time is not on our side here. We need you moving ASAP. Once you have things pinned down, let Barb know so she can make the arrangements."

A subdued murmur filled the room as the teams went over their mission parameters. They worked in unhurried discussions, each member putting forward suggestions. Brognola left them to it, withdrawing from the table to pour himself a mug of coffee from one of the thermos jugs supplied. As he stood there, Kurtzman spun his wheelchair around and powered it to where the big Fed stood.

"Never fails to impress me, watching them figure out a battle plan," he said. He was refilling his mug from the infamous pot of his special brew. It was said Kurtzman's coffee had the same strength as industrial paint stripper, and no one at Stony Man would ever deny that statement. "They're a unique crew."

"Damn right there, Aaron. It's a shame when you think how many times they've pulled this country back from the brink, and no one apart from the SOG will ever know it."

"The President knows. So did his predecessors." Kurtzman paused, then added, "And I guess he knows that truth, as well. He can't say anything, because Stony Man doesn't officially exist, so if he spills the beans he's just as guilty by default."

Brognola chuckled softly. "Hell of a way to make a living."

An hour later decisions had been made. Both teams had their objectives. In-depth discussions had been completed. Barbara Price had left and was already elsewhere, making travel arrangements and handing out assignments to her teams. The support staff at the Farm were responsible for travel and documentation, arranging equipment and weapons Phoenix Force and Able Team might need.

Once they were on their own, the Stony Man teams would, as usual, rely on skill and determination to get them through whatever came up.

MCCARTER GAVE Phoenix Force their orders.

"Gary, you and Rafe take Pakistan. Go scope out the situation. The rest of us will head to London. We can dig into the U.K. mob and see what we can find. Once we reach a conclusion we'll head out to join you. Barb will arrange transport. Gary and Rafe need to cross over from Afghanistan unannounced. We can work out a cover story for them so they can snoop around Peshawar. Maybe something to do with the New Relief charity?"

Price nodded. "There's a contact we can use in the city. A guy working undercover for British security. He's been in place for a while. Knows Peshawar. He could ease the way in."

"Okay. The rest of us need a ride to the U.K. Usual arrangements via the Air Force would be handy. Ferry us to a base near London."

"I can sort that. We'll organize documents for Gary and Rafe. Passports and visas all stamped with current dates. I'll get that set up for them."

"Ordnance," Encizo said. "Pakistan cops might not look too favorably on foreigners supposed to be working for a charity who are walking around loaded for bear."

"Make up a pack and hide it once you're across the border, before you go into the city," McCarter said. "Something to fall back on if things get hot."

"And knowing our luck, that's likely to happen," James said.

"Bloody bloke is such a party pooper," McCarter said.

"You guys need anything special for London?" Price asked.

"Pocket translator?" T. J. Hawkins said, grinning. "Way those Brits talk it might as well be Cantonese."

"Coming from you that's rich," McCarter said. "Barb, just fix us up with a decent hotel, love. We might not be there long, but let's be comfortable while we are."

BOSTON WAS ABLE TEAM'S destination. Khalil Amir was their target of interest. The man's connection to Jabir Rahman and Samman Prem brought him into the spotlight for the Able Team trio.

Once destinations had been settled the Stony Man support departments swung into action, leaving the teams to spend the next few hours reviewing their mission files, discussing how they were going to handle the operations.

Weapons were talked over, with visits to the armory in the lower section of the building, where they could test and check the ordnance chosen.

Barbara Price handed each man his personal folder holding passports, cash and credit cards. Later that evening the passports for Manning and Encizo were delivered, along with all the documentation they would need in Pakistan if they were asked to produce it. Dates and stamps had been added, and Price was able to say with confidence that no one would be able to spot they were forgeries.

The communication section provided the teams with current high spec satellite phones with global capabilities. Each phone had a built-in GPS system and, more importantly, a direct speed dial to the Farm.

"Able, I've arranged a private flight for you to Logan. Your credentials will ID you as Justice Department agents on special assignment. Your weapons will be in a separate, secure case. When you touch down you can go direct to the Hertz rental stand, where a vehicle has already been booked for you. It's in your cover name, Carl. And rooms are also booked at the Boston Marriott."

Price turned to McCarter. "David, there's an Air Force supply flight due to leave at seven tomorrow morning. We can have Phoenix Force there in time. You will touch down at RAF Mildenhall. Orders have been cut that will get you on board and delivered safely, no questions asked. Car will be waiting for you to pick up on base. After that you're on your own. When you want to move on, a USAF plane will fly you on a regular supply run to Afghanistan, where you'll be shipped out to the forward Marine base close to the border with Pakistan."

"What about Gary and Rafe?" McCarter asked.

"They'll be flown to the same base and choppered in across the border at night for a rendezvous with our contact. He'll drive them into Peshawar to where they're staying. This guy can give only limited assistance, so when he drops you at your hotel and gets you settled, he'll move on."

"Sounds playable," McCarter said.

"Just to make sure you all have your cover names correct," Price said. "David, you're Jack Coyle, because your guy in London knows you from previous meetings. Samuel Allen?" Manning held up a hand. Rafe—Fredo Constantine, and Cal, you are Roy Landis."

"Do I look like a Roy?" James asked.

"What the hell does a Roy look like?" McCarter retorted.

"T.J.?" Price said, moving on before the banter gained momentum.

"Daniel Rankin at your service, ma'am."

CHAPTER TWO

London

"I have a feeling the old town isn't what it used to be," David McCarter said.

While James drove the BMW, Hawkins at his side, the Briton, sitting in the rear, was staring out the window of the rental SUV Stony Man had arranged for them. They were heading toward the East End, where McCarter had arranged to meet up with Greg Henning. The man was part of a Scotland Yard Special Branch counterterrorist unit. Phoenix Force had come into contact with Henning a couple years back, during an operation that had taken them to the U.K. McCarter and the tough cop had sparred on their first meeting, but as the mission moved on they came to respect each other. Henning, a hard-nosed cop from the old school, had little tolerance for anyone classed as a terrorist. He and McCarter had met up a number of times when the Briton was visiting London and the man from Scotland Yard had made it clear he was ready to help if assistance was needed. When McCarter called him, Henning had agreed to meet in his favorite East End pub.

"Drop me off," McCarter said when the rendezvous point came into sight, "and carry on to the hotel. Get checked in and relax. I'll be in touch."

"Watch your back, boss," Hawkins said. "Looks like a rough area."

McCarter grinned, patting him on the shoulder. "You don't know the half of it, T.J."

James and Hawkins watched McCarter's tall figure cross the street, pause briefly at the door, then vanish inside the pub.

"Maybe we should hang around," Hawkins suggested.

"No need," James said as he pulled away. "He'll be fine. David's on home ground here. He's a lot safer than we are."

McCarter slipped off his topcoat as he moved inside the pub. At this time of day the place was quiet, with only a dozen customers scattered around. The interior didn't appear to have changed in the past ten years. The only thing missing were the wreaths of cigarette smoke. Since the government had banned smoking in buildings, the air might be cleaner, but the ambience had vanished along with the tobacco smoke.

Greg Henning waved when he spotted McCarter, then he pushed himself to his feet and reached out to shake his hand. "Pint, is it?" he asked.

McCarter nodded and sat down, watching Henning cross to the bar and order his drink.

"Bit scary, all this clean air," McCarter said when Henning placed his glass on the table and resumed his seat.

"Bloody nanny mentality," the cop muttered. He watched McCarter swallow a good third of the beer. "Looks like you needed that."

"You'll never know," McCarter said. "Can't get a decent glass of beer in America. It's like the proverbial gnat's piss."

Henning laughed, a deep hearty sound. He was a well-built man with a craggy, lived-in face, and he was wearing his dark hair longer than he had the last time McCarter saw him.

"So what's so urgent, Jack?"

Jack Coyle was the cover name McCarter had used the first time he and Henning met, and he'd retained it ever since. Henning understood it was a false identity, but it didn't seem to bother him, and he never probed for information. He knew McCarter was part of an American covert group that undertook difficult, high-risk operations. Henning had a blunt, no-nonsense attitude and a deep dislike of anything that hinted at terrorism. In his job as part of London's antiterrorist unit he had seen the results firsthand and hated what the bombers and radicals could do. As far as he was concerned such thugs warranted no consideration.

"We're trying to connect dots," McCarter said. "There are indications of a possible bomb threat against the U.S. and Pakistan, designed to make some kind of statement about U.S. presence and what we've made out to be payback for involvement with the Pakistani administration. You've probably heard about the recent killings in Peshawar and the bombing of the aid agency there."

"It was all over the news," Henning said. "A bloody business. Heard about the assassinations here and in the U.S., too. Were those events in line with what you're looking into?"

McCarter nodded. "We reckon so. All part of a buildup to the main event. Our initial intel gave us some leads, including a few names of people sympathetic to the bombing campaign."

"Here in London?"

"Yeah. Some of the extremists are on U.S. and U.K. watch lists. As usual, no one has anything hard enough to move on." McCarter paused. "But we're not bound by anything like that, Gregory, my old chum."

Henning smiled. He knew exactly what McCarter was hinting at. "If it looks like a duck, quacks like a duck, it most probably is a duck," he said. "Too many of these *known* individuals are being allowed to wander around free and clear."

"I just need some guidance," McCarter said. "From someone with up-to-date local intel. It's worth another pint, Gregory."

"First time I met you I knew you were cheap," Henning said. "And it's always the same."

"Hey, last time I bought you two pints."

Henning grinned. "You know, I'd almost forgotten about that. I suppose anything you want has to be under the radar?"

"I don't want anything landing back at your door."

"You think I'm worried about that? Don't. I've seen the results of bombings. The damage done to people. Faces shattered beyond recognition. Not pretty. And don't ever excuse it by giving these bastards a name—except terrorists. Murderers. Heartless sons of bitches. Any potential threat taken off the streets is fine by me. Where doesn't matter. Bloody hell, Jack, we're all in this whether we want to be or not."

Henning drained his beer and lapsed into silence. McCarter went to the bar and ordered two more pints, brought them back and placed one in front of the cop. Henning laid his open hands on the table. Cleared his throat.

"I think I went off on one there. Sorry."

McCarter raised his glass. "Do not apologize, Gregory," he said. "Too many people out there making excuses for those pricks. Time we had a few who call it like it is."

The cop shook his head wryly. "If anyone, including the commissioner of police, called me 'Gregory' I would lay one on him. Only my old mum is allowed to use that name. How come I let you get away with it?"

"I'm not your old mum, for sure, Gregory. So it has to be my winning personality."

"Cheeky sod. Now who are these ungodly buggers you need to track down?"

McCarter passed across a folded paper with the names of interest written on it. He had also jotted his cell number and details of the hotel where Phoenix Force were staying.

Henning scanned the names. McCarter noticed the fleeting expression of discomfort that crossed his friend's face.

"There a problem? Look, Greg, if I'm putting you on the spot here, let's forget it. Last thing I'd do is ask for—"

"It's not that," Henning said. "Past couple of weeks we've had a few ops go bad. Mainly surveillance. Everything okay until the suspects just cut and run. Left us high and dry. Looks like we have someone tipping our subjects off, so they've broken away before we could catch them in the act. I figure we have someone in the department letting our subjects know we've been watching them. On their payroll."

"It's been known to happen," McCarter said.

"What bothers me is the thought that a tipoff might turn nasty one day and someone in our team gets hurt."

"Any thoughts on who might be the mole?"

Henning hunched his shoulders. "I have my suspicions. I'm running this on my own until I get it pinned down. Nothing strong enough to point the official finger. If I show my hand too soon the bastard could cover his tracks and vanish."

"When you read those names I gave you," McCarter said, "it meant something."

"Yeah. The names are allied to the ops we were scuppered over."

"Your mole could be working for them?"

Henning nodded. "Let me check them out. Get you some

local info on them. If these blokes are the ones involved in these suspected attacks, we have to make the effort."

"Thanks, Greg."

"And I suppose you want the info ASAP, if not sooner?"

McCarter swallowed his beer. "Not trying to put any pressure on, mate, but yes. I told you about a bomb plot. What I didn't mention was it looks like they could be nuclear devices."

HENNING ARRIVED at the hotel in the early evening. The desk called McCarter's room and the Phoenix Force trio joined the cop in the lounge bar. Once drinks had been delivered, the group settled down to listen to what Henning had to tell them.

"I've been calling in favors like they're going out of fashion," the cop said. He raised his glass to McCarter. "My God, Jack, you owe me bloody big."

McCarter simply grinned at him. "Stop being a drama queen, Gregory."

"How do you blokes put up with him?"

"We have to," James said. "He signs our expenses slips."

"I guessed it would be something like that." Henning reached into his coat, took out a folded sheaf of papers and handed them to McCarter. "According to my sources, Samman Prem is a man of many parts. He runs a business based here in the city. He also has a storage facility on Tilbury docks. Bloke called Saeeda Hussein owns the company. Runs freighters from there. Prem has cargo and container ships coming and going, supplied by Hussein,"

"Ties in with what our initial searches came up with," McCarter said. "We're on the same track."

"Surveillance has Rahman and this Umer Qazi spotted at Prem's head office in the East End during their last visit. Looking really cozy."

McCarter grunted. "Makes you wonder what kind of deal they were cooking up."

"Could be anything. Legit or otherwise. The East End is pretty upmarket these days, Jack. It isn't all cobbled streets and back-to-back houses. A thriving multicultural scene now."

"So Rahman and Qazi wouldn't look out of place," Hawkins observed.

"They'd fit right in."

"Right," McCarter said. "Looks like we need to make a visit to Tilbury. Go shake Prem up a bit."

Tilbury Docks

LYING ON THE NORTH SIDE of the River Thames, the Tilbury docks complex was the third largest container port in the U.K. Oceangoing vessels carried a constant flow of goods to and from destinations around the globe. Warehouses and storage units lined the length of the facility and vast compounds of metal containers dominated the area.

The ID cards obtained for them by Greg Henning had got them inside the perimeter fence and the security-manned main gate. McCarter's story for the guard detail had them down as making a check on the quality of the service being provided. The Briton had spun a plausible yarn to the guy on the gate, praising him for his alertness at checking them out.

"That's what we're here for, mate. Just observing how people do their job. You know how it is these days. All to do with statistics. But they never ask blokes like you, the ones who have to do the work."

"Too right," the security guard said. "They sit in those nice warm offices pressing bleedin' buttons, and reckon they've done a good day's work."

"Lazy sods," McCarter declared. "Don't let on I said that." He checked out the man's name tag. "Listen, George, we shouldn't be here long. Can we park over there? If we need to walk about I'll come and check with you first. You're the bloke in charge."

George puffed up with pride. "You take your time. I could make you and your mates a nice hot cuppa later."

"That would great, George. Appreciate the thought."

George waved them through, watching as McCarter drove to the parking area.

"Charm the birds off the trees," James said.

"Got to give the man his due," Hawkins agreed.

"Watch and learn, my children," McCarter said, grinning.

From their position they could see the warehouses belonging to Saeeda Hussein's firm. The company name was evident on many of the stacked metal containers in view.

"Hope we don't have to check out every damn box on this dock," Hawkins said.

"Just keep your eyes and ears open," McCarter replied. "This is a bit of a long shot, so we need to stay sharp."

"'"T'was ever thus,'" James said.

"Say what?" Hawkins asked.

"He's showing off his classical side," McCarter said. "Shakespeare used it in *Twelfth Night*."

"English, please."

"Sort of *this is how it always is*," James explained.

"So why not damn well say so?" Hawkins asked.

"He just wants us to know he once read a book," McCarter said lightly.

"Oh, Mr. Smarty Ass," Hawkins grunted.

"There, you figured him out," McCarter said.

James's laugh was cut short when he leaned forward to

check out someone he'd seen. "Hey, isn't that our buddy Samman Prem?"

"It is," Hawkins confirmed.

The man had emerged from the warehouse and was standing on the edge of the dock, staring out across the water. A minute later another man appeared. He joined Prem and they fell into an intense conversation. It was Saeeda Hussein, easily identified from the photographs Phoenix Force had studied.

James picked up the zoom-lens digital camera they had brought along. From his position in the passenger seat next to McCarter he had a clear and unobstructed view. He raised the device, focused in and ran off a number of speed shots.

"Get a good photo?" McCarter asked.

"Prize-winning," James said.

"More for the party," McCarter said.

Another man, tall and thin, with long dark hair that reached his shoulders, came into view. When he joined the others he stood listening to the conversation. James took more photos.

The three talked for a few minutes before wandering off along the dock. They gathered again alongside a container ship being loaded.

"I'll send these to Stony Man," James said.

He opened the slide cover and took out the camera's memory chip. Picking up his digital sat phone, he inserted the chip into the access port and let it load. Once the contents of the chip were in place James used the coded number that gave him a satellite link to the Farm.

"Hey, Barb," he said when his call was picked up. "I'm sending some images for Bear to check out. Get him to run facial scans on the men. We pretty well know who they are, but it does no harm to double-check."

"Will do. How are things in merry England?"

"I'll let you know as soon as we do."

"Okay."

"Hey, boss, I think we might have been spotted," Hawkins said.

McCarter watched as the three men they had been checking out all turned to stare in the direction of the Phoenix Force car.

"What do you want to do?" James asked. He slipped the camera and sat phone out of sight beneath his seat.

McCarter opened his door and stepped out of the SUV. Leaning against the vehicle, he casually took out his pack of Player's cigarettes and lit one.

"Man, he loves doing this," James said. "It's like a game of chicken, but without the cars." He slid his hand inside his coat to ease his shoulder-holstered Beretta.

Hawkins noticed the move and said, "This going to turn into a shooting match?"

"I hope not, but with Commander I-love-taking-a-risk McCarter it's safer to stay cautious."

Samman Prem walked back along the dock and headed in their direction. He was not a tall man, but carried himself with an arrogant bearing that told the world he was important and not to be trifled with. He wore his thick black hair long, almost to his shoulders. Under the jacket of his expensive suit he wore a thin-striped shirt and matching tie. The heavy watch on his wrist gleamed dull gold.

"Who are you people?" he demanded. "What are you doing on this dock? Do you realize who I am?"

"We're just doing our job, Mr. Prem," McCarter said.

"How do you know my name?"

"I told you we're doing our job, and knowing who you are is part of it." McCarter examined the glowing end of his cigarette. "You know, I'm sure they don't make these as thick as they used to."

Prem's face flushed with righteous anger. "I demand to know who you are and how you got into this facility."

"That's easy," McCarter said. He took out his ID card and showed it to Prem, keeping it just beyond the man's reach. "No need to touch," he said. "It's official. All you need to know. Gives me and my team the right to check out security on this dock."

"You have no right to..."

"To what?" McCarter asked pleasantly, but with just enough of a suggestion in his tone to needle the businessman. "I hope you have nothing to hide, Mr. Prem. I'd hate to have to send for help. The backup team gets a little testy if they get called out this late in the day."

"I will take this up with—"

McCarter eased his long form away from the side of the car, leaning forward a little so he could look Prem in the eye.

"Now you go ahead, mate. Take it up with whoever you want. Your local MP. Lawyer. Anyone in your old boys' club. But bear in mind that we know a lot about you and your friends. What you've been up to and what you have planned. Think on what I've said and watch your back."

As McCarter straightened up, he saw that the other two men had appeared behind Prem. The Briton nodded in their direction. "Mr. Prem will bring you up to date, gents. When you see him next time, give my regards to Colonel Rahman. You are familiar with the name I'm sure."

McCarter turned and opened the door of the BMW, then climbed in. After starting the engine, he swung the SUV around and drove to the security gate. George the gateman opened up for him.

"You're doing a nice job, George," he said. "Sorry we

can't stay for that tea. You know how it is when duty calls. Just keep your eye on the rough element they seem to be letting onto this dock. "

George grinned. "I'll do that," he said.

McCarter drove away and picked up the main road leading back to the city.

"Where I come from," Hawkins said, "that would be known as baiting the bull."

"Poking a stick in a hornets" nest," James said.

McCarter smiled. "Lads, it helps to stir the pot sometimes. Bloody hell, I'd give anything to be a fly on Mr. Prem's office wall right now."

"Never mind Prem," Hawkins said from the rear seat. "We've got our own problem. It's black, has three guys in it and has a Citroën badge on the hood. It just rolled in behind us. I saw it exit the dock gate when you turned onto the main road. Fellers, we have a tail."

CHAPTER THREE

Samman Prem summoned three of his waiting soldiers and gave them instructions. Without questions they left the warehouse, commandeered one of the parked vehicles and drove off the dock.

Prem made his way back to Hussein's office, slammed the door and crossed to the desk. His face was taut with anger.

"He mentioned Colonel Rahman," he said angrily. "Who are these people? What do they know? This could be a threat to us all."

"Why?" Hussein said. He had witnessed only the tail end of Prem's confrontation with the tall Englishman. "The Barracuda is out of the country. It could already be in Rahman's hands. What can one policeman do to us now?"

"I wish it was a simple thing to dismiss this whole matter," Prem said. "We know the British authorities have been looking at our business. If there is a possibility these people are getting close to us they could harm our whole U.K. setup. Don't you realize the extent of our organization here? Our people like Qazi." He indicated the third man in the office. "A brilliant recruiter. A teacher. It was Qazi who found Anwar Fazeel and coached him in the ways of Allah. Fazeel is now in Pakistan and, using his computer and electronic skills, he will be the one to control and guide the Barracuda. There are others like Qazi who are spreading our message and bringing new followers.

"If the U.K. authorities destroy us, our organization will have been for nothing," Prem continued. "Over the years we have created cells of followers ready to do our bidding. There are safe houses. Stores of supplies and weapons. People who will assist. Money from our al Qaeda brothers."

"So what do we do? Why not let the British fumble around, trying to investigate us?"

"Because there is too much to lose. If the brothers who are following those three fail to stop them, I must prepare to use our main asset."

Qazi sat down. "Winch?"

"Yes. A turncoat who has a terrible greed for money. An English antiterrorist agent who has worked for me a long time. Admittedly, he is a dog on two legs. A betrayer of his own, but one who has been extremely useful to us."

"Is he the one who directed our brothers in Peshawar? Who gave up the CIA agents?"

"The very one. He has many contacts within the security department of the U.K. and contact with the Americans through his position as a liaison officer for the European task force on terrorism."

"Was he responsible for the Washington and London kills, too?" Hussein asked.

"Yes. Winch has access to mercenary units who were contracted to provide men. Many of them are ex-military. His knowledge of these people has proved very useful."

Hussein still expressed doubt. "This man is not of our faith. He is a Westerner. How can he be trusted?"

"Because he is a Westerner and he lives by their corrupt ways. His life is centered around acquiring personal wealth. As long as it is on offer he will forgo any loyalty to his own. The man has no religion. No higher authority. Like his faithless society, his creed is to serve himself only.

So while he remains useful to me I will take advantage of his vile expectations."

"Use the serpent, but be wary of his fangs," Qazi said.

Prem, picking up his phone, nodded. "Winch has proved extremely adept at providing sensitive information. The man has gained the confidences of many in the security community." He paused, allowing himself a smile. "Saeeda, where do you think we got our hands on the scheduling that allowed us to hijack the Barracuda UAV?"

"That was Winch? Ah, a valuable asset, then," Hussein agreed.

"And a very rich one. His hidden bank accounts must be extremely healthy by now."

Prem made his call. When it was answered, he spoke briefly at first, to establish safe contact. "I hope we are able to talk freely."

"This is the safe number I gave you," Winch said. "Do we have a problem?"

"There has been a development that might become worrying. A short time ago three men came to the dock. They identified themselves as security personnel. The ID they showed me said they were from the police. London Metropolitan CTS attachment."

"Was there an authorization signature?"

"G. Henning—senior agent. Does the name mean anything to you?"

"Yes. Were they just snooping around, or did they have a definite purpose?"

"The one I spoke to said they knew all about us. That they were watching closely."

"Sounds like they were fishing."

"Did I not mention that Colonel Rahman was identified by name? Does that suggest *fishing,* Mr. Winch?" Prem's tone had lost any pretense of friendliness. "I suggest you look into this. Find out what is going on. Agent Henning needs to be dealt with if he is sending in people to check me out. I do not like to be investigated in such a way. It is why I employ you, Winch. And pay you handsomely to prevent this kind of thing from happening." He paused. "You agree?"

"Yes."

"I dispatched three of my people to follow and deal with these men. If they do not succeed it will be down to you to engage your mercenaries to handle them. I will let you know what unfolds. In the meantime your task is to make certain Mr. Henning is unable to conduct his inquiries further. Do you understand?"

"Understood," Winch said. "It will be handled immediately. Personally."

"Do not contact me until the matter is concluded."

"The usual arrangement?"

"Of course, Mr. Winch. Do not worry about it. You will definitely get what is coming to you."

Winch failed to recognize the irony in Prem's words.

Prem ended the call and replaced the handset.

"He can do this?" Qazi asked.

"I believe so. He has never failed me yet and I see no reason why it should be any different this time. It must not be different. Our purpose here in the U.K. is much more than assisting in Rahman's operation, important as it is. Our whole network could be jeopardized. I will not allow that to happen." Prem picked up the phone again. "I must call Colonel Rahman and update him on the situation. If matters escalate he will not be pleased if he has not been advised."

"Tell him I will be leaving on the evening flight back to Pakistan," Qazi said. "There is nothing else here for me to do."

THE CITROËN ACCELERATED as the road narrowed, bounded on either side by older houses in various stages of redevelopment. The French-built car powered up to within a foot of the Phoenix Force vehicle.

"Naughty, naughty," McCarter muttered. "I hate tailgaters. But I have a way of dealing with them."

The Briton stomped on the brake. As the Phoenix Force BMW slowed, the driver of the Citroën was forced to do the same. The car lurched, tires squealing as it dropped back, smoke whipping from the tires. McCarter pushed his foot down again and took the BMW up to the maximum he could risk on a public road.

"Never a cop around when you need one," he grumbled. "Any other time the place would be crawling with patrol cars and the road lined with speed cameras."

"I think these guys know that, too," Hawkins said. "And I don't reckon they're about to quit and go home to Momma."

"You think I went too far with Prem?" McCarter asked.

James glanced at the Briton and didn't miss the slight smirk on his lips. "You wanted him to react, didn't you?"

"Was that what I did?"

"Dammit, David, you know how these guys hate anyone pissing them off. Right now you've probably been issued with a fatwa all your own."

"Bloody hell, me on a level with Salman Rushdie. Next thing, the queen will be offering me an OBE."

Tires screeched as the Citroën swept into the opposite lane and started to draw level with the SUV.

"That guy behind the wheel is one reckless dude," James said.

"You think?" Hawkins commented. "Oh, great..."

"What?"

"Gun," Hawkins yelled.

The BMW shuddered as a stream of slugs struck the right-hand rear side panel.

McCarter responded with a jerk to the wheel that sent the BMW into the path of the chase car. There was a hard thump as the two collided. The Citroën rocked under the impact. The shooter, leaning out of the rear window, was knocked back inside the car, giving Hawkins the chance he needed. He had already powered down his window, giving him a clear shot as he leveled his Beretta and triggered a triple volley. The shooter, righting himself, caught the 9 mm slugs in his throat and jaw. Hawkins caught a brief glimpse of the guy jerking back from the window, blood spurting from his torn flesh.

Swinging the wheel again, McCarter slammed the Citroën a second time. It swung away, hitting the far curb. The impact bounced the Citroën up onto the sidewalk, the wheels turning despite the driver's attempt to maintain a straight course. The car plowed into piles of building materials in of one of the houses. Hawkins, watching through the rear window, saw the vehicle slide, then flip over onto its side, crashing headlong through the stacks of lumber and sheeting.

McCarter raised his eyes to the rearview mirror.

"Oops," he said. He met Calvin James's eyes. "Cal, call Henning and let him know what just happened. Tell him we need to get this car off the streets. He'll know somewhere we can meet up without any kind of audience."

"ANY DAMAGE?" Henning asked. He had met Phoenix Force at a basement garage of a closed office block off the Bayswater Road. The garage was gloomy, with water dripping from the low concrete ceiling.

"Only to the car," James said. "And one of the opposition ran into a couple of bullets."

"Good." Henning peered at the buckled front end and the ragged bullet holes at the rear. "Business as usual, Jack. Never fails. Minute you set foot in the old town, all hell breaks loose."

"He has that effect wherever he goes," James said.

"I believe you." The cop leaned against the hood of the BMW. "I take it all this was a result of you going to visit Samman Prem? How did you find him?"

"Tetchy," McCarter said. "Thinks a lot of himself. Didn't take it too well, me hinting we have the goods on him."

"He wouldn't. Not a winning personality, our Mr. Prem. I'd go as far as saying he is an arrogant little jerk."

"Poking him with a stick didn't help his disposition," James added, glancing sideways at McCarter.

The Briton feigned innocence. "I was just keeping the conversation going."

"How did he react to that?"

"Stamped his little feet when he walked away," McCarter said.

"Then sent a tail car after us," Hawkins interjected. "They tried to push us off the road, then started shooting."

"Christ, Jack, when you blokes start something you really start something."

"One way of putting it," McCarter said. "We're punching in the dark here, Gregory. We have the threat of a hit, but we don't know when or where, so no time for being subtle or checking the rule books. If that means kicking arses to make things happen, then we kick."

"I'll handle the car for you. Get it moved where no questions are the order of the day," Henning said. "Give you a ride back to your hotel?"

"Thanks, mate. Your tip about Prem looks like it paid off. That bugger is involved in something. I'll bet my pension on that. We can have our people check out his company. Maybe they'll come up with something useful. If they don't I'll most likely go back and beat it out of him before I set fire to his warehouses."

"Maybe the day hasn't been a total waste, then," Henning said.

"McCarter might not be joking," Hawkins said.

"Oh, I know that," the cop acknowledged. "Listen, I think I have a lead on who might have been selling us out. I had my suspicions and was going to follow them through, but I was given an assignment and had to drop what I was doing. When you called and brought me up to date, certain things you said tied in with my own theory. So expect a call if I hit pay dirt."

McCarter nodded. "You watch your back, Gregory. Rats may be squirmy little buggers, but they have sharp teeth when they're backed into a corner."

Henning led them to his parked SUV and they all climbed in. He swung the vehicle around and drove out of the garage. As he pushed into the traffic, he activated his car phone and punched in a speed dial number. When his call was answered Henning gave explicit instructions to whoever was on the line, making it clear what he needed done. He finished the call and sat back, smiling.

"Your wheels will disappear in the next couple of hours. Never to be seen again. I'll insert a stolen-vehicle report for you. Call the rental firm and tell them the car was nicked earlier this afternoon. There's a pad on the dash there. Write down this number and quote it to the rental company. They'll use it when they contact the local cops. It's a crime case number. Rental company can use it when they make a claim on their insurance."

McCarter wrote down the information and tucked the

paper in his jacket. "Always knew the Met was a bloody good outfit."

"'Met?'" Hawkins repeated.

"Metropolitan Police," Henning said. "London's city police force. Go all the way back to 1829. They always say those were the good old days. With what we have to deal with now I'm starting to think that could be true."

"Gregory, we live in parlous times," McCarter said. "All we can do is keep up the good work."

"Hey, you two, "James said, "enough of the down-home philosophy. It's like listening to a couple of old-timers rocking on the porch."

Back at the hotel McCarter contacted Stony Man and spoke with Barbara Price. He gave her an update, including the fate of their rental.

"Well, at least letting your pal handle the disappearance should avoid awkward questions about bullet holes," Price said. "I'll make a call and sort out another car for you."

"Thanks. We need some in-depth information about Samman Prem and his company. Shipping. Any connections. Hell, you know the drill."

CHAPTER FOUR

Greg Henning's earlier investigation went back a couple weeks. Even then he'd been aware he was breaking every rule in the book, but his conviction that he had the right man dictated he do something about it. Operating in the counterterrorist unit had exposed him to the inner workings of the terrorist mind, and the things he had seen and heard only proved what he suspected. Terrorism, in all its twisted forms, was the scourge of the twenty-first century. It fed on hypocrisy, hid its evil under religious dogma, using the logic of persuasion and in most cases blatant brainwashing of vulnerable minds. The hate fostered by the al Qaeda generation of terrormongers was done via the teachers and advisors, men who stayed away from the results of their haranguing, never exposing themselves to risk. They remained in safety, dispatching their acolytes to kill and maim, and in many instances to be killed themselves in suicide attacks, willing to destroy with the promises of eternal life in paradise.

Nine/eleven, the London bombings and countless other atrocities were claimed as victories for the jihad. Each strike was celebrated by cheering, howling mobs, while the innocent victims were grieved by the survivors. There was little sense to it all, but in the aftermath, the Western governments realized this was going to be a long battle. The security agencies slowly began to understand the complexities of this new kind of war, and after false starts gathered themselves unto some semblance of coordination.

Perfection was still a distance away, but antiterrorist organizations slowly emerged. Greg Henning volunteered for the U.K.'s counterterrorist squad the day he heard it was being formed. He saw it as a total necessity, and pushed himself to the limit once he had been fully accredited. It was a job that demanded every agent give total attention, then more. Henning had been married in his younger years, but the partnership hadn't lasted, ending in divorce after six years. His work in the new unit meant he needed to be there on a 24/7 basis. It suited him.

His understanding of the job and its requirements was cause for concern when it became suspected there could be a leak within the unit. He found the concept of a traitor repulsive. The squad was manned by professional men and women who put themselves on the line and worked endless shifts to keep ahead of the terrorists. To have one of their own passing information, weakening the group's ability to stay focused, was unthinkable and totally unacceptable.

Being in the top echelon within the department, Henning was given a briefing by his immediate superiors. They had suspicions but no proof. Initial investigation had been difficult. If there was a traitor inside the unit, any checking had to be undertaken with great care, for fear of alerting the mole. It was one of those near impossible situations. It could have easily broken up the team, each member suspicious of his or her partners. Any prolonged procedure would damage trust and imperil the smooth workings of the department.

Henning had already fixed his attention on a single member of the unit, having been alerted by the man's behavior. He closed in on the individual in his own surreptitious way, quietly and with an almost indifferent attitude.

The man's name was Lewis Winch. A smart and confident agent, he held a high ranking in the unit. His brief was to act not only as a U.K. operative, but also to liaise with European and American agencies. Winch had made this his prime role and had built a reputation as a brilliant negotiator when it came to handling awkward international conflicts. There were still territorial stumbling blocks to deal with when it came to diplomacy directives, and Winch seemed to have the techniques for smoothing things over. Within the department he was almost a law unto himself. He came and went, making frequent visits to the Continent and even the U.S.A. He was often out of the department on consultations, as he put it.

Henning wasn't sure how or when he began to have an unsettling feeling where Winch was concerned. His suspicions might have been aroused by the man's increasing attitude of what Henning could only call twitchy. Winch seemed to be looking over his shoulder metaphorically, reacting awkwardly whenever someone approached him, almost with paranoia. Henning told himself he was looking too hard, seeing things that meant very little, but he found he was studying Winch whenever the man was around.

A definite sign appeared the day the reports started coming in about the killing and bombing in Peshawar. Henning saw Winch's reaction as the large wall-mounted plasma TV began to show the images. The whole of the main office was watching, so Winch's response was noticed only by Henning. He saw Winch turn away and hurry to his own office, where he took out a cell phone. Seated at in his own desk, Henning witnessed Winch's actions through the open blinds. He couldn't hear what the man was saying, but from his expression it was plain he was agitated. The call went on for a couple of minutes before he cut the conversation and dropped the cell phone back into the desk drawer, then snatched his coat off its hook and exited.

Henning went to his office window, which overlooked the street. As he had somehow expected, Winch stepped into view from the building and hailed a taxi. Henning's office was only one floor up so he was able to read the number on the cab's license plate. He turned and jotted it on his desk pad.

Nothing unusual in someone taking a taxi.

Except that this was Lewis Winch.

And Winch hated any kind of public transport. He never, ever used taxis. Always drove his own car, which would be parked, even now, in the basement garage under the building. The whole scenario jarred. Henning sat down, staring at the number he had written on his desk pad.

Winch had reacted sharply at the TV report. It wasn't anything they hadn't seen before. But this time Winch had been clearly taken by surprise.

Why?

And who had he called so urgently?

Henning sat back, understanding he had to follow this through. It might not lead him anywhere. Winch's behavior could have been an innocent reaction to the events unfolding on the screen. But it felt like something entirely different to Greg Henning.

He wanted to be proved wrong.

Genuinely proved wrong.

The recent problems the department had been experiencing, the operations having to be called off due to compromising situations and the fact that prior warning had been leaked to parties under observation—all these needed to be answered.

And this unusual behavior warranted investigation, no matter what the outcome.

That afternoon, Winch didn't return for a couple hours. On arrival, he went directly to his office and closed the door, then sat at his desk for a while before he turned on his laptop and began to work.

Henning watched him covertly from his own office. His hopes of not being seen were marred when he saw Winch watching *him.* This happened a couple times.

Winch finished early, pulling on his coat and walking out of his office. He flicked off the light and closed the door.

It seemed he was about to head over to Henning's office, but he stared for a moment, then turned and left the department.

Back at his office window, Henning waited, finally seeing his colleague's car nose out from the basement garage and merge with the busy London traffic. He stayed at the window until the vehicle was out of sight.

Winch's behavior left Henning with a feeling of disquiet, an unsettling sensation that wouldn't leave him.

He was ready to take those suspicions a step forward. That was when his telephone rang and Henning was assigned a call to duty. He had to put the Winch matter on the back burner until he had cleared his assignment, because he refused to expose his feelings until he could prove his case.

The day he returned to the department, and before he could even check his computer, the phone rang and the man he knew as Jack Coyle was asking him to meet for a drink and a chat.

ON HIS RETURN TO his office following his meeting with Jack Coyle, Henning went over their conversation. The subjects they had covered had rekindled his earlier suspicions about Lewis Winch—the man's reaction to the bombing scenes in Pakistan, his sudden departure from the office and his extremely odd behavior with the taxi.

If Henning was wrong about him, no harm would have been done. If his suspicions proved sound, that was another matter. He admitted he was acting purely on instinct, but he trusted his senses. They had proved reliable on other occasions.

Henning located the license number of the taxi he had written down. The antiterrorism squad had an extensive and top-of-the-line cyber unit. Their ability to seek and find was unrivaled in London. Henning logged on using his password. He tapped in the vehicle number and ran a check on its details. The search provided him with the cab company, and from that Henning was able to access the logs of each vehicle. He inputted the taxi's license number and the date he was interested in. In less than a minute he had a list of all the fares the cab had picked up that day. Henning scrolled down it until he located the one that had originated outside their building. The time tallied with when he had seen Winch climb into the taxi.

Henning studied the address where his colleagues had completed his journey.

The London office of Samman Prem.

Henning sat and stared at the monitor, trying to come up with any legitimate reason for Lewis Winch to visit the office of a man like Prem. He failed. Then he pondered whether, just because Winch had been dropped off outside Prem's building, it was fair to assume the man had gone inside. Henning decided it was too much of a stretch to believe Winch had been dropped off at Prem's place of business and not gone inside.

Samman Prem was one of the men on the watch list. A man who had been followed from time to time and considered a person of interest. If the unit had unlimited funds, it might have placed Prem under full-time observation, but true to the way things happened, the counterterrorist squad had to spread its allocations of men and money thinly over a large area. So Prem was no longer under watch.

Henning tried another route, via the extensive network of TV cameras that were installed all over London. He used the system to locate the address he wanted, and discovered there were two cameras on the East End street where Samman Prem's office building stood. Henning tapped in date and time and waited, hoping that any recorded views had not been wiped from the digital records.

The first camera had been cleared, but Henning's second attempt provided what he wanted. The long shot showed the taxi pulling up outside the building. Even at that distance, he recognized Winch as the man stepped out of the taxi, paid the driver, turned and went in through the main door. Henning ran the action back until he had a full shot of him, then used the zoom facility to bring the image closer. This time there was no doubt in Henning's mind; the man on his monitor screen was Lewis Winch. Before he logged out, Henning saved the image and stored it on his own computer.

He leaned back in his chair and stared at the face of the man he had just watched enter the office building of a suspect individual.

Looking over the top of his monitor, Henning was able to see Winch in his own office.

So what now?

Did he go across and confront the man?

Or take his findings to his superiors?

Henning knew he had to proceed carefully. Confronting Winch might backfire on him. The man would undoubtedly deny any wrongdoing, might even come up with a logical explanation.

Henning dismissed that thought immediately. There was no logical explanation that would clear up the fact that Winch had been seen entering Prem's building.

Something was nagging away at the back of Henning's mind, demanding an answer. He allowed it to take form.

If Winch was a mole, why would he risk a daylight visit to the office of a suspected terrorist?

There was no sense in risking exposure.

Henning recalled the way Winch had reacted to the TV coverage of the Pakistani bombing report. Perhaps seeing the results of information he may have passed along had unnerved him. Maybe this was the first time he had been witness to what his traitorous dealings had done. A touch of conscience, a realization that what he was involved in was far from a harmless game? Perhaps time had caught up and Winch realized he had become part of what was not a game but a brutal reality. Seeing death and human suffering, Winch may have felt the need to confront his paymasters. It was no big leap to move to the inevitable conclusion that his colleague was selling information for cash. Henning didn't view him as idealistic. There was no visible altruistic reason why Winch would be passing along sensitive information without receiving some kind of reward.

Henning brought himself back to the present. He played with the details he had, using his desk pad to list them, then stared at the penciled notations.

Lewis Winch—supposedly on Henning's side of the fence, though emerging facts were suggesting otherwise.

Samman Prem—a suspect who had received a personal visit from Winch a couple weeks back.

Jack Coyle's face-to-face with Prem, which had been followed by a violent attack on Coyle and his team.

Henning doodled with his pencil, still unsure of the full intent of his gathered information. When he glanced at his watch he saw it was late. He threw the pencil down and stood up, clicking off his computer. He tore the sheet of paper from his pad and slid it into the office shredder, grabbed his coat and headed out. The department was empty except for the evening team.

Winch had left much earlier.

In the elevator Henning leaned against the side of the car, glad to leave the office behind. The image of a tender steak and a foamy pint of beer crossed his mind. He was still thinking about food as he climbed into his car and drove out of the basement garage. Light rain had wet the road, and multicolored reflections of street and store lights spread across the tarmac. There was heavy rush-hour traffic and it took Henning forty-five minutes to negotiate the distance to his home.

Reaching his destination, he turned in at the archway that fronted the residential mews where he lived. He came to a stop a few yards from his front door, cut the engine, climbed out and locked his car.

And that was when he heard someone call his name.

CHAPTER FIVE

Greg Henning paused as he searched in his pocket for his house key. Stalling by pretending he couldn't find it, he slid his right hand inside his coat, located the butt of his handgun and released the breakaway strap. His already alerted senses ratcheted up a notch when he heard his name being spoken again.

He knew now he hadn't been mistaken.

Someone was standing in the deep shadow at the end of the cul-de-sac. Under Henning's coat his hand closed around the butt of his 9 mm Glock. He took out his key and inserted it into the lock.

Henning turned the key. Felt the lock give. He pushed against the door and it swung inward. At the same time he pulled his Glock, angling it across his body as he made a swift turn.

He caught a fragmented glimpse of the figure closing in fast. He heard the subdued snap of a suppressed shot and felt a hard blow just below his left shoulder. The impact tipped him off balance. He hit the edge of the door frame, stumbling partway inside. Henning struggled to stay upright as he triggered a shot from the Glock. The report sounded extremely loud in the quiet surroundings.

The other shooter's weapon fired again, twice. Henning gasped in shock as the slugs struck home. He fired again himself, pulling the trigger as many time as he could. He saw the shooter stop in midstride, and knew he'd scored some kind of hit. The man turned aside, pulling away, and as he passed through the light thrown from the wall lamp above the door Henning saw his face in profile. It was only for a fleeting second but long enough for him to recognize the man.

It was Lewis Winch.

Henning went down in a heavy sprawl, blood pulsing from the bullet wounds in his chest. He didn't really register hitting the ground, just saw the strange angle of the open door looming above him. The night sky was sprinkled with stars. There was a rush of pain, then a comforting numbness that spread with alarming speed. He picked up sounds far off.

Unconnected.

Henning fumbled his cell from his coat, peering at the screen as he pressed keys for a text message. The effort cost him, pain making him gasp, fingers feeling thick and clumsy. When he located the number for Jack Coyle, he sent a text.

He felt the phone slip from his hand. He sensed people around him, bending over him, anxious voices. Henning couldn't make sense of any of it. He hoped his text had got through. That was the last thing he remembered.

McCarter took out his cell, checking the incoming call. It was from Stony Man. He answered and heard Barbara Price's voice.

"Text message rerouted via the cover number," she said. "From your cop buddy in London. Henning. He's in trouble. Something about being shot and knowing who the mole is."

"I'm on it, Barb."

"Merry England isn't sounding too merry."

"You don't know the half."

"Progress?"

"We're picking up scraps here and there. Names you guys supplied are tying up, but nothing too definite yet. Just feed us anything you find." McCarter paused. "Heard from the others yet?"

"Only that they've located themselves and it's hot."

McCarter smiled. "That will be our Canadian member," he said. "He prefers snow and ice."

"Let us know about Henning."

"Thanks, love, I'll keep you updated."

McCarter managed to maintain his composure in the face of hospital protocol. It took all his patience and persuasion to even get to the nurses' station on Henning's floor. The young woman in charge, an attractive redhead, at least had an engaging personality. She listened to McCarter's story in silence, lips pursed in a gentle smile.

"You must understand hospital rules," she said finally. "We can't have people wandering in unannounced. Mr. Henning is lucky to be alive. He was shot three times. One bullet clipped his left lung. He lost a great deal of blood before the ambulance crew arrived, and he's had serious surgery."

"You know he's a security officer?" McCarter said.

The nurse chuckled at that. "Don't I know it. Seems as if we've had half the Met in here. There's even an officer on duty outside his room. Look, we've been told no one is allowed in unless they've been vetted, so there isn't much I can do."

McCarter took a breath. He peered at the name tag on the young woman's uniform. "Nurse Jenny…"

"Actually, it's *Sister* Jenny."

"Sorry," McCarter said. "Look, Sister Jenny, I'm in the same business. Working undercover with Greg Henning.

I'm pretty sure his shooting was because of the case we're involved with. Right now my only contact is through Greg. I can't go any higher because our investigation concerns leaks within the security department itself."

McCarter took out his cell and opened Henning's text message. He showed it to Jenny. She checked it out, and murmured, "The time on that message is five minutes before the ambulance arrived at Mr. Henning's address."

"He must have sent it just after he'd been shot. He was trying to let me know something."

"I still can't let you into his room."

"But you can go in."

She eyed him warily. "Yes…"

"If he's awake, ask him if he has anything for me. Just tell him Jack Coyle wants to know."

Jenny's expression told McCarter he'd made a connection. "You're Jack Coyle?"

"Yes. Why?"

"He asked me if you'd been around. As soon as he woke up."

McCarter smiled. "Good old Gregory."

She frowned. "Gregory?"

"Mention that to him. It'll prove who I am. No one else calls him that." McCarter touched her arm. "It's important, love."

"Okay." The nurse relented.

"So you'll ask him?"

"Only if you stay right here."

"Word of honor, Sister Jenny."

McCarter watched her as she crossed the room, pushed through the double doors and vanished down the corridor. She made the nurse's uniform look good on her trim, shapely figure. If anything could make Henning sit up and take notice it would be Sister Jenny.

Fifteen minutes later she returned. McCarter was sitting one of the plastic visitor chairs, nursing a can of Coke he'd purchased from the vending machine. He glanced up when she appeared.

"How is he?"

"Weak. In considerable pain. But stubborn and determined. And set on sending you this message." She held out a sheet of notepaper. "He dictated it, I wrote it. He could barely speak, but he made me listen."

McCarter took the note and scanned the neat writing.

"Is it helpful?"

"It's certainly that, Jenny, my girl." McCarter grabbed her by her shoulders and laid a gentle kiss on her cheek. "Thanks."

HENNING'S NOTE TO McCarter was characterized by precise detail. The Briton could only marvel at Henning's ability to be so comprehensive in his current condition.

The mole was revealed to be Lewis Winch, an agent on Henning's team. Henning had found proof that Winch had been in contact with Samman Prem at the man's London office. Winch's operational position at the counterterrorism unit would have given him the opportunity to know about U.S. and U.K. personnel who were victims in the recent wave of assassinations and the Peshawar bombing.

The note also detailed Winch's home address in London.

Henning had signed the note "Gregory."

McCarter called ahead. By the time he reached the hotel, James and Hawkins were waiting. They climbed into the new rental and McCarter pulled back into the traffic. He had already fed Winch's address into the built-in sat-nav unit.

McCarter handed the note to James so he and Hawkins could read Henning's information.

"How is he?" James asked.

"Not too good right now," McCarter said, "but he'll survive. This bastard Winch shot him on his own doorstep. Luckily for Greg, the bugger didn't check his work." McCarter muttered something under his breath, then said, "Next to sneaky buggers I hate amateurs."

"Do we know if this Winch guy has backup?" Hawkins asked.

"Let's assume he does," McCarter said.

"Way you said that I take it you *hope* he does," James said.

McCarter glanced at him, his face taut. "Is it a problem?"

James shook his head. "No. You shouldn't need to ask, David."

McCarter let out a hard breath. "No, I shouldn't. It's been a hell of a night."

Winch lived in southwest London in, an older house standing back off the residential street. The frontage was studded with trees and hedges, with a short driveway leading up to the front door. A couple cars were parked in the drive. McCarter drove by, circled and turned back. He parked four houses short of Winch's.

"Lights on all floors," James said. "He's got guests or he's nervous. You want us to go around back? Come in from the rear?"

"Yeah," McCarter said. "Put phones on vibrate and give me a call when you're in position."

Once out of the car, they moved along the sidewalk, James and Hawkins slipping out of sight along the low dividing wall at the side of the house next to Winch's, leaving McCarter to his frontal approach.

The two agents pushed their way through thick hedges running the length of the house, trying to ignore the fine spray of rain that flicked off the vegetation as they disturbed it. They were glad they had decided to don waterproof topcoats from the car.

"Hold it," James said, pressing a hand to Hawkins's shoulder.

"Company?"

"Yeah." Light from the rear of the house cast a semicircle of illumination across the lawn, and James had spotted the dark-clad figure pacing back and forth. "And that isn't a garden tool he's toting."

In fact the man, clad in a bulky weatherproof jacket, was carrying a squat SMG.

Hawkins peered across his partner's shoulder. "Looks like a suppressed MP-5," he said. "And here we are with nothing but our faithful 9 mm Berettas."

They wore the 92-F pistols, complete with suppressors, under their coats.

"Maybe this guy is part of the neighborhood watch," James said.

"Right," Hawkins said.

"We can't stand here all night. David will start paging us any minute."

"Let him know we're in position and he can start the show," Hawkins suggested. "If he makes some noise it might draw that guy toward the house."

James took out his cell and tapped the speed dial for McCarter's phone. "Hey, David, in position. Only we have a guy armed with an MP-5 blocking our way in."

After James disconnected, Hawkins asked, "What did he say?"

"'Watch and learn,'" James answered.

McCarter pocketed his cell, took out his suppressed Browning Hi-Power and went up the steps. He scanned the door, assessing its makeup, and decided it wouldn't present all that much of a problem. He took a couple steps back, then launched himself, shoulder first, at the barrier. There was toned muscle under the Briton's coat. The impact broke the inner latch, sending the door wide open, smashing the glass panels inlaid in the upper section. McCarter followed on, the Browning held in both hands. The muzzle swept back and forth, searching the entrance hall.

An armed figure burst into view, attracted by the noise. The guy swept his SMG round to target the intruder. McCarter's Hi-Power fired twice. Nine millimeter slugs slammed into the guy's chest, over his heart, punching him back against the frame of the door he had just exited.

A figure moved at the head of the stairs ahead of McCarter. The Phoenix Force leader recognized him from the image Stony Man had sent.

"Winch, hold it right there," he yelled, raising his Browning.

"No chance," Winch said, and stepped to the side, vanishing behind the edge of wall.

McCarter went up the stairs fast, pulling out his cell and hitting speed dial.

"Don't hang about," he said into the phone. "It's going down now."

"LET'S MOVE, T.J.," James said, and stepped from cover, his Beretta raised.

The armed guard spotted the Phoenix Force warrior. To his credit he was fast to react, the MP-5 arcing around, his finger already stroking the trigger. A stream of suppressed 9 mm slugs went over James's head, taking chunks out of the brickwork. He felt slivers pepper the back of his neck.

"Down," Hawkins yelled. As the black Phoenix Force commando dropped to a crouch, Hawkins tracked in with his Beretta and hit the moving gunner with a trio of 9 mm slugs.

The man went down, hitting the rain-soaked lawn on his back, the MP-5 spilling from his hands.

"As David would say, nice one, mate," James said.

They moved quickly now, heading for French windows that stood partly open. The room beyond was dimly illuminated, but there was enough light to show James and Hawkins the armed figure approaching. The guy opened up with a stream of hissing 9 mm slugs that shattered glass and splintered wood in their faces….

CHAPTER SIX

McCarter reached the top of the stairs and swung to the right, where Winch had gone.

As he faced the corridor, a bulky figure launched itself in his direction. The guy was broad, with a shaved head and a thick mustache. He was not Lewis Winch. A short-bladed knife caught the light as he slashed at McCarter.

The Briton ducked under the sweeping blade, ramming his shoulder into the attacker's midsection. The guy grunted as he felt the force of the lunge. McCarter kept pushing, wanting to knock him off balance. The problem was his adversary was not just broad, he was solid and well muscled. And quick. His free arm swept down and chopped at McCarter's gun hand, knocking it aside. McCarter blocked the next swing of the knife, curling his own fingers around the man's thick wrist and forcing the blade away from his body. They held each other motionless for seconds, each attempting to gain control.

McCarter had no intention of allowing the stalemate to continue. He had no time for delay. Every second wasted gave Winch more of an opportunity to evade capture. There was no way the Briton would allow that to happen.

He let go of his pistol, turned his body toward his opponent, brought up his right arm and executed a swift hip throw. The guy left the floor, a startled cry bursting from his lips as he was slammed down on his back. McCarter followed through, levering the man's knife arm across his thigh until he heard bone crack. The knife slipped from his opponent's fingers and McCarter scooped it up, half turned and sliced the blade across the exposed throat, cutting deep. Dropping the knife, he snatched up his Browning and sprinted along the corridor in pursuit of Winch.

Ahead of McCarter a door was swinging shut. The Briton reached it and booted it open, plunging through with a reckless disregard for his own safety. In the split second it took to cross the threshold, he saw he was entering a study all tricked out with computers and terminals. Winch was at a wide, curving desk, reaching for a phone, his finger already pressing a speed dial number. The security agent threw a startled glance over his shoulder and saw McCarter charging across the room like a runaway locomotive.

McCarter hit Winch head-on, spinning the traitor along the side of the desk, arms and legs windmilling. Winch tried to club him with his autopistol, but McCarter twisted his upper body and the blow missed. There was no restraint in McCarter's punch as his left first connected with Winch's jaw. The blow crunched home with a solid sound, the force knocking the man to the floor. He landed hard, losing his grip on the pistol, and watched it bounced out of reach across the carpet. Winch rolled, scrabbling his way in the direction of the fallen weapon. McCarter gave him no chance. He tossed his Browning on the desk, reached down and grabbed Winch by his jacket, then hauled him upright. Winch's bleeding mouth spurted even more blood as McCarter drove him across the room with his pounding fists, until he slammed into the wall.

"You can't do this," Winch yelled. "Breaking into someone's home and—"

"Oh, that's right," McCarter said. "I should have waited until you were on your doorstep and then shot you. That the way you bastards do it around here?"

Realization gleamed in the security agent's eyes. He spit blood, sucking in air through his battered nose. "I should have guessed. You're one of those fucks Henning sent out to look over Prem's place. Much good it's done him. At least they can say he died doing his duty to queen and country."

"Wrong there, sunshine. You might be a smart snitch, but as a hit man you failed the test. Henning is still alive. And under so much protection even the queen couldn't get in to see him."

"You're lying."

"You should have stayed around to make sure he was dead. You're a bloody amateur, Winch. Admittedly a creepy one, but just an amateur."

Winch uttered an enraged cry. He dropped his right hand into his pocket, jerked it back out, showing the butterfly knife he held. His hand and wrist flicked in a controlled action and the naked blade sprang into view, locking in place.

McCarter stayed exactly where he was, no flicker of emotion crossing his face.

"Is this where I'm supposed to be scared to death? Isn't going to work, chum. Come ahead if you think you can carve me up with that little boy's knife."

White lines formed at the corners of Winch's taut mouth. "I'll show you," he said, his voice rising.

McCarter saw the bunching of muscles under Winch's shirt, then the slight lean forward before he launched himself. The man was no knife fighter; the way he rushed McCarter showed his lack of expertise. Also his absence of judgment. His headlong lunge might as well have been in slow motion, since every scrap of movement was telegraphed to McCarter. The Phoenix Force commander held his position until the last moment, then turned his lean body, right hand snapping around to grasp Winch's wrist. McCarter slid his left arm under Winch's just below the elbow joint. He bore down on the wrist, heaved up with his left arm and snapped the forearm bone. Winch screamed in a high falsetto as the jagged end of the broken bone tore through the flesh, gleaming white against the bloody flesh. McCarter dragged him forward, turning him, and slammed Winch facefirst into the wall. The brutal impact crushed his nose and split his cheek. Winch slumped to his knees, sobbing in agony, hugging his ruined arm. Blood coursed down his face. The butterfly knife was on the floor beside him. McCarter snatched it up and closed it. He hadn't even broken a sweat.

"The thought that you turned on Henning pisses me off," the Phoenix Force commander said. "I really don't like people who do that to my mates."

"They'll get you. Get you all," Winch rasped through clenched teeth. "You won't stop…Prem…or Rahman…."

"One thing for sure, mate, you won't be around to see it either way." McCarter raised his right leg and slammed his foot into the back of his opponent's neck. Winch's spine was severed by the blow, the force driving his face into the wall with a sodden crunch. His body arched and then slumped to the floor, all resistance vanishing in death.

"That was for Gregory," McCarter muttered.

Where Winch's jacket had fallen open, McCarter saw the bloodstain over his ribs, the shirt torn where a bullet had cleaved his side. Henning had clipped him for sure.

"Good one, mate," McCarter said.

T. J. HAWKINS DROPPED AND rolled, his Beretta extended and tracking the silhouetted figure on the other side of the shattered French windows. His target had taken a step closer when Hawkins opened fire, hitting the chest and throat with half the contents of his Baretta's magazine. The guy fell back, jerking in spasms as his body took the full brunt of the 92-F's load.

"That was impressive," James remarked as he joined his partner. "You been watching those *Walker, Texas Ranger* reruns again?"

Hawkins stood, shaking off slivers of glass from his wet coat. "Humor me, man, I just experienced a personal trauma."

They cleared the room and, covering each other, made their way to the hall, where they found the front door wide open and a body on the floor. James closed the door. The inner latch had been torn from its housing, so he secured the panal using the bolts fixed to top and bottom.

They heard sounds from above and went up the stairs. On the landing was another body, throat sliced open and a large patch of spreading blood.

"He's up here," James said.

They made their way to the one open door and saw McCarter checking out a telephone on the big desk that dominated the room. A still, bloody figure lay slumped against one wall.

"David?" James said.

McCarter glance over his shoulder at the pair. "The cyber team would have a bloody field day with all this computer hardware," he stated. "We need to open it up and let Aaron download the hard drives."

"He can gain access with one of his little programs," Hawkins agreed. He crossed to the desk and took a look at the electronic setup. "I can connect with Stony Man and let him in."

"Do it," McCarter said. "I don't want to hang around here too long. Cal, let's run a quick check on this place."

HAWKINS CALLED STONY MAN and spoke to Akira Tokaido. The young cyber expert took him through the process necessary to access the computer system. Hawkins watched as the monitor screen responded to the hack program that quickly inserted itself into Winch's hard drives, sucking out the data stored there.

"We can strip search his files. He may have deleted stuff, but once I sit down with this data I can find out all his little secrets," Akira said confidently.

McCarter and James were back in the room. The Briton said, "If I get the chance I'll tell Hal you should get a big raise."

"You just did tell Hal," Brognola said over the connection, "and no, he can't have a raise. He's getting too much as it is."

"Have you been monitoring our calls?" McCarter asked in an aggrieved tone.

"Yeah. How do you think I always know what you guys are up to?"

"Sneaky boss," McCarter said.

"Aren't I just." Brognola's gruff tones segued into a chuckle. "So what's the situation?"

"Greg Henning is in hospital recovering from bullet wounds. He gave me a heads-up on the mole in his department, and soon after was ambushed outside his own home. The shooter screwed up and Greg survived. Even got a look at the bastard and passed the guy's name to me."

"And you went looking for him?"

"Damn right. Turns out this bloke didn't want to come quietly. He even had an armed and hostile home-protection team waiting. But his days as a mole are over for good. As you heard, we gave Akira access to Winch's computer setup so he can check out the bugger's data."

"All right. Call in if you need anything."

"You got an update on the others?"

"Nothing current. Don't you guys do anything crazy."

McCarter laughed. "As if we would."

McCarter and James had found substantial amounts of cash hidden in Winch's bedroom. Thick rolls of banknotes were concealed in socks at the back of a drawer. There were U.K. pounds and U.S. dollars. Also Euros.

"Man, this guy wasn't exactly subtle," James said.

"Looks like handy cash," McCarter said. "On tap for emergency payouts."

They had also located a slim attaché case under the king-size bed. Inside, along with a number of preloaded magazines, was a 9 mm autopistol and suppressor. McCarter didn't touch the weapon. When they returned to the office, he placed the open case on the desk.

James leaned over to sniff the barrel. "Been fired very recently."

"Bet you a roll of those notes this is the gun he used on Greg."

"I told you last time I'm never betting with you again," James said. "You cheat."

McCarter looked suitably aggrieved. "That is a terrible thing to say to a man who has hauled your arse out of the fire on countless occasions."

The Briton's expression was so forlorn that James was unable to hold back a burst of laughter.

"Guys," Hawkins said, "we're done here. Akira has pulled everything off this computer. He's going to get the team to analyze the stuff, and they'll come back to us with any results."

McCarter used his sat phone to speak with Brognola again.

"We're getting out now. Give us a half hour, then put in an anonymous call to Greg's department. Give them

Winch's address and tell them they can find the gun that was used to shoot Greg Henning. Tell them about the cash and advise them they no longer have a leak in the department. Suggest they check out the identities of the dead hardmen Winch was using as bodyguards. Damn sure they won't be upstanding citizens."

"Leave that with me," Brognola said. "You going back to your hotel?"

"Something we have to do first. Then we can take it easy."

"I'm not even going to ask," he muttered.

"Oh, you'll hear about it soon enough," McCarter said.

"If this Winch guy turns out to be the one responsible for orchestrating the Pakistan killings and the ones in Washington and London, the President will be happy," Brognola said.

"Get him to up our expenses," McCarter said, "and I'll be happy, as well."

Brognola ignored the remark. "We still have the bomb threats."

"Don't think we've forgotten that. Once we clear things up here we'll head out to join Gary and Rafe. Sooner we team up again the better I'll like it. We need to pin down these threats pronto."

"I JUST KNEW WE WERE going to end up here," James said.

"Is that a problem?"

"No, just an observation."

"Let's get this done," McCarter said.

They climbed out of the rental and crossed the street, gathering outside Samman Prem's London office building.

"You think he's home?" Hawkins asked.

"Let's find out. T.J., you want the back door?"

"Front, back, all the same to me." Hawkins moved down the alley at the side of the building.

"What do think, Cal? Shall we make an unannounced call?"

"Isn't the first and it won't be the last."

The building's main entrance featured a pair of wooden doors with inset glass panels. James tried the handle, pushed. The doors gave but didn't open. He tried his shoulder with the same result.

"It's been a crap day, evening, and it's bloody raining," McCarter said.

He took a step back, raised his right foot and slammed it against the doors at lock level. Something cracked. McCarter repeated the action and this time the doors parted and swung open.

"It's just technique, James, old son."

They went through, pistols in their hands, and crossed the entrance foyer.

"I think someone heard," James said.

They strode along a corridor that had wood-paneled walls and hard tiles on the floor. The decor was years old.

The SMG in the hands of the man who burst into view from a hastily opened door was far from ancient.

He saw McCarter and James and opened fire instantly. He had a slack grip on the front of the SMG and the rise in the muzzle took the 9 mm slugs over McCarter and James as they dropped to the tiled floor.

McCarter's Browning Hi-Power snapped out a pair of accurately placed 9 mm slugs that targeted one of the shooter's legs. He gave a howl of agony as his wounded limb collapsed under him, tipping him to the floor, where he lay moaning, clutching his shattered leg and bleeding across the tiles.

"Gun," James yelled as he spotted a barrel pushing into

view from the open door. He rose up onto one knee and drew down with his Beretta. As the man carrying the SMG showed himself, James triggered two fast shots that ripped into his right shoulder, breaking bone. The guy squealed, dropping the weapon and clutching at his bleeding shoulder.

McCarter went in through the open door, to discover a large office.

And also Samman Prem and Saeeda Hussein.

The pair were moving to the rear of the room, toward a door set in the extreme corner.

"Don't even try," McCarter warned.

Prem raised his hands in a gesture of surrender.

Saeeda Hussein kept moving, intent on reaching the exit.

"Give it up, Hussein," McCarter yelled.

The man stopped, started to turn. His hands began to drop to his sides. His right hand diverted, slipping under his jacket, only to reappear curled around the butt of a squat autopistol. His expression was hateful.

A burst of protest in his own tongue exploded from his lips as he leveled the pistol, finger already pressing against the trigger.

McCarter fired, James a second later. Hussein skittered back against the door he wanted to escape through, sliding to the floor. The front of his shirt began to show blood from the bullet wounds in his chest.

Samman Prem stared at the crumpled form, his face stiff with shock, his eyes wide. He was shaking, his entire body reacting to what he had just seen, and a spreading wet patch on the front of his pants defined his condition.

"You guys okay?" Hawkins asked as he appeared in the doorway. "Nothing out the back except a pile of trash."

McCarter holstered his Hi-Power. "We've got plenty of that in here," he said. "Isn't that right, *Mr.* Prem?"

Prem's previous arrogance had vanished, leaving a scared little man in an expensive suit. He visibly cowered when McCarter stood over him. "You are going to kill me. Please do not hurt me."

"We're not going to do that, Prem, but you might wish it had happened by the time all this is over. You made a big mistake when you sent those idiots after us in that car. One's dead, the others are locked up in a police cell. And the car they were in belongs to your company."

"Winch fingered you and Rahman," James added, not revealing Winch was dead.

Prem shook his head. "This was not supposed to happen." He raised his head and said to McCarter, "My solicitors will help me." He almost smiled. "I will be out on the street in the morning."

"The Met think otherwise, Prem. They don't take it kindly when one of their own is gunned down. This gives them the chance to dig very deep into your affairs, and dig they will. I have a feeling you will find yourself locked away for a long time while they build a case around your terrorist activities."

"You cannot prove anything."

McCarter smiled and crossed to the far side of the office. He took out his sat phone and made a call.

"Fantastic what they can do tracking phone accounts, pulling up call lists," James said. "CCTV cameras on the streets record comings and goings. How will you explain away Lewis Winch visiting you here? It's all going to add up. Your association with Hussein and what you've been sending out on his ships."

Prem looked at the three Phoenix Force men, fast realizing that this time his high-priced London lawyers were going to struggle earning their ridiculously expensive fees.

"The counterterrorism squad is on its way, Prem. No Lewis Winch to bail you out this time. And by the way, your office is closed for business."

"In good old, plain English, buddy," Hawkins said, "you be screwed."

Two hours later the Phoenix Force trio was on its way back the hotel. Investigators were still stripping Prem's office building as they gathered information. His computers, cell phones and anything that might yield data were being confiscated. Samman Prem had already been whisked away to a holding suite in the building, and when he had demanded he be allowed to speak to his lawyer, all he received was a flat refusal from the head officer.

"Not in the public interest to allow that to happen," the agent said.

Prem was handcuffed and led away.

"Can you do that?" James had asked. "Is it legal?"

The agent smiled. "How the bloody hell would I know?" he said. "I just made it up on the spot."

McCarter had slapped the man on his shoulder. "Gregory would love that. Oops, I meant Agent Henning."

SETTLED IN AT THE HOTEL, McCarter called up Stony Man and spoke briefly to Barbara Price. "Fix us up with a flight to Pakistan, love," he said. "But not too early. We need a good night's sleep before we go trekking in the hills."

"Stony Air will do its best to bring you a comfortable flight, sir," she said in a rich, plummy voice. "If I was there in London I would make sure you were all tucked in safe and sound."

"Now that isn't fair," McCarter said. "I'll be dreaming about that all night."

He heard Price's throaty chuckle just before the phone was taken from her hand and Brognola's gruff tones shattered any illusions he was having.

"Okay, sonny, wet dream over."

"Perish the thought, boss. Did we do good?"

"Apart from skimming through U.K. procedures, using firearms contrary to the law and creating a fair amount of mayhem, I think we can say yes. The Met is unofficially delighted now they have Prem in their grasp, even though it's the thin end of the wedge. Getting their hands on his electronic files is something they've been struggling to achieve. It's going to take them a hell of a time to unravel everything, but they will. What they've already managed to unearth is spilling out names and locations regarding extremist cells in the U.K. The guys in the car that tailed you are just low-rent thugs, so something may come from them. Latest update says Henning is making a slow recovery. He'll be out of action for some time but he'll make it."

"That's good to hear."

Brognola coughed. "A message sent via Sister Jenny says to warn you Henning is after your blood. Apparently you let it slip about his name. *Gregory?* What's that all about, David?"

"Just a private joke," McCarter said.

"Well, Henning is so pissed he isn't going to invite you along on his first date with Sister Jenny."

"Good for Greg. I knew he'd crack it."

"I don't get all this English stuff," Hal grumbled.

"I'll explain when we get back from Pakistan."

"Watch your backs out there," Brognola said. "Rough country."

"Will do, boss."

CHAPTER SEVEN

"They weren't joking when they said it got cold come nighttime," Manning commented.

"If the local Taliban chapter finds out we're here it will get hot," Encizo said.

"Thanks for that morale-boosting little homily, partner."

"Hey, anytime, hombre."

Manning checked his watch. "Our guy should be here by now."

"Gary, this is border country here. No taxi service on tap. He's only forty minutes over."

"Thirty-nine minutes too long," Manning said.

Encizo removed the GPS unit from his attaché case and scanned the readout. "We're still on location. If our ride doesn't show up the only other thing we can do is thumb a lift, but there's no way I'm pulling up my pants and showing a leg."

Manning had stood up and was staring along the moonlit landscape. He had spotted dim headlights moving along the road. As the vehicle neared their position it began to slow, then flashed its lights.

"Let's go," Manning said.

They cleared the brush and headed for the dusty strip of the road, both Phoenix Force warriors resting their hands on the butts of their handguns.

The car was a Citroën that had seen better days, but at

least the motor purred quietly. The driver's door opened and a tall, fair-haired man stepped out to meet them.

"Mr. Allen. Mr. Constantine," he said, holding out a lean hand.

"Roy Bannister?" Manning said.

"No." The man backed up. "Who the bloody hell is Roy Bannister?"

"Not the man we're supposed to meet, Steve Hutchins."

The man held his position for a moment, studying the Phoenix pair. "You checking *me* out?"

"Let's say we're a long way from home if we make a mistake."

Hutchins relaxed, a grin lighting up his face. "Bloody security," he said, his British accent coming through stronger now. "Tell me, what would have happened if I had been one of the bad guys?"

Manning and Encizo eased their coats aside to expose the holstered autopistols on their hips. Hutchings took a considered look, nodding his head in acknowledgment.

"Serves me right for asking." He glanced around, then suggested, "Time we got out of here. Not the most friendly part of the country."

He opened the trunk so Manning and Encizo could place their luggage inside. Encizo took the wide rear seat, Manning taking the passenger seat next to Hutchins, who drove off, working his way through the gears.

"Anything you can tell us about the situation?" Manning asked.

"The *situation*, as you call it," Hutchins said, "is about as fluid as you can get. Since that first bomb blast in the Sarafa bazaar, intelligence and security has been all over the place. Look, you blokes must know the situation regarding agencies. We're all supposed to be working together to deal with terrorism. CIA, MI-5, MI-6, Pakistani intelligence. Lord knows who else. I guess I don't have to tell you what a crock that is. No one wants to give too much away to other agencies. There are territorial issues. Interdepartment rivalries. You name it, we've got it. So right now it's a lot of strands all tangled up, and no one knows where the end is."

"You were told why we're here?" Manning asked.

Hutchins nodded. "More or less on a need-to-know. My instructions are to pick you up and run you to your hotel in Peshawar. Rooms have been booked in your names. I assume you have all the necessary paperwork?"

"Yes," Encizo said. "Current visas and stamped passports all arranged by our people via the U.S. Justice Department."

"Our cover is that we work for the New Relief charity that was bombed," Manning said. "Our task is to simply assess the situation with regard to the organization. Pretty low-key, which is how we want to handle it unless circumstances change."

"But you're armed?"

Manning nodded. "Just handguns. That a problem?"

"Not for me," Hutchins said. "But if you are found with weapons it could quickly become a problem. The local cops are a nervous lot. They don't approve of foreigners with guns. They can be extremely volatile. Shoot-first policy, so be bloody careful."

"Thanks for the warning," Encizo said. "We'll try and stay out of the way of Peshawar's finest."

"You do understand we can't give away much detail about our mission?" Manning said. "We're working on information received that implies a possible threat against the U.S. and Pakistan."

"That much I do know," Hutchins said. "I was given my instructions via London, so I guessed this must be a matter sanctioned by both our governments. Look, I'm not going to embarrass you by asking too many questions. Just to let you know I'm here to offer whatever assistance I can."

"We appreciate that, Steve," Manning said. "I take it you've been here for some time?"

"Almost two years."

"You happy with that?" Encizo asked.

"Times when I wish I was back home, but this is still an interesting place. It can be hairy at times. Bombs and bullets. Intriguing."

"What do you think about Colonel Rahman?" Manning asked.

"He's powerful. Has the ear of a lot of influential people. The man is untouchable. He'd like nothing better than to oust the current president and take over. Believe me, he's very dangerous. An extremely duplicitous man. If I was in the same room I would not turn my back on him."

"Sounds as if you don't trust him," Encizo said.

"The man plays politics like it's a game—a game that uses other people as pawns. Rahman has extreme notions. He makes it clear he doesn't like the U.K. or the U.S. He condemns any and all Western concepts. Treats people as if they were dirt underfoot. He works the Pakistani citizenry with fiery speeches. Gets then worked up into a frenzy. Then he'll turn up at some government benefit and charm everyone there, including guests from the very countries he castigates."

"Doesn't that make you uncomfortable?" Manning asked. "Having to live and work here?"

"All part of the job. I was told from day one this assignment has its risks." Hutchins laughed out loud. "A polite way of saying I could get my head blown off. Still, it's a little less boring than sitting behind a desk back in London."

"I know what you mean," Encizo said.

"Sit back and take it easy," Hutchins advised. "We should arrive at the hotel in time for breakfast."

HUTCHINS WAS AS GOOD as his word. It was just after 8:00 a.m. when he pulled onto the hotel forecourt. He led the way inside and the Phoenix Force operatives checked in. The desk clerk, a slim young man, handed over their room key cards.

"I wish your reason for coming here was not so sad," he said. "It was a terrible thing that happened to your people."

"We live in difficult times." Manning said.

"But so cruel when your people were here only to offer help to others less fortunate. I hope you do not believe we are all like those murderers."

"Not at all," Hutchins said. "Now I will go to the restaurant and arrange breakfast for our guests."

"We'll join you in a few minutes," Encizo told him.

A porter in white carried their bags up to their rooms. After freshening up, Manning and Encizo made their way back downstairs and found the restaurant. The ornate room, with ceiling fans turning slowly overhead, was half-full. Hutchins beckoned to them and they joined him.

"My mother always told me breakfast was the most important meal of the day," he said. "So, can I tempt you?"

"Why not," Manning said.

THE RENTAL CAR WAS a year-old Toyota. Manning drove, Encizo at his side. The hotel was no more than a couple of miles from the site of the bombing. The offices of the New Relief charity organization were in a relatively old part of Peshawar. Manning had to drive slowly along the crowded, dusty street, finally stopping just short of the wrecked building. He and Encizo sat looking the place over. Little had been done to repair the damage, which was substantial.

"They were serious," Encizo said. "That must have been some blast."

Buildings on either side of the bombed offices had taken hits, as well. There were cracks in walls and some windows were still missing glass.

"Reports said this explosion was simply an example. A warning."

"More than twenty dead and thirty wounded," Manning reminded his partner. "They made their point."

They exited the car, Manning locking it. Crossing the street, they feigned interest in the demolished building. Encizo took out a slim digital camera and began to shoot photos. While he did that Manning carefully watched to see if anyone was observing them. The Canadian scanned the crowded street surreptitiously. Part of the Phoenix pair's strategy was to attempt to draw interest in their presence. The information they had to go on was thin. They had names and little else, so drawing attention to themselves might promote some kind of reaction. It wasn't much to go on, but there were times when a gamble paid off.

Manning led the way around to the rear of the buildings. The back wall of the charity offices had been breached, the brick and concrete split and shattered. The back lot was an untidy section of land overrun with trash and abandoned crates and barrels.

Encizo kept on taking pictures while Manning poked around among the trash, still observing.

He was not surprised when a slight man appeared, dressed in a white suit and crisp shirt and tie. Manning had spotted him watching them while they were out on the street. He stood at the back corner of the buildings now, the white Panama hat he had been wearing in one hand, while the other held a cotton handkerchief he was using to wipe his forehead. His brown skin gleamed with sweat as he moved in their direction.

"Company," Manning said quietly. He stepped forward to intercept him.

"May I ask who you are?" the man asked. His English was perfect, overlaid with a Pakistani accent. He finished wiping his face and replaced the Panama with a quick movement of his left hand. The handkerchief was pushed into his jacket pocket. "Who gave you permission to take pictures?"

The tone of his voice indicated he was used to being in charge and deferred to by those he challenged.

"I apologize if we are out of line, Mr....?"

"Jahil Karim. I represent the local community on behalf of the authorities."

"My name is Allen," Manning said. "Samuel Allen. And this is Mr. Fredo Constantine." He took a card, prepared by Stony Man, from his inside pocket. "We are from the board of the New Relief charity. Our organization sent us to look the site over and submit a report for our insurance concerning rebuilding the offices."

Encizo smiled. "I hope that creates no problem. Since our people were killed in the explosion there has been some confusion and a breakdown in communication. We spent the last few days in Islamabad at our headquarters. Our charity is hoping to set up other offices in your country. Three days ago we received a telephone call from back home, instructing us to make the trip here."

"Perhaps that is why I was not informed," Karim said. He hesitated. "But surely the site has been visited already by American officials. Why would you need to look again?"

"Mr. Karim, I'm sure you are familiar with the way organizations work. These days we need reports in duplicate. One for this department, another for someone else. As tedious as it becomes, we are slaves to the needs of others. There has been some problem in negotiations with the charity's insurance company, so we need to resubmit a damage summary for the claims adjuster."

"We will be gone in a few minutes, Mr. Karim," Encizo said, using his disarming smile again.

"We will, of course, be available if you need to speak with us again, sir," Manning added. "We are staying at the Pearl Continental while we are in Peshawar. You are welcome to contact us there."

Karin stood watching as Manning and Encizo returned to their supposed inspection of the building, talking to each other and pointing out details. The Pakistani official was unsettled by the presence of the two Americans. Karim had an extremely suspicious nature. It suited his work. The information he had given the two Americans was far from the truth. He worked for Colonel Jabir Rahman as a security agent.

Karim's presence at the bomb site was no accident. Ever since the charity was bombed, under orders from Rahman, Jahil Karim spent much of his time in the vicinity. His standing orders were to observe and report—in fact he had to submit a written report on everything he saw and heard every two days, to update the colonel.

Rahman, for all his power and authority, had a slight case of paranoia. The destruction of the charity building, which had become identified as a listening post for the CIA, was part of Rahman's scheme to upset the Americans. The bombing would make them aware that as powerful as they were, they could be attacked. The bomb in the building and the assassination of operatives in Pakistan, London and even America had been orchestrated to unsettle the U.S. authorities prior to the even larger attacks Rahman was planning. He hoped it might distract them from the bigger picture.

Yet despite his triumph with the initial phase, Rahman still worried about U.S. reactions. His thinking was that if there was any follow-up, it was in his best interest to be aware. So Karim was to watch out for any suspicious individuals and pass along such information to his leader.

Karim's self-importance grew with the mission. He was not well-liked within the ranks of his profession, being such a sycophantic character. Totally dedicated to Rahman, whom he had elevated to godlike stature, Karim was on a high when he was working for the colonel on a special assignment. It was suspected, but not proved, that he had turned in a couple of former agents, who were accused of being traitors. Both men had later been found dead. They had been brutally tortured before having their hands wired behind their backs, and being shot in the head. Their naked bodies had been dumped at night in the middle of a main street, so they could be seen by everyone who walked by the following morning.

In private, Karim had been thanked, personally, by Rahman. He was promoted as the colonel's covert watcher and listener. Karim became very good at his job.

"IT IS KARIM. Two Americans are staying at the Pearl Continental. Under the names of Constantine and Allen. They say they are here to make a report on the New Relief charity building bombing."

"You do not believe them?"

"They do not seem the type to work for such an enterprise. Something about them is out of place. Charity workers do not carry themselves with such confidence. As the Americans would say, these are *hardmen*."

"CIA looking into Crawford's death?" Rahman suggested. "The Agency would like to find out who killed him and the others. Just as I suspected they might. It appears, Karim, that our observations are proving correct."

"Something tells me these are not CIA. Maybe they are from one of the American Special Forces units the President has allowed to operate inside our border. Shall I observe in case they make contact with anyone?"

"No, we cannot risk that. Can't take the chance they might speak to someone with a sympathetic ear. Karim, I am not foolish or arrogant enough to believe everyone favors my ambitions. There are those who would be delighted to gain evidence of what we are planning. So we must not allow those bastards to have the opportunity of turning us in. We must do what is necessary to protect ourselves."

"Then we should kill them immediately. I will arrange it personally, Colonel."

Rahman might have agreed with Karim's solution, but his flesh crawled at the man's slavish emphasis over the pronouncement. He had always suspected Karim's devotion to violent acts, which he carried out with too obvious pleasure.

"Yes, Karim. But get them out of the city before you do anything. We do not need witnesses. Karim, do you know what *discretion* means?"

There was a slight, thoughtful hesitation before he said, "Yes, Colonel."

"Then employ it, Karim, please."

CHAPTER EIGHT

Manning and Encizo were back in the vicinity of the bombing the following day, speaking to anyone willing to be seen with Americans. Many of the Pakistanis refused to come close to the Phoenix Force pair, moving away when approached. There were others who behaved differently. The number of Pakistanis who spoke English was surprisingly high. Some talked openly about their suspicions and the connection between the bombing and anti-U.S. sentiment. Rahman's name came up a couple times, and Manning and Encizo got the feeling the man was not entirely popular. Reading into the conversations, they realized Colonel Rahman might easily be the power behind the recent attacks. There were no outright accusations, just hints, and a suggestion that Rahman was not a man to be trusted. It was obvious that no one wanted to be linked to any disparaging remarks about the man. It was made clear to Manning and Encizo that Jabir Rahman wielded great power and influence. He was not a man to be crossed.

By midday the Phoenix Force pair had the feeling there was little else they could learn. The day was stifling, the heat oppressive, the air dusty.

"I don't see that we're going to find out much more," Encizo said. "All I want now is to get back to the hotel, have a shower and sit down with a cold drink."

"I'll vote for that," Manning agreed.

"The more I hear about this Rahman, the less I like him," Encizo said.

"Not like you to make snap decisions about someone you haven't even met." Manning grinned as they headed back to where they had left their car.

"I have my moments," the Cuban said.

A figure materialized out of the shadows of the building near where the car stood. The lean figure was dressed in an off-white suit, his black hair hanging to the frayed collar of his jacket. His brown skin showed a sheen of sweat.

"May I speak with you?" he asked. The man looked nervous, plucking at his skinny neck with bony fingers.

"Go ahead," Manning said.

"I hear you are asking questions about the bombing. I believe I can be of service." Now he was pulling at the collar of his wrinkled shirt, his eyes flicking back and forth.

"This going to cost us?" asked the ever cynical Encizo.

"That would be for you to decide," the nervous guy said.

"You have some information we might be interested in?" Manning said. "I'm listening."

The man stepped away from the Phoenix pair. "Not here on the street. There are too many eyes and ears." He gestured behind him, to the open door of a store displaying locally made baskets. "We can go through to the rear and talk out of sight."

Manning glanced at Encizo. He understood his partner's questioning expression.

A trap?

An excuse to get them in an awkward situation?

Or a genuine offer made by a man who needed to protect himself?

Manning eased his jacket aside and placed his hand on the Beretta in its hip holster. Although he didn't show the weapon, it was clear he intended to be ready. Without looking, the Canadian knew Encizo would have done the same.

The Pakistani noticed the gestures and nodded nervously. "You are cautious. I understand."

"Understand who stands to lose if things go wrong," Manning said. "Now get moving, *friend*."

As they followed the man into the cool interior of the basket store, Manning was telling himself that with every mission, seeking information brought with it risk. He and Encizo had entered the country illegally, which was a big risk on its own. They were wandering the streets of Peshawar carrying unauthorized weapons. Another risky maneuver. The man they were following to the rear of the store might have vital mission information. He could also be leading them into harm's way.

Manning's first two risk assessments were positive. Unfortunately, so was his third.

"I have good information about Colonel Rahman," the man said. "How he is involved in what has happened. But it must not go any further." He paused, turning around to face Manning and Encizo. "And of course it never will," he added, a knowing smile crossing his lean face.

Son of a bitch, Manning thought as realization hit. *We walked right into this.* His hand went for his autopistol.

"Mr. Allen. Mr. Constantine. Here we are once more."

Jahil Karim emerged from cover, a Glock 19 in his thin hand. From the opposite side of the storeroom a second man stepped into view, a 9 mm H&K MP-5 aimed at the Phoenix Force operatives. He was large and his shirt strained against the bulge of his thick shoulders.

"Please do not be so foolish. You would never manage it," Karim said.

Manning held his hands clear of his holstered weapon,

fully aware that any overt move could only lead to fatal results. He heard Encizo let out a hard breath of frustration.

"Ishmal, take their weapons," Karim said, and the nervous man became abruptly efficient. Showing a confident side, he quickly took the handguns from Manning and Encizo and dropped them into the pockets of his jacket.

"You have walked into something of great importance," Karim stated. "So important you must be removed before you learn anything that might jeopardize Colonel Rahman's operation."

"These guys are all the same," Manning said. "They can't help giving away names."

Karim's face darkened with an embarrassed flush. Then he shrugged. "No matter. You will carry that information to your graves. Once we have you out of town you are going to die."

They don't want to risk discovery by killing us here. Manning recognized a thin opportunity.

Ishmal pushed by the Canadian, deliberately driving his bony shoulder against him.

"Hey," Manning said, letting his anger build. As the man turned to stare at him, the Phoenix Force warrior launched his big right fist into his face. With considerable force it slammed into Ishmal's nose, cracking cartilage. He uttered a stunned cry, stepping back as blood started to gush from his collapsed nose. It streamed down his face and onto his white shirt and suit.

"I never did like sneaky buggers," Manning said, stepping back and holding up his hands in a show of compliance to Karim's pistol, which was still trained on him.

Karim held Manning's unflinching stare, then glanced at Ishmal, who was leaning against the wall as he tried vainly to stem the blood streaming from his crushed nose.

"Dhotar," he said to the hulking man wielding the MP-5,

"take those pistols from Ishmal. I do not think he will be joining us in the car."

He did as ordered, tucking the Berettas into the broad belt around his waist.

Karim spoke to Ishmal without taking his eyes off Manning and Encizo. "Go. To your home. Anywhere. Just out of sight." He addressed himself to Manning. "I understand your feelings toward Ishmal. Betrayal is not an experience many people accept. And he should not have been so careless. Your actions, however, will not affect what lies ahead." He gestured with the Glock. "Out through the door. Your ride is waiting."

With Dhotar behind, Manning and Encizo were escorted to the store's back lot. It was a dusty, weed-choked plot littered with all kinds of debris. A dusty SUV stood under the hot sun.

"You will climb onto the rear seat," Karim said.

"Maybe we'd rather go back to our hotel," Encizo said.

"Do as I say." Karim moved the Glock's muzzle to emphasis his request. "On behalf of my colonel—Jabir Rahman—I insist you join me for a ride."

"Isn't this a little extreme for tourist relations?" Manning asked.

"I would prefer to do this somewhere more private," Karim said. "But if you do not do as I tell you, I will kill you here."

"At least we get a choice," Encizo said.

The Phoenix pair climbed into the SUV as ordered. Dhotar covered them while Karim took the front passenger seat, then turned half around so he could keep his Glock on them. Then Dhotar settled himself behind the wheel, the MP-5 placed on the floor by his feet.

"Go," Karim ordered. "Get us out of the city."

"A guided tour," Manning said. "Very thoughtful, Karim."

The Pakistani scowled. "Why do you insist on this childish attitude?"

Manning shrugged. "Just my nature," he said. "Doesn't look like you people have a sense of humor. Must be miserable being so grim all the time. What do think, Fredo?"

"At the beck and call of someone like Rahman, wouldn't you be miserable?"

"Enough!" Karim shouted.

"Now you've gone and upset him," Manning said. "Maybe we should just sit back and admire the scenery."

"Mmm, I think you're right."

They lapsed into silence for a while. The road out of Peshawar took them north, in the direction of the border area. Manning and Encizo recognized it as the same road they had traveled coming into the city. Karim saw they had identified the road. He smiled.

"Yes," he said. "Where you came in. Your late friend Steve Hutchins was kind enough to tell me exactly how and where he met you."

If news of Hutchins's death was a shock, neither Phoenix Force warrior expressed it. It was enough they knew who was responsible. The fact had been noted and would be remembered.

"It took some time to extract the information," Karim said, warming to the subject. "Your infidel Englishman was not a man to suffer in silence. He screamed like a woman." The words came softly from Karim's lips, his eyes betraying his inner satisfaction as he recalled what he had done. "Was it not so, Dhotar?"

The driver nodded. "He almost tore the ropes holding him down."

Manning felt Encizo tense beside him as the Cuban listened to Karim. If only the Pakistani knew who he was talking to. Rafael Encizo had endured torture himself during his time in a Cuban prison. Anyone who had the temerity to gloat about inflicting torture on another human being would be marked in Encizo's book for future reference.

Fifty minutes later Dhotar eased his foot onto the SUV's brake, reducing speed.

"We are here," he said in English for the duo's benefit.

Looking out the windshield, the Phoenix Force pair saw a battered panel truck parked at an angle across the road. A group of armed figures was ranged along the length of the vehicle. One raised a hand in greeting when he recognized Karim.

"This is where you get out," Karim said. He failed to suppress a toothy grin. "Get out to die."

"No more choices?" Manning asked. "No? Why don't you go first."

From the front seat the driver, Dhotar, made an angry noise in his throat. "Let me shoot them here," he said.

He leaned forward and picked up the MP-5, flourishing the weapon in a dramatic fashion.

"Idiot," Karim snapped. "Be careful with that thing in here."

His reprimand annoyed Dhotar. "Do not speak to me like I am one of these infidel pigs."

For a second or two Karim and Dhotar allowed their concentration to wander as they glared at each other. It was a foolish mistake—and a fatal one.

Encizo leaned forward and snapped a powerful arm around Dhotar's neck. He applied pressure, hauling the Pakistani up off his seat. Dhotar began to choke as his air was cut off, struggling against the Cuban's grip. Encizo reached out with his free, right hand, taking hold of the MP-5. Dhotar had only a light grasp on it and when Encizo slid his finger inside the trigger guard and clasped the pistol grip he was able to snatch the weapon free. Continuing his motion, Encizo let go of the gasping Dhotar, leaned back to jam the MP-5's muzzle against the back of the driver's seat and pulled the trigger. The SMG snapped out a 3-round burst that drove a trio of 9 mm slugs into Dhotar's spine. The terrorist managed a hoarse cry as the bullets ripped through him, bursting out his chest in a bloody spray that spattered the windshield.

Encizo's unexpected move caught Karim off guard. As the Cuban triggered the MP-5, Manning made his own move. He took hold of Karim's gun arm, dragged him half over the seat, then twisted the man's wrist and bore down on it. The brawny Canadian possessed a great deal of strength. His unrestrained action snapped Karim's arm midway between elbow and wrist. The Pakistani screamed, the sound trailing away into a sob.

There was no resistance when Manning took the Glock out of Karim's limp hand, not when he reversed the weapon and clubbed him alongside his head. Manning repeated the blow a few times, and Karim sagged forward, blood streaming from his skull.

Reaching over the seat, Encizo retrieved the Berettas from Dhotar's belt, passing one to Manning. They holstered the weapons.

"That was the easy part," Encizo grumbled as he freed the rear door handle on his side. "We getting out or what?"

"Advisable," his partner agreed.

Seeing what had happened, the armed men lined up by the truck—five in all—moved in an uncoordinated run toward the 4x4. They opened fire, riddling the front of the SUV with bullets. As Encizo and Manning rolled out their individual doors, dropping to the road and scooting to the rear of the vehicle, they heard the solid thud of shots striking the SUV. The windshield shattered. A side mirror was blown off its mount, to clatter on the road.

Braced against the rear of the SUV, Encizo raised the MP-5 and took quick aim. The H&K, now on full auto, crackled as the Phoenix warrior opened fire. One of the hardmen went down kicking and screaming. The others scattered.

Manning leaned out, picking up one of the thugs as he veered to the Canadian's side of the road. Manning gripped the Glock two-handed, led the moving target, then triggered two fast shots at his target's chest. The man stumbled, lost his balance and plunged facedown.

One of the remaining thugs decided to make a run for the SUV, firing as he moved, fumbling a frag grenade from his coat as he came. He let his SMG hang from its strap as he pulled the pin and drew his arm back, ready to throw. His shirtfront blossomed with blood as Encizo rose from cover long enough to hit the attacker with a hard burst. The impact of the shots spun the man around, his legs losing coordination. He tumbled to the ground, still clutching the grenade, and it detonated just before he landed. The blast tore him apart, bloody debris erupting across the road. Steel splinters from the burst caught one of the remaining hardmen, tearing flesh from his thigh.

Before the opposition could recover, Encizo and Manning opened fire together, taking down the last of the attackers.

"You okay?" Manning asked, glancing at his partner.

Encizo nodded. He turned to check out the SUV and found both Dhotar and Karim dead. Both had been hit numerous times when their own men had riddled the vehicle.

"That was bloody," Manning said. "These guys really had it in for us."

"And we can thank a certain Colonel Rahman for that," Encizo said. "He wants us dead, buried and forgotten."

"Pleased to be able to disappoint him," Manning said. "No tolerance in that guy at all."

"Vehicle inbound," Encizo warned.

They watched a dusty, late-model Toyota 4x4 come barreling in their direction. It slowed as it neared the scene, braked and stopped. A tall, lean Pakistani climbed out and walked toward them. He wore a neat, dark suit. With black hair, and a trimmed mustache, he had the good looks that would have got him into a Bollywood movie. Both hands were held away from his body.

He stopped and took a long look around, then advanced until he was close to Manning and Encizo.

"You are Allen and Constantine." It was not a question.

"How did I figure you would know that?" Manning said.

"I also know that you are not charity workers," the man said. "And that you have caused Colonel Rahman some concern. Which is why he sent his pet dog after you. Where is Karim?"

"In the SUV," Encizo said. "Kind of dead."

"Karim is—was—Rahman's killing hand. You have done many people a favor by removing him."

"He was set to do the same with us," Encizo said.

The man nodded. "Rahman ordered your execution personally. I was in the room when he gave the order. I was delayed when I set out to follow you from Peshawar. But I see now you did not need my help."

Manning kept his pistol in sight. He still was not entirely sure he could trust this newcomer. "Don't be surprised if we take this slowly. Just who are you? What are you doing out here?"

"My name is Nasir Hanafi. Captain Hanafi. I am an agent in the ISI."

"Inter Services Intelligence?" Encizo said.

Hanafi nodded. "Yes. On active undercover duty in Colonel Rahman's covert group."

"Doing exactly what?" Manning asked.

"Gathering information on Rahman's organization. His illegal activities working with the Taliban and possibly al Qaeda."

"We take your word on that?" Encizo said.

Hanafi maintained his composure. "As I take your word you are representatives of the New Relief charity and not illegally working within Pakistan's borders on some unauthorized mission."

Encizo folded his arms across his chest, glancing at Manning. "I guess we hung ourselves out to dry with that story."

"You think?"

"Would it not be advisable for us to remove ourselves from this place while we discuss our relationship?" Hanafi said. He opened his jacket to reveal a holstered autopistol. "Here, take this as a gesture of goodwill." He removed the pistol and handed it to Manning. "Please, shall we go?"

Manning and Encizo took the rear seat. Hanafi started the engine and they drove away from the scene.

"Is there any particular location you wish to visit?"

Encizo glanced at his partner. Manning nodded.

"A rendezvous point," Manning said. "Just keep driving in the direction of the border for now."

He took out his sat phone and hit the speed dial number that would connect him with McCarter.

"You want to drop in," he said when the Phoenix Force leader came on the line, "make it ASAP. Things have kind of racked themselves up over here."

"You okay?"

"Yeah. Oh, don't bother with formal wear. I think we're going to need working clothes."

"What have you blokes been up to?"

"Tell you later. Just stay on your toes. We've got hostiles around."

"You don't say."

"Ask the chopper guys to drop you at the same location. We can be in the area in a couple of hours. Wait until dark. We'll link up."

"Try not to get bored while you wait," McCarter said.

"See you soon," Manning said, and cut the call.

He caught Hanafi watching him through the rearview mirror. "You have more men to come to you?"

"The rest of our team."

"This could turn out to be interesting," Hanafi said.

CHAPTER NINE

Nothing they carried indicated a U.S. origin. The clothing they changed into was unmarked and from foreign sources. Their weapons were the same. AK-47 rifles and Swiss-made combat knives. They carried their own handguns: 9 mm Berettas and McCarter's Browning Hi-Power. Grenades, both fragmentation and concussion, were non-U.S. They all carried Japanese-manufactured sat phones.

"If I was a suspicious character," Major Jessup observed, "I'd say this operation is so below the radar it's submarine."

McCarter grinned. "Pretty close, mate," he said. "To be truthful, we are not even here and you are talking to yourself."

"Could be my ticket out of here," Jessup said. "By reason of insanity."

"Major, we're all crazy anyhow," James stated.

"Can you insert us close to where you placed our other guys?" McCarter asked, leaning over the trestle table as he studied the map.

"All under way," Jessup said. He circled the designated area on the map. "That is one hot zone. You'll be inside Pakistan territory. Place is a shitload of trouble. Taliban use it to work their drug trade, so you'll have those bastards everywhere. It's a known area where Pakistani militants hang out. Radicals who don't like anyone walking across their turf. Not even their own regular military."

"So you've heard of Colonel Jabir Rahman?" McCarter asked.

Jessup spit in the dust. "You'd need to be deaf, dumb and blind not to have heard that name. Now I can't give credence to the scuttlebutt, since it comes from every source known to man, but the way it goes, Rahman runs his own little kingdom in this 'hood. The man is part soldier, part radical and all fucked up."

"The local lunatic," Hawkins said. "We always get the dingbats."

"Son," Jessup said, "this is one mean dirtbag. If he's anything to do with your mission I only have one suggestion. Get him in your crosshairs and take him down."

Jessup was around thirty-five, but he looked older. His combat fatigues hung loosely on his six-foot frame, and his face bore testimony to the stress and fatigue of being in a constant war zone, where the relentless grind never allowed Marines to lower their guard. Despite it, they fought on, true to their Marine code, and always to the betterment of the Corps.

"What's the situation regarding the security of this area?" McCarter asked.

"These people don't have much in the way of high-tech equipment. Pretty much a ragtag setup. Plenty of light ordnance but no electronic hardware. Hand-launched stuff. LAWs. RPG-7s. Our intelligence has tagged them as having supplies of U.S. light weapons that come in across the border. Nothing to worry about where wheeled vehicles are concerned. This isn't exactly the kind of terrain that welcomes ground vehicles. Not up in these hills. Mostly dirt track roads."

"You have much truck with them?" Hawkins asked.

"Thankfully, no. We stay on our side of the border. Hell, we have enough problems of our own with the Afghan Taliban and other nonfriendly's. Pakistan is not in our purview." Jessup paused. "Not yet, anyhow. They're supposed to be on our side right now. Unless you guys have any updates on that."

"No change as far as we understand," McCarter said. "Our mates are having some problems already. Sooner we link up the better."

"Yeah. No offense, fellers, but I'll be happy to see you go. We got our own priorities and this area is primed to go ballistic. Sooner I can off-load you, the better I'll feel."

"Understood," McCarter said. "Thanks for the hospitality, Major."

"Good luck with whatever you're here for. Hit the pickup alarm if you need lifting out. If we can accommodate we will. No guarantees."

McCarter reached out and shook Jessup's hand. "Thanks. Stay safe, Major. Semper fi."

The major moved out of the tent, leaving Phoenix Force to complete their preparations.

"Ever get the feeling you're out in the cold?" Manning said.

"Always," James grinned.

McCarter used his sat phone to check in with Stony Man, giving Barbara Price their current sit-rep.

"We'll be going in any minute," he finished up.

"God bless," Price said. "You all come back safe. That's an order."

"Yes, ma'am."

McCarter switched off. He connected the sat phone to one of the power points in the tent, leaving it there to fully charge before they left.

Standing outside, feeling the dry wind coming in off the high ground, he stared across the isolated American camp. The complement of U.S. Marines defending this dangerous ground faced daily threats from Taliban hostiles. Mortar bombardments were regular as clockwork. Sudden strikes by Taliban insurgents could come at any time. There was little relief for any of the men here. Under pressure 24/7, the combatants stood their ground and fought back when danger presented itself. McCarter had nothing but respect for these beleaguered young men, far from home and family, fighting an action that must at times seem pointless and without end. McCarter had served in the military. He understood the mind-set. The need to stay the course and give the enemy a hell of a fight.

"Man, they deserve the best," James said from where he had stepped up alongside the Briton. "Those boys really do."

"Amen to that, mate."

TWENTY MINUTES LATER the three-man Phoenix Force team was aboard the CH-46 helicopter as it went airborne. It was full dark, the night chill already dissipating the day's heat. The chopper flew in dark mode, the pilot working simply by his knowledge of the terrain and the display on his radar screen. The aircraft had a crew of three. Pilot and copilot. The third was the door gunner, manning a .50-caliber machine gun fixed to a door-mounted pintle. The gunner was a young Marine corporal from Corpus Christi, Texas. He and Hawkins spent most of the two-hour flight talking about home.

James curled up on the deck and dozed.

McCarter sat back against the bulkhead, his AK-47 cradled across his legs. His mind was on Manning and Encizo, wondering what they had been through. Reconnecting with them would be a relief. He didn't like being separated from his team like this. McCarter accepted that one-to-one contact under such conditions didn't always work to plan, but even so, he worried. They were in what could be termed enemy territory, and that was not ideal. The sooner Phoenix Force was a whole unit again, the better he would feel.

"Hey, I can't wait to see their ugly faces," James said, raising his head. "Take more than the Taliban to kick that pair into touch."

"LZ in ten," the pilot called over the intercom."

"Final checks, lads. Make sure your popguns are loaded and you have a spare supply of corks."

THE CHOPPER HOVERED, the rotors driving dust into the night air.

"Good luck, guys," the pilot said.

"Give 'em hell," the Texan gunner added.

Phoenix Force went EVA. The CH-46 banked away and gained height, the rotor sound fading quickly. The three commandos were truly on their own.

"Let's find cover," McCarter said, leading the way off the high ground. "Gary and Encizo should connect anytime if they heard that bird."

MANNING INTRODUCED HANAFI as soon as he and Encizo linked up with the rest of Phoenix Force. Manning gave McCarter a full rundown on what had happened since they'd touched down in Pakistan, including the death of Steve Hutchins.

They located the ordnance pack they had concealed on their arrival, and quickly changed from their suits into combat gear.

Manning also explained Hanafi's presence and relayed what the man had revealed about himself.

"Captain Hanafi," McCarter said, keeping his tone respectful, "we're in a difficult position here. To be truthful we need help, and right now our lives may depend on what you say and do."

Hanafi looked from man to man, his gaze penetrating, and the moment stretched into a long silence until he spoke. "Colonel Rahman presents a believable image of you all as nothing more than puppets of the U.S. President sent here to carry out assassinations on behalf of the American government."

"And what do you think, Captain?" Manning asked.

"His language is colorful and his use of inflammatory phrases like something out of a comic book," Hanafi said. "On the other hand, his rhetoric *will* appeal to a certain group. Personally, to use one of your American sayings, I think he is talking through his ass."

"Close enough," McCarter said, "but where does it leave us? From what my people tell me, Rahman has us down as a threat and has already tried to take two of my team out."

"Since you showed up in the U.K. Rahman has been unsettled. Nervous. Now that his operation is moving ahead, the pressure is growing. I have seen him in hurried conferences with his men. Your presence here will be something he could do without."

"Without trying to appear skeptical," McCarter said, "for all we know you could be in with Rahman. Maybe this visit is a ploy to fool us into believing you're on our side."

Hanafi smiled. "I would be less than impressed if you didn't think that way. The truth is I am an ISI agent, appointed by the president of Pakistan to collect evidence against Rahman. Suspicions of him being in league with the Taliban have never been substantiated. However, he controls territory along the Pakistan-Waziristan border area, long known to be a district where dealings between certain elements take place."

"So you're working undercover," McCarter stated, "playing along with Rahman while you gather intel."

"Exactly so," Hanafi said. He glanced around at Phoenix Force. "Did you not receive information that indicated Rahman was the one suspected to be behind this nuclear threat? Where did you think it came from? And once more you instantly doubt me, because I could be lying to you. I have no more proof than my own word. No documents to show you. No badge of office."

McCarter sighed, scrubbing a big hand through his hair. "Hanafi, consider it from where we stand. Allen and Constantine have lost the first guy helping them. Then they get screwed by Karim, who turned out to be Rahman's pet rottweiler. Not a good start. We'd already figured out that Rahman was one of the bad guys, so that's no surprise. Now here you are, pleading your case, and all we need to do is hold out our hands and say let's be best mates. In my position what would you do?"

"Try to establish if the man was telling the truth?"

"Easier said than done," Hawkins said. "It isn't as if we can pick up a phone and ask someone."

"You have satellite phones?" Hanafi said.

McCarter produced his. "Who do I call? The President?"

"You must have a contact. Call and tell them Paladin needs confirmation from the White House. Nasir Hanafi needs confirmation."

To his credit McCarter offered no reaction.

"Nothing to lose except a little time," Manning conceded.

Stepping away from the group, McCarter tapped the speed dial for Stony Man and waited while the connection was made half the world away. When the call was picked up by Barbara Price, he spoke without wasting time on pleasantries.

"Put him on."

Brognola's gruff voice came on the line seconds later. "What is it? You guys in trouble again?"

"You need to call the President. Ask him what Paladin means. Nasir Hanafi. I'll expect your call."

BROGNOLA STARED AT his phone for a few seconds before he hit a number that would connect him directly to the White House. Less than three minutes later he was speaking to the President of the United States, who confirmed that Paladin was indeed the code name for Nasir Hanafi. The ISI agent had been working directly for the Pakistani president, trying to expose Taliban infiltration of the military.

Brognola phoned McCarter back with the confirmation.

"Hanafi is your man," Brognola said. "Deep-cover agent."

"Bloody cheek," McCarter said.

"Find out what this guy Hanafi has and use it if you can. You know what's at stake," the big Fed directed.

"Okay, *jefe*."

"Serve me right for asking, but just how are things going over there?"

"As you would expect," McCarter said.

"Like I said, I did ask."

McCarter put the sat phone away. He rejoined his team.

"No hard feelings, mate, but I needed to check," he said to Hanafi, and put out his hand. "We can't afford too many mistakes on this."

Hanafi nodded in agreement and shook hands. "Understandable."

McCarter made the introductions, using the cover names

Phoenix Force had adopted for the mission. Then they got down to business.

"If Rahman is planning some kind of nuclear attack," McCarter said, "he needs the goods first. That kind of material isn't easily available. Question is where would Rahman get his hands on it—here in Pakistan or from some outside source?"

"There is a nuclear facility at Kanupp. I have heard Rahman speak of it. But Kanupp is restricted and guarded."

"What about material transfers?" James asked. "Waste materials?"

"Used rods have to be kept in specially designed pools to prevent any leaks, right?" Encizo said.

"I need to make a call," Hanafi said.

He took a cell from his jacket and punched in a number. The call was answered quickly and the ISI undercover agent began a conversation that ranged from casual to heated, then to a steady monologue with angry undertones. All this was conducted in Pashto, so none of it meant a thing to Phoenix Force. The call lasted for long minutes, with a couple of tense silences as Hanafi waited for a response. He paced back and forth, his left hand clenching and unclenching in frustration. Finally the call was ended. Hanafi stood in silence for a few moments before he turned to face Phoenix Force again.

"There are times when being an ISI agent has great advantages," he said. "This was one of them. I have just spoken with one of my contacts who owes me many favors. He works within a department privy to many levels of security. One of the levels is concerned with movement of sensitive materials. Under my order he accessed a high-level section and discovered that a consignment of nuclear rods from Kanupp is being transferred by road to a military installation for classified testing somewhere in the northwest."

"Right where we're standing is the northwest," Hawkins said.

"The military authority of the area asked for this transfer. The command is within Rahman's purview, and the commander who initiated the operation I know to be sympathetic to Jabir Rahman's cause. With Rahman's high ranking and influence, the transfer has been kept low-key. Very few outside the local military district will have been informed."

"The more I hear about this the less I like it," McCarter declared.

"All sounds highly suspect," Manning said. "But even Rahman wouldn't be stupid enough to step in and steal this consignment."

"I doubt if Rahman would involve himself openly," Hanafi said. "If he does intend stealing it he will devise a way of disguising such a risky venture. Something that will keep his hands clean."

"A hijack carried out by local radicals? Taliban hit?" Encizo suggested.

"Maybe. There are those around who would help Rahman," the ISI agent said. "Now, according to my source there will be three vehicles in the convoy. Two trucks carrying security men, with a protected vehicle carrying the rods in the middle."

"If there are armed security men guarding the consignment, any attack on it might not be successful," James said. "They'd get one chance to make it work."

"Unless someone has come up with a sure way of doing it," Encizo said.

"Any date and route?" McCarter asked.

Hanafi shook his head. "Even my contact can't find that out."

"Who would Rahman use to hijack the convoy?" McCarter queried. "Okay, he has his military personnel, but could he guarantee they would all be faithful? Only takes one to blow the whistle."

"Outside help?" Hawkins said. "Isn't he in contact with the Taliban?"

"Most likely," Hanafi agreed. "And one in particular. Naj Hajik has local warlord status. Runs this area like his own kingdom. Very fierce. Very tough. If a strike could be successful Hajik could do it."

"My kind of bloke," McCarter said airily.

"You think so?" Hanafi smiled. "Hajik kills without compassion. No conscience. No pity."

Manning stifled a chuckle. "Like you said, boss, your kind of guy."

"If we moved out now we could reach one of Hajik's bases in the morning," Hanafi said.

"By car?" James asked.

Hanafi shook his head. "My vehicle could not cross the terrain we have to negotiate." He smiled again. "We walk."

"I think he enjoyed telling us that," Hawkins muttered.

"Let's do it," McCarter said. "Listen up. We're going on the assumption Rahman and this Hajik may be in partnership. Theorizing is all well and good, but walking halfway across Pakistan could turn out to offer us bugger all."

"Boss," Hawkins argued, "right now we don't have much of a choice. If this does turn out to be a crock at least we gave her a try. We have Rahman down as the main man in all this, so let's see if we can catch the bum with a match ready to light the fuse."

"T.J., I'd have to say that's the longest speech you ever made," Manning said.

"Saddle up," McCarter said, "and fall in behind Nasir. Ears and eyes open. This isn't a stroll down Oxford Street."

Hanafi collected his backpack from his vehicle and slung it across his shoulders, then led Phoenix Force into the Pakistani night.

CHAPTER TEN

Rahman's Residence

"Sit down, Luba," Jabir Rahman said.

Luba Radesh crossed the room. A tall, athletic figure with hawkish dark looks, the Serbian glanced at his surroundings approvingly. He was a fighter rather than a homemaker, but he recognized good things. He chose a comfortable leather recliner and glanced around the wide, well-appointed room.

"Drink?" Rahman crossed to a carved wood cabinet and opened the doors, reaching inside for a bottle of fresh fruit juice and a thick tumbler. He filled it and brought it to Radesh. The Serb took it, not revealing that his preference would have been for something stronger.

"Is everything going to plan?" Rahman queried.

The cool juice was refreshing, sliding easily down Radesh's throat. He decided he could live with the juice for now. He watched as Rahman sat across from him.

"Are you worried about the merchandise?" Radesh asked.

"Without it all our plans become redundant. Of course I am concerned."

"Don't be," Radesh said. "Colonel, with an operation like this there are going to be obstacles to overcome. Finance, contingency plans, the logistics involved. But I can assure you everything is in place. We all need to have patience. Nothing can be rushed. To ensure smooth running, everyone has to be in place at the right time. The people I have brought together are the best. They know their jobs. They understand the importance of working as a team. They will not let you down. *I* will not let you down."

"With a presentation like that you should be in sales."

Radesh smiled. "I've done that, too," he said. "I worked a car dealership in Paris. If you can sell cars in Paris you have it made."

"That must have been stifling for someone like you. After the war in Kosovo."

"Paris was only a stopgap while I looked for something better."

Rahman smiled. "And now you have found it."

"Yes, Colonel. Now I have found it. With my brothers again in a fight I understand, and where I can offer my skills."

"Your team are all of the faith?"

Radesh nodded. "All true Serbian Muslins. Brothers who know why we are fighting, and who will lay down their lives for the cause. Your cause, Colonel is one we are all committed to."

Rahman leaned back in his seat, propping his fingertips together. "Are you all good Muslims?"

"To a man. We say our prayers every day and we honor what we do in the name of Allah."

"This operation I am mounting—you fully understand what I hope to achieve?"

"Yes. A statement that will shock both the American and Pakistani governments." Radesh leaned forward, eyes gleaming. "We must succeed, Colonel. The time is right to make such a statement, to show that a partnership with the U.S. will not be tolerated. The Americans have been weighing down upon us for too long. Interfering, coercing others into their way of thinking. They believe that their position as the wealthiest, most powerful nation on earth allows them to crush our will. And Pakistan's government simply allows this to go on, even stands alongside them and allows American military onto Pakistani soil. Lets them operate in secret while they commit slaughter in Afghanistan."

"America and its allies will not stop until they are made to realize the folly of their ways," Rahman stated. "An extreme act may do that."

"I have received information about the nuclear rods," Radesh said. "They are on the move as we anticipated."

Rahman nodded. "This is wonderful news, Luba. Now, is everything else ready? The transport to take the rods into America?"

"I have everything on standby. The JetStar conversion is complete. All the passenger seats removed and extra fuel tanks fitted. Refueling points from here to Morocco are set up. As soon as we gain control of the cargo it will be split into two consignments. One will go to the hangar the UAV will return to, and the other will be taken to the airstrip where the plane and crew are waiting."

"Good. Let us go, my brother. My helicopter is waiting to take us, so we can watch the Barracuda do its work. I feel we are getting closer to our goal with every passing minute."

THEY REACHED THE AREA where the base was situated about an hour after full light. Hanafi led them down off a stony ridge and they crouched behind a scattering of stones and shriveled, dusty undergrowth.

"The Taliban moved the people out of this village because they wanted a base to operate from," the ISI agent murmured. "Naj Hajik made the citizens a simple offer—

stay and we will kill you, or pack your belongings and leave the village. When the headman protested, Hajik made good his promise. He took his pistol and shot him in the skull in front of the villagers. After that there was no more protest. The village was empty by nightfall. That is how the Taliban operate. They were supposed to be freedom fighters. Now they bully and kill to get what they want."

"It's an old story, Nasir," Encizo said.

McCarter told them all to don the lightweight comm sets from their packs. He pulled out a backup set and handed it to Hanafi. They donned the devices and ran quick checks to make certain all were working.

"Make sure you let everyone know if you spot anything. No mistakes, ladies. I want you on your feet and in good working order when this is over."

They scoped out the sprawl of buildings, most of them now derelict. The village had the look of having long been abandoned. The area was littered with scrapped oil drums and cannibalized vehicles.

But a few moving figures showed—armed men in a mix of traditional dark robes and headdresses, some wearing combat fatigues, the majority of them bearded. The one constant was the AK-47 rifle each man carried.

"They look a surly lot," McCarter commented.

"Wouldn't you?" Manning said. "Having to stay in a place like this. No running water and probably no room service."

Before Phoenix Force had an opportunity to formulate a workable plan of action, they were interrupted by the unexpected appearance of a Taliban sentry.

The guy came out of nowhere, rounding an outcropping of rock only yards from where the SOG team knelt.

For a split second they all stared at one another.

The Taliban soldier let go a powerful yell that carried across the village.

He went for the Kalashnikov slung from his shoulder.

Hawkins was faster on the uptake. His own weapon, already in his hands, swept online, targeting the Taliban. He stroked the trigger and hit the man with a short burst that slapped the intruder off his feet and onto the rocky ground.

"Bloody great," McCarter said. "Let's get to it, fellers. No time for standing around and wondering what if...."

Phoenix Force, with Hanafi in their ranks, broke cover and charged the village as armed Taliban responded to the warning shout and raced for the spot where their brother had been shot.

"Spread!" McCarter yelled. "Take positions. Give 'em too many targets to take on. Circle around. Don't let them bunch us together."

McCarter sprinted for the closest building, slamming against the crumbling wall, the clamor of autofire heavy in the air. A hail of slugs hammered into the stucco inches from the Briton. The wall exploded from the impact, fragments of stone and dust misting the air. McCarter, cursing like a trooper, rolled back into cover around the end of the wall. The left side of his face stung from the peppering debris. He spit dust from his mouth as he picked up the sound of men running toward his position.

"No, you bloody well don't," he muttered.

McCarter dropped to one knee, peering from his hiding place. He saw armed figures bearing down on his location. He counted three, but had a nagging feeling there were more of them around.

"All right, chums, come to Daddy," he said.

McCarter rose to his feet, angling the barrel of the AK-47 around the wall. He brought his sights on line and triggered a sustained burst, the savage crackle of the weapon loud in his ears. He raked the two men in the lead, his volley of slugs cutting bloody swathes through the running figures. They stumbled, bodies twisting, the impact stunning them.

McCarter didn't hold back. He held the Kalashnikov on his targets and they crashed hard to the dusty ground. The third man opened up as he saw his companions go down, his weapon firing in short, erratic bursts that sent slugs wide. He saw his error and skidded to a stop, adjusting his aim, but didn't get the opportunity to fire. McCarter hit him first, then came a secondary blast from Calvin James that hit the guy in the lower back, shattering his spine. The Taliban fighter went down screaming, flopping in the bloody dirt until a short burst from McCarter cleaved his skull and spilled his brains into the dust.

"Coming in from the east side of the village." Encizo's call came over McCarter's comm set. "I see more."

As his voice broke off, the crackle of autofire came from his direction. The Cuban's steady shooting warned the rest of Phoenix Force they were not getting out lightly.

"Eyes sharp, lads," McCarter said into his mic, then swung around and took the rear exit from his cover.

He saw fast-moving figures converging, heard the sudden cacophony of a number of weapons firing at once, and knew that the battle had started in earnest.

ENCIZO SAW HIS FIRST targets go down in a bloody flurry, bodies raising dust as they were hammered to the ground. He ducked behind a low, crumbling wall, hearing the solid thud of bullets hitting the stone. He crawled to the left, peering around the shattered structure, and saw two armed Taliban advancing on his position. He muttered to himself in Spanish, pulling his AK-47 into firing position, then rolled out from the wall, stretching flat on his stomach. The

Taliban, caught by this sudden move, swung their weapons in his direction. Propped on his elbows, Encizo hit them with savage fire from the Soviet killing machine. The Kalashnikov exploded with powerful bursts, and the Taliban fighters were slammed to the ground, gasping their final breaths in stunned silence. As they hit the ground Encizo pushed himself to his feet and moved away from cover. He triggered short bursts into the downed men's skulls to finish the job. The stocky Cuban had too much respect for his own life to walk by wounded men who might still have enough life left for a final shot at him. As he walked past the bloody bodies Encizo crouched and pulled a couple loaded magazines from them, tucking them behind his belt.

He heard shots coming from over on his right and angled in that direction.

T.J. HAWKINS HAD TAKEN cover beneath an old truck. Slugs slammed into the wrecked bodywork and whined off the steel chassis. He was down in a hollow beneath the abandoned vehicle, and could feel water and oil that had leaked from the engine soaking into his combat pants and shirt. He ignored that, considering it the least of his worries. Already a ricocheting slug had seared his right shoulder in passing. It had left a stinging burn in its wake. Hawkins was wondering how long before a similar slug might find a deeper hole to bury itself in.

"Goddamn it," he yelled. "This ain't no way for a Texas boy to behave."

He squirmed around in the soggy dirt, sliding by one of the rear wheels, the steel bulk shielding him briefly. He dragged a frag grenade from his harness and pulled the pin. Holding his rifle in his left hand, Hawkins dived around the wheel and rolled clear, ignoring the continuous fire coming in his direction. He rose to his knees, powering forward toward the front the truck, then hurled the grenade in a powerful throw. It spun as it flew, then dropped to the ground, exploding a microsecond after it landed. The detonation slammed shrapnel against the group of Taliban fighters. High screams erupted as the blast tore into their bodies.

Hawkins ran forward, rifle in his hands, and closed in on the enemy position. He knew he would have no more than a few seconds, so he hightailed it, firing at anyone who moved through the dust and smoke, which was dissipating fast. Two Taliban went down yelling as Hawkins's hard bursts caught them. He saw a figure lurch out of the dust, arms flailing. The guy had caught the full force of the grenade. His body was shredded and torn, his face a shattered mask of blood and flesh. His gaping mouth showed where his teeth had been torn from his gums, and there didn't appear to be very much left of his eyes. Hawkins pumped a burst into the guy's bleeding skull, toppling him backward into oblivion.

"David, working my way to your position. You holding?" T.J. asked.

McCarter's voice rasped through the comm set. "These buggers are coming out of the walls."

ON THE FAR SIDE of the village Gary Manning snapped a fresh magazine into his AK-47, turning back to confront the three shooters advancing on his position. The Canadian demolitions expert had already put two Taliban down, leaving a third in the dirt clutching his right leg, where shattered bone protruded from the bloody wound in his thigh.

One of the advancing Taliban set up covering fire as his two companions broke off in different directions. They clearly intended to catch Manning in a crossfire.

"Not going to happen, guys," he said quietly. "Not on your best day."

The Phoenix Force warrior set his rifle for single shot, raised it and chose his first target. Manning led the moving figure, then gently squeezed the trigger. His slug caught the running man center mass, in the chest. The Taliban stumbled awkwardly, then toppled forward, face scraping the hard earth as he fell. Even as the guy went down Manning switched his aim, picking up on the second flanker. His shot was almost identical to the first, pitching the target off to one side, the slug tearing its way through, to exit after severing the spine. As his target crashed to the ground, Manning settled his rifle on the center guy. The Canadian pulled to the left as slugs pounded the low wall he was using for cover. Ignoring the dusty fragments filling the air, Manning held his aim, triggered his shot and saw the man arch back. He fired twice more, seeing the hits raise blossoms of dust from the Taliban's tunic. The guy struggled to stay upright. Held himself for long seconds before he went backward onto the dry earth, his rifle clattering as it struck the ground.

Manning turned and saw a group of armed figures running across open ground in the direction of the village. He judged it would be about a minute before they came within range.

"Check the eastern approach," he said into his comm set. "More hostiles moving our way. I see maybe eight, ten of them. Anytime now we'll be knee deep in Rahman's buddies. I'm heading your way."

"Hear you loud and clear," McCarter acknowledged. "Yeah, we see them now. Lock and load, boys, we have uninvited guests on the way."

The Taliban let loose, sending crackling bursts of autofire converging on the Phoenix Force position. Slugs whined and slammed into the already crumbling stonework. Splinters filled the air, along with the snap of shots thudding against the walls.

"Hey, you guys need backup?" Calvin James asked.

CHAPTER ELEVEN

The black Phoenix Force commando had been working his way around the village perimeter to bring himself to the rear of the advancing attack group. Now he was flat in the dirt, watching as the Taliban as made their run in the direction of his companions.

Beside James lay the inert body of the Taliban who had been at the rear of the group. The terrorist, who had a couple of U.S. LAW hand-launch missiles strapped across his back, had died from a single, accurate cut made by the tanto combat knife in James's hand. He had died quickly, held motionless by James until he breathed his last. Moving rapidly, James tugged the LAWs free, extending the tube of the first as he rose to one knee.

"Guys, take cover in case my aim's off," he announced over his comm set. "Missile incoming."

James shouldered the armed tube, swinging the muzzle to aim at the ground just behind the advancing Taliban. He touched the trigger button, felt the kickback as the rocket launched, stabilizing fins springing out as it sped in the direction of the intended targets. The missile struck less than five feet from the moving Taliban, the explosion throwing up a mushroom of dirt and human debris. Bodies were hurled into the air, the solid boom of the exploding missile drowning out every other sound.

James pushed to his feet, hanging the second LAW from his shoulder and grabbing up his Kalashnikov as he closed in on the downed attackers. Most of the group were sprawled on the ground, dirt raining down on them, smoke swirling in thick clouds. As James entered the dust he saw at least two Taliban still upright, dazed but able to move. He swung the AK-47 in their direction, stroking back the trigger and punching 7.62 mm slugs into them. The figures stumbled, falling under the sustained burst from James's weapon.

The rest of Phoenix Force emerged from cover, closing in on Calvin James.

"Caught them napping," McCarter said. "Times like these, Cal, makes me realize you're not always a bloody hindrance."

"It's praise like that makes me want to get up in the morning."

"T.J., take a look round. See if there are any more of these buggers still lurking out there."

"I'll go with him," Encizo said.

The pair moved out, reloading their weapons as they went.

"Am I the only one beginning to suspect we're not exactly being welcomed with open arms?" Manning observed.

"Looks like the word is out," James said.

"You think?" McCarter was turning in a three-sixty arc, eyes scanning every building. Every shadow. The Phoenix Force leader wasn't happy over their situation. McCarter never took anything for granted. Combat situations were constantly evolving. There was no such thing as a stable condition. A high state of alertness was needed. Dropping guard could often lead to disaster. And disaster could become a permanent matter. "What is it about this place that needed so much guarding? Look at it. Two steps away from a slum. Got to be something here we aren't seeing."

"Want to check it out?" Manning asked.

"Something odd..." McCarter mused.

"What?" James asked. "This is a deserted village. Tumbledown buildings. Trash strewn around. What's to see?"

McCarter stood still, his gaze centered on a structure directly ahead of him. "That's the one," he stated.

He was right. The building, when closely viewed, stood out from the rest. Though built in the same style, it had a look of permanence that the rest of the village lacked. The closer they got, the more evident it became that was in much better condition—a solid structure despite its rough facade. When McCarter slammed his boot against the wooden door it resisted. The barrier was no flimsy construction; it took a half-dozen of McCarter's kicks to break the interior lock and send the heavy panel swinging back against the wall.

"I think we've found their home base," the Briton said.

It consisted of one large room. Living quarters and kitchen area. A number of wooden cots and blankets. A long communal table with benches either side. Remains of food were scattered across the table.

McCarter paced the room, dissatisfied until he stripped back a blanket curtain to expose a wide opening with stone steps cut into the rock, leading down.

"Bloody knew it," he said triumphantly.

Hawkins moved toward the steps, but McCarter put up a big hand to hold him back, shaking his head. He glanced across at Encizo, who anticipated his need. The Cuban freed a flash-bang grenade from his harness and tossed it to McCarter. Their commander pulled the tab, waved everyone away, then threw the canister down the steps so it struck the stone floor at the bottom and bounced out of sight. The Phoenix Force commandos turned away, covering their ears to minimize the effects of the concussion grenade.

The moment the brilliant flash of light and the high-impact sound faded McCarter went down the steps fast, Hawkins at his rear. Only Manning stayed behind, acting as the team's backstop.

The stairway opened up into a large underground space with an uneven rock ceiling and floor. It took only moments for them to realize this was a natural formation, not manmade.

There were three armed figures, all suffering from the effects of the grenade, eyes staring at the ghostly images of Phoenix Force appearing in front of them. The one at the farthest point swung up his AK-47 and opened fire. His spray of slugs howled off the basement walls, whining as they bounced away. One of the flash-blinded men dropped as a flattened slug cored into the side of his skull. He went down in a spray of splintered bone and torn flesh.

McCarter triggered a burst that slammed the shooter to the floor.

The surviving Taliban made no offer of resistance. He simply knelt on the hard floor, hands clutched over his ears, moaning to himself.

"Deal with him, T.J.," McCarter directed.

Hawkins secured the prisoner with plastic ties around his wrists, then followed the rest of the team as they inspected the basement cavern.

"Clever move to build over this," Encizo said. "Gave them a hell of a storage facility."

In a side cave was a modern generator, providing power for the lamps strung out across the chamber. McCarter saw that diesel fumes produced by the machine were vented via a flexible pipe that had been threaded to the outside through a narrow gap in the cave ceiling.

"Yeah," James said. "Look at what they've been hoarding."

As Phoenix Force moved through the cavern they located piles of packed white powder—pure heroin. All neatly bound and sealed in plastic. There was more as they moved farther in. Then they encountered stacks of brown heroin used for heating up for smoking.

"These guys are nothing if not versatile," Hawkins said. "Something for everyone. Enough stuff here to bring in millions."

"It finances their operations," Hanafi stated.

"And buys their weapons." James waved for his partners to join him.

They stared at the crated AK-47 rifles, handguns, stacks of ammunition, land mines, grenades and LAW launchers and heavy machine guns. Boxes of plastic explosive in solid bricks sat next to cartons of fuses.

"All this so they can keep on killing allied soldiers," Encizo said, a bitter edge to his voice.

"Sam, you clear up there?" McCarter asked Manning.

His comm set buzzed as the Canadian's voice came through.

"No problems. Anything interesting down there?"

"Oh, yes. Enough drugs to feed the markets for a long time. And ordnance by the crateload. Listen, I'll send Danny to take over up there. You get down here and work your magic. I want this place brought down and the merchandise reduced to ashes."

"On my way," Manning said.

"Take that bastard up with you," McCarter said to Hawkins, indicating the prisoner.

"I will go with him," Hanafi said. "Perhaps I can get some information from him."

"Good idea, Nasir."

Hawkins and Hanafi escorted the prisoner out of the cavern.

"David, come take a look at this," Encizo called.

McCarter joined him and they stood looking at two long, narrow crates. One container was longer than its neighbor. They were all empty.

"Pretty big," Hawkins said. "This must be at least sixty feet. The other around thirty."

"Another one here," James said, pointing out a ten-foot-square container.

"Missile?" Encizo suggested.

James was walking around the container, absorbed in his inspection.

"Cal?" McCarter asked.

"Looks like the padded inserts might have held wing sections. About twenty-five feet each."

"Fifty-foot span?" Encizo said as he joined them.

Manning appeared, taking in the stacked material in the cavern.

McCarter had spotted lettering on the side of the main container.

"Lansing & Bedloe, U.K.," he read. "Some kind of serial number, as well. I'm going up top to call this in. See if Stony Man can find out what was in these crates. Gary, rig this place to blow. I don't want anything left for those buggers to salvage."

"Okay," Manning said. "Rafe, Cal, give me a hand."

Before McCarter made his way out he checked the smaller container. It had the same company name on the side and another serial number. McCarter went up the steps and exited the building. Hawkins had their prisoner under guard while Hanafi talked to him in Pashto. The Briton took out his sat phone and made the connection with Stony Man, speaking to Barbara Price.

"Take this down, Barb," he said, quoting her the name and serial numbers. "Get the team to run it through their databases and see what comes up."

"You found something?"

"All we have at the moment is the wrapping paper. I need to find out what was inside."

"I'll get back to you."

"Busy day," Hawkins said, when McCarter rejoined him. He jerked a thumb in the direction of the building. "Things folks keep in the basement."

McCarter grinned. "Make one hell of a garage sale."

They were still waiting for Stony Man to call when Manning, Encizo and James came back outside. The explosives expert joined McCarter.

"All set," he said. "I think we should get as far away as we can. There was a hell of lot of explosive down there. I've rigged it so the whole lot will go. Set it on a fifteen-minute timer."

"Bloody hell," McCarter said. "Is it going to be that big a bang?"

Manning grinned. "Huge bang," he confirmed. "If the wind's right they'll hear it at the Farm." He shrugged. "Not really."

"Yeah, I get the idea, mate. Heads up, fellers, we need to get away from here. Sammy here is going to blow this section of Pakistan off the map."

"What about our buddy?" Hawkins asked.

"Haul his bony arse along for now. We'll cut him loose later and let him run home to Rahman."

They hustled away from the village, making fast time despite the rough terrain. McCarter kept checking his watch, counting down the minutes. They had been walking for a good ten minutes before Manning called a halt.

"Did we need to clear this far?" James asked, wiping sweat from his face with his sleeve.

"No, we could have stopped way back," Manning said.

"Why all this way, then?" Encizo asked.

"I like to see the fear in your eyes."

"Ah, that good old Canadian sense of humor," McCarter said. "You got us going there, mate."

"Funny. Really funny," James said, dropping to the ground. "Remind me to buy you a cold beer for that."

McCarter's sat phone rang and he listened to Price's information. "Oh, hell," he said initially. He calmed down after that. "Thanks, love. I'll fill you in later."

The ground shook, the vibration was so strong. When they looked back in the direction of the distant village they saw the dust and smoke cloud rising into the hot air. The sound of the explosion reached them seconds later, a long, deep rumble. The widening cloud of smoke made a massive impression. The earth continued to vibrate under their feet.

"No more underground stash," Manning said.

"I'd guess no more village," McCarter added.

"It was due for redevelopment," the Canadian said. "I did the zone planners a favor."

"Previous owners are liable to be a mite unappreciative," Hawkins said.

"Tough," McCarter said. "Pity they weren't home at the time. Okay, boys, let's get out of Dodge before the neighbors come to see what all the noise was about." He turned about suddenly, his expression solemn. "I think we might have another problem."

That got the attention of Phoenix Force.

"Those crates we saw held a Barracuda, a UAV. Pilotless flying drone. Large crates held the fuselage and the wing assemblies. The smallest crate held its control console, which the operator could use to steer the thing."

"I'm guessing Rahman's bunch didn't buy it over the internet," James said.

"It was taken in a hijack. The unit was being transported from the U.K. factory to an airbase in Norfolk. Two of the manufacturer's truckers were beaten pretty badly during the theft. One is still in a coma. The attack took place on a stretch of road way out in the sticks. Always pretty deserted at night. It's why the route is used to move this kind of gear. Never happened before."

"When did it go down?" Manning asked.

"Three weeks ago," McCarter said. "The theft was kept under wraps because no one wants to admit something like a Barracuda has gone missing. Public hears enough about terrorist threats. Last thing they need is to be told someone has a flying robot weapon in their hands."

"This thing is armed?" Encizo asked, not believing he was going to like the answer.

"You'll love this," McCarter said. "Carries four hardpoints fitted with air-to-ground Hellfire missiles."

"Sorry I asked," Encizo said.

"This could be where Prem and Saeeda Hussein fit into the scheme," Manning said. "Prem could have gotten details about the movement of the UAV from Winch. He works the hijack, then moves the merchandise to Tilbury, where it's loaded onto one of Hussein's freighters."

"Rahman takes over when the freighter docks. Brings the UAV up here and keeps it concealed until he's ready to use it," James added.

"Let's think what that means," Manning said. "Rahman has a UAV loaded with missiles. He can program it to go wherever he wants. Our intel, in fact the reason we're here, is that he's planning on using some kind of nuclear devices. Here in Pakistan and also in the U.S. What's he going to do, load the missiles with nuclear warheads?"

"He couldn't do that," James said. "It's not possible."

"Exactly my point," Manning said. "So what the hell is he playing at?"

"The UAV must be part of his plan to get his hands on the nuclear material," Hawkins suggested. "Maybe he's going to steal it using the drone as a flying can opener."

"We have a theory, Nasir," McCarter said as the team rejoined the ISI agent, who was again interrogating the Taliban captive. "Rahman has got his hands on a UAV. Basically, an unmanned aircraft that can be used to spy on subjects from the air."

"What would he do with it?"

"This drone is armed with air-to-ground Hellfire seek-and-destroy missiles. It could track a vehicle convoy. Even take out escort vehicles so the main cargo truck would be isolated. If that was done Rahman's people could move in and take over."

"My God," Hanafi said. "He has kept that close to his chest. Nothing was spoken about such an exercise in my presence."

"Not surprising," McCarter said, "they'd want to keep it under wraps."

"What about home?" Encizo interjected. "Get the cyber team to run some scans. See if they can come up with anything. Maybe they can pick something up through satellite surveillance. Use Zero One's system."

"It's worth a try," Manning agreed.

"Better than us just sitting around with nowhere to go," Hawkins said.

McCarter tapped in the Stony Man code and waited. "Here goes nothing," he said. "Let's hope we haven't run out of time."

After he made his call, alerting Stony Man to their theory, Phoenix Force, Hanafi and their prisoner moved out.

McCarter wanted to get away from the immediate area in case further Taliban activity began.

THEY HAD BEEN ON THE MOVE for almost an hour, Hanafi trying to get them clear of the local Taliban neighborhood. Moving higher, they crossed a moonscape of eroded rock and loose shale. Dust rose from under their feet. The heat bore down with relentless determination. Even Hanafi was sweating.

The Taliban prisoner, whose name Hanafi had established as Paduh, had lapsed into a sullen silence. Hanafi had long since given up trying to draw any information from him, telling McCarter the man refused to give anything but his name. All Paduh did was rant at his captors in an unceasing litany of threats and curses. Hanafi had translated some of the epithets until McCarter said he got the idea and they should let Paduh wear out his vocal cords if that was what he wanted.

As they negotiated a dusty slope Hanafi spotted movement just ahead. He stared for a few seconds to make certain he was not mistaken, then yelled a warning.

"Taliban. Up ahead."

McCarter followed his pointing finger, saw the figures and the weapons they carried.

"Damn," he said. "Heads up..."

Phoenix Force saw the enemy and brought their weapons to bear.

And Paduh recognized his brother warriors and broke his silence, screaming wildly to attract their attention.

Encizo was closest to the man and saw his triumphant smile as more armed Taliban stepped into view.

"You are dead now," Paduh said, abruptly developing the ability to speak English. He swung around to raise his arms, signaling his friends forward, yelling wildly in Pashto.

"He's telling them to cut our throats like the pigs we are," Hanafi said.

"You will die, infidel pigs," Paduh screamed in English. "You will all go to hell."

He lunged at Encizo.

As he moved, his right hand clawing at Encizo's face, the Cuban's own fist slashed forward, slamming into his throat with full force. The blow was brutal, crushing the Taliban thug's windpipe and cartilage. Paduh dropped to his knees, clutching his throat, croaking sounds erupting from his slack mouth.

"You first," Encizo said, bringing his Kalashnikov on target, as did the rest of Phoenix Force.

The defile echoed with the sound of autofire, slugs burning through the air, empty shell casings catching the light as they blew from ejection ports.

"Take cover," McCarter yelled.

Phoenix Force and Hanafi scattered even as the first of the Taliban went down.

McCarter, Hawkins and Manning broke left, clearing a low ridge edging the trail. They slithered and stumbled down a dusty, rock-strewed slope, dragging loose shale with them. They could hear the crackle of autofire. As they reached bottom a line of slugs from distant guns chased them, followed by the whine and detonation of a mortar. The solid thump preceded an erupting mushroom of earth and stones. For long seconds everything was obscured by the cloud of debris and drifting smoke.

SEPARATED FROM THE OTHERS by the mortar blast, James, Encizo and Hanafi were forced to backtrack, aware that the

Taliban were following. Autofire sent slugs in their wake, hits kicking up spouts of dirt and pebbles.

"These guys just keep coming out of the rocks," James said.

"You think?" Encizo muttered.

The approaching hum of another mortar warned them to move.

"Incoming," James yelled, and they spread, diving for cover.

The shell landed well short, but the explosion hammered at their ears. A rain of dirt showered over them.

"Let's go," James said. "They drop many more, they're going to range in."

As he led the others away, a second mortar landed close enough to shake the ground beneath their feet.

"Over there!" Hanafi called, gesturing ahead.

They scrambled over slabs of eroded rock, falling into a basin dotted with dusty shrubs and brittle grass.

More mortar shells landed, still behind them but getting closer as the launch crew ranged in.

"Here," Hanafi said.

They veered off course, ducking beneath an overhang that led into a head-high cave. In cover for a moment, they regrouped, checking weapons and themselves.

"Anyone hit?" James asked.

Apart from the odd graze from flying debris, they had avoided any major injuries.

"We need to get back to the others," Encizo said.

James nodded. "And fast, before they're overrun."

"We can circle around," Hanafi said. "I know this area. There is a way we can—"

A mortar landed just short of the overhang. The sound reverberated inside the cave, followed by a swelling cloud of dust and stone fragments. The concussion knocked them off their feet. As the noise of the blast faded they heard a rising rumble of grating rock. Sharp splintering was accompanied by the rattle of more falling rocks, and then the jutting overhang collapsed.

It happened in a few seconds. The immense weight of tons of shattered slabs dropped; the rumble of shifting stone increased. Thick dust filled the cave, leave them gasping for breath, and all light vanished as the cave entrance became buried by the rock fall.

They were left in darkness, without a glimmer of light showing.

The rumbling of shifting rocks faded.

Calvin James regained his feet.

"You guys okay?" he asked.

He received affirmative responses from Encizo and Hanafi.

"It depends how you define *okay,*" Encizo added.

James slipped off his backpack and delved inside. He brought out a medium-size flashlight, flicking it on. The beam played across the rockfall.

"No way we can dig ourselves through that," he said.

"Let's check the back door," Encizo suggested.

"If there is one," Hanafi added.

James pulled on his backpack, hung his rifle by its shoulder strap and headed into the cave.

"Just our luck if it's only a few feet deep," Encizo said.

James let his flashlight point the way. They walked a great deal farther than a few feet. It appeared the cave cut deep into the hillside. They walked for almost a quarter hour before a slope of tumbled rock barred their way. James checked out the jagged mass. His flashlight beam traced the heap to where it ended some twenty feet above them.

"More rock here than the other end," Hanafi said. He

squatted on his heels, wiping sweat from his face. "Have we come all this way for nothing?"

"I don't think so, man," James said. "Look."

He switched off the flashlight. At the top of the slope sunlight showed between the uppermost chunks of rock. A few thin beams of light lanced into the gloom.

"Nicest thing I've seen all day," Encizo said.

James put away his flashlight. "We do this slowly," he said. "No way of knowing how firm those boulders are. Last thing we need is to start a rockslide and end up buried under it."

"He always looks on the bright side," Encizo told Hanafi. "Don't let it bother you."

James led, testing each step as he began the climb. He used both hands to check the way, diverting if a section seemed suspect. The others followed in his wake, using the same rocks he had stepped on. They stayed well apart, aware that one misplaced footstep might start a slide that would end their climb quickly. Occasionally a small chunk of stone would roll from under their feet, clattering noisily as it bounced downward. Fine dust misted the air, disturbed by their passing. After ten minutes they were still only a third of the way up the slope, and their clothing was soaked with sweat. It ran down their faces, stinging their eyes and leaving a pasty taste in their mouths. James called a halt, giving them all a chance to catch their breath.

"What if we break through and find we're on a sheer rock face with a hundred-foot drop?" Encizo asked.

James chuckled at the thought. "If we have to jump, at least we'll feel some cool air on the way down."

"What did I tell you about seeing the good in any situation?" Encizo said.

"But what if he is right?" Hanafi asked. "It could be a long way down."

"Great," Encizo said. "Now I got two pessimists on my case. You make a good double act."

James shook his head. "Comics. Let's go, guys, before I laugh myself to death."

They climbed. Slowly. Carefully. Always with the knowledge that their passage could loosen some slab of rock and the slide might collapse beneath them. When movement was detected they froze until the moment passed. But their patience was rewarded when James was able to ease his body into a position level with the top of the slide, pressing his face to one of the gaps so he could feel the comparatively fresh air passing through it.

"Save some for us, hombre," Encizo said.

They bunched together, finding firm footholds. James put his hands on a wide chunk of rock and tested its stability. At first nothing happened. He applied more pressure, feeling his aching muscles strain. The stone moved a fraction, with a grating sound. Encizo moved in closer and added his muscle to the effort. The rock began to shift.

"Be ready to go if this makes a large enough gap," James advised.

"A very good suggestion," Hanafi said.

They checked the curving rock above the opening. From what James could make out it looked to be solid and unbroken.

"Let's do it," he said. "I'm done crawling around in the dark."

With Encizo's help James dislodge the slab. It slid away and they heard it land with a thump just beyond the opening. With Encizo at his side James shoved at more rocks, widening the hole.

"Enough," Encizo said.

"Go," James yelled, pushing his partner through the opening.

Encizo wriggled over the rocks and vanished from sight. James heard him land.

Reaching out to grab hold of Hanafi's shirt James half dragged the Pakistani to the gap. "Go now," he shouted. "Move your ass, man."

As Hanafi vanished in turn through the opening, James heard a rising rumble beneath him. He felt the rocks start to slide, threw out a hand. But everything he tried to grab was already moving, and he was going with it.... Then a vise caught his left wrist. Fingers clamped down hard, taking all James's weight as the sliding rocks pummeled his body.

When he looked up he saw Hanafi's dirt-streaked, glistening face peering down at him. The Pakistani's lips were peeled back as he grimaced with the effort of holding on. A moment later Encizo appeared, his own arm thrusting outward. James threw his other hand up, and his partner grabbed it, and with Hanafi hung on to James as the rocks tumbled away into the cave below, leaving the Phoenix Force warrior dangling in empty air.

"You going to hang about all day?" Encizo asked.

Between them, the Cuban and Hanafi hauled Calvin James to the lip of the gap, dragged him unceremoniously into the clear and let him slump to the ground. The three of them lay spread-eagled, panting for breath, listening to the rumble of falling rocks inside the cave. Pale dust smoked from the fissure they had clambered through.

"That's something I don't want to go through again in a hurry," James said.

"Not ever," Encizo said.

"Even longer," Hanafi agreed.

"Guys, thanks for the hand," James said. "Both of them."

"We couldn't let you go," Encizo said. "You've got the medi kit."

"All heart," James said, grinning.

They climbed to their feet, staring at each other. They were sweat-stained, covered in dust, faces smeared and grazed.

But they were alive.

"Nasir, can you figure out where we might be?" James asked.

Hanafi nodded, glancing around the landscape. James and Encizo left him to it while they checked their ordnance. The weapons didn't appear to have suffered any damage, but the Phoenix Force pros inspected them thoroughly. It would have been remiss of them not to make sure their arms were still functional.

Hanafi had moved off some distance, scanning the terrain.

"You worried about the others?" Encizo asked.

"I will be until I see them in one piece," James said.

"Let's hope Nasir can get us back on track."

The Pakistani rejoined them, indicating the route they needed to follow. "I think we should be able to make our way back to where we were separated," he said. "I'd estimate we are maybe two, three miles east of our former position."

"You lead," James said. He reached out to touch Hanafi's sleeve. "But first check your weapons. See there's been no damage. If we have to use them, it's too late if you find out that AK-47 doesn't work."

"Yes. You are right, my friend."

SMOKE WAS STILL CLEARING after the mortar explosion. McCarter had seen James, Encizo and Hanafi just before it hit. He felt relief afterward spotting no bodies on the ground.

But there was no happy outcome, as more Taliban swarmed into view, weapons up and ready to fire. David

McCarter would readily admit to having a reckless, unpredictable nature, but he was not suicidal. There were too many even for three Phoenix Force commandos to take on.

"Okay, lads, time out," he said. "For now."

The Taliban surrounded them, disarmed them and bound their arms behind them. There was a great deal of jostling and unfriendly punching of the captives. Among the hostile warriors the Phoenix Force pros could do nothing but accept their treatment.

They were force marched for miles, over rugged, sun-bleached terrain, dust swirling around them from the boots of their captors. Night fell, and while the Taliban ate and drank, the Phoenix Force trio was forced to lie in the dirt, given neither food nor water.

"I don't remember this being in the brochure," McCarter muttered. "Nothing about a fast-track diet by starvation."

"David," Manning said.

"What?"

"Just shut up."

The following morning they marched again, reaching their destination by midday. The prisoners were roughly herded into a cramped building, their bonds cut away before they were pushed unceremoniously into a stone cell and the heavy wooden door slammed shut.

They all realized it was far from over yet.

CHAPTER TWELVE

'The course is set," Anwar Fazeel said. "The drone will make its own corrections once it is fully locked in."

As well as being able to set computer-controlled flight instructions, Fazeel had a manual control stick to override if needed.

"Excellent," Rahman said. He stood directly behind him in the hangar where the UAV control center was housed.

To Fazeel's right was a large flat-screen monitor relaying an image from the video camera mounted on the nose of the UAV. As he observed the screen, Rahman was surprised at how clear the picture was.

"How long before we reach the target area?" Luba Radesh asked.

"Based on speed and course correction, less than eighteen minutes," Fazeel said. "If prevailing winds alter, the drone will send details back here and the computer will adjust."

"Are the missiles armed?" Rahman asked.

"Once the target comes in sight I will do that," Fazeel answered. "At the same time the designated targets will be assessed by the UAV's onboard sensors and the information fed into its memory. The data will also be sent here for acknowledgment and final target acquisition. After that we need to do nothing except watch the monitor."

The screen showed that the UAV was flying over featureless, dun-colored terrain. The undulating ranks of low, rocky hills offered little vegetation to relieve the dusty drabness. The picture showed a wide expanse of land and sky, with just the tip of the UAV's nose cone visible.

"The image is very sharp," Rahman said.

"Digital technology," Radesh pointed out. "If you look closely you can see the detail below, even at such a height."

"If nothing else," Rahman said, "we must give the British full marks for the quality of the Barracuda."

"Pity they can't actually see the result of their product in action."

"Perhaps we could send them a copy of the flight video, Colonel," Fazeel suggested.

"Only if we achieve the result we want," Radesh said.

"Have faith, my brother," Rahman told him.

On screen the UAV made a gradual arc as the course was changed, the landscape tilting at an angle. The digital readouts on Fazeel's control module sped through alternating sequences.

Rahman leaned forward, gripping the back of Fazeel's seat. "What is happening?"

"The computer has locked on to the final course change. The target is fully registering now," Fazeel explained. He pointed to the monitor screen. "See? There. There is the target."

As the UAV leveled into its final approach, an uneven ribbon of road appeared below. And less than a half mile ahead they could see the three-vehicle convoy. Dust trailed behind the trucks.

Fazeel adjusted the camera lens, zooming in to offer a closer look. The images loomed larger, sharp detail resolving itself. It was possible to see the faces of the armed security force sitting in the rear of the last vehicle.

"Can they see the drone?" Rahman asked.

"No, Colonel," Fazeel said. "It is too high and its configuration blends in with the sky."

"I doubt they will realize what has hit them," Radesh said.

They studied the convoy, noting that there was some considerable distance between trucks. The wide gaps between the escorts and the container vehicle were visible reminder of what was being transported.

"How long before the missiles are fired?" Radesh asked.

Fazeel activated a key, and display lights showed on the module. "Missiles are activated," he said. He worked some more instructions via his keyboard. "The computer has now instructed the UAV to gain target acquisition. Front and rear vehicles. The firing sequence will now initiate."

Radesh spoke into his radio handset, passing instructions to the waiting strike force, who had been monitoring the convoy's progress from their parallel course on the ground. They were close by, hidden on the higher slopes, within a few hundred feet of the vehicles.

"As soon as the escort trucks are hit, move in. Finish off any survivors. Surround the container vehicle and kill the driver and codriver."

His message was confirmed. As Radesh turned back to the monitor, he sensed a flash of something streaking from the UAV. Twin trails appeared as a pair of Hellfire missiles sprang from the left and right missile pods. The thin white snakes curved down toward the moving convoy. It might have seemed as if everything was in slow motion, but only seconds passed in reality. The front truck vanished in a sudden burst of writhing flame that curled up into the sky. The vehicle disintegrated, parts hurled in every direction. The sight was all the more eerie due to the total absence of sound. A moment later the rear truck was delivered a similar blow. As it blew, the stricken vehicle slewed off course, rolling to the side of the road. Burning fuel spattered the ground. Bodies were toppled from the shattered rear of the truck, some of them aflame, thrashing around as their flesh and clothing were consumed by the hungry flames.

The UAV flew on, overshooting the destruction.

"Bring it around," Rahman said. "Show us the scene."

Fazeel tapped instructions into the computer, bringing the drone full circle so its camera could scan the site.

The escort vehicles were burning furiously. Bodies were scattered across the ground. Armed figures were emerging from either side of the road, weapons raised. A number approached the container vehicle. Doors were pulled open. The driver and his partner were dragged from the cab and thrown to the ground. Weapons were turned on them, autofire tearing into them.

Radesh spoke to the ground commander, Naj Hajik. "You know what to do. Get that container truck away from there. Follow the plan. Make sure no one is left alive. Let us know once you have the truck hidden safely."

Rahman was jubilant, his face flushed with excitement. "Brothers, we have succeeded in the first phase of our operation. Now we can move on to the next." He turned to Fazeel. "Bring the drone home. We have work to do. And well done, Anwar Fazeel. This success is due to you, my brother, and I salute you."

Rahman dialed his sat phone. When Umer Qazi answered, Rahman had to calm himself before he spoke.

"It is done. Are you at the airport?"

"We board in ten minutes." Qazi added, "Congratulations."

"To us all," Rahman said.

He completed the call. Everything was going to plan.

The nuclear rods were in his possession.

Qazi was on his way to Boston. He would make contact

with the sleeper who would handle the rods and create the explosive device that would release the radioactive poison in the city.

Allahu Akbar.

MCCARTER STARED AROUND the dusty room. Stone walls and floor. A barred window showing a view of the bleak exterior. The space was devoid of furniture. When the heavy wooden door slammed, the Briton turned to face his three captors.

"I don't suppose I could ask for a change of room," he said. "This one doesn't have much ambience, but it's better than that cell."

The three Taliban, hard faces showing no emotion, spread out, the thick canes in their hands swishing back and forth. The one in the center stepped forward.

"Why have you come here?" His English was stilted, accented, but his intent was evident. He launched into a wild speech, half in fractured English, half in Pashto. Standing motionless, McCarter let the guy tire himself out.

"Go to hell," he finally answered, feeling more than a little aggrieved.

The speaker's hand moved and the cane cracked viciously across McCarter's body. The Briton stepped back, flesh stinging from the blow.

"Bugger," he said. "Going to take three of you bearded wonders to deal with me, is it? Well, come on, then, you bloody jokers."

The cane slashed out again. Before it landed, McCarter sidestepped, hands snapping up to grab the guard's wrist. McCarter yanked the startled man forward and as he stumbled, the Briton slammed his fist into his attacker's face, splitting his lips. The other two Taliban sprang forward, canes landing brutal blows on McCarter's shoulders and back, while the first man stepped away, pawing at his bloody mouth. He released a stream of invective, urging his companions to punish their captive.

McCarter protected his face and head with his raised arms, refusing to let his attackers get the better of him. Resolutely, he stayed on his feet, taking his beating with stubborn resistance.

When the blows stopped McCarter was bloody but unbowed. A couple slashes had caught him across the side of his head. A raw gash on his left cheek bled profusely.

Dabbing at his torn lips, the first Taliban guard thrust a finger at McCarter. "We know you were sent by the American government. You have come to kill our brave warriors. This will not happen. We will defeat you all. America will go down on its knees when the Taliban is victorious."

"I'll remember that," McCarter said. Especially next time I'm blowing your arses away.

"Take him back," the lead Taliban ordered. "Let his companions see what we have in store for them. Then we will bring the next one here."

McCarter was escorted back to the cell, helped along by repeated slashes from the canes his captors still wielded. The armed guard opened the door and McCarter was pushed inside the tiny cell. As he slumped against the rough stone wall he heard the door slam shut behind him.

Manning took a look at his shredded and bloody shirt. "You been upsetting the staff again?"

"Buggers just don't have a sense of humor," McCarter said. He shook his head. "Christ, it bloody hurts, though," he said. "If I get the chance, this bunch are going to hell in a handcart."

"Still preaching brotherly love and forgiveness, then," Hawkins said. "Ready to hold out the hand of friendship."

McCarter grinned. "Only if I have an AK-47 in it."

He was almost face-to-face with his partners, having little room to maneuver.

"If you were young, blonde and blue eyed, answered to the name Tammy and had a habit of leaving your clothes on the floor, I'd be happy to have you this close," Hawkins said.

"You think so?" McCarter replied. "Well, chum, if I was all those things I'd be cuddling up to one of our guards to get us out of here."

"Appears to me," Manning said, "you're both going to be disappointed."

The stone cell, with no window except a tiny slit high in the wall, had been designed for single occupancy, so the three Phoenix Force members were forced into extremely close proximity. There was barely enough room to sit, and no chance to lie full length. Light came through the high slit and the barred opening in the wooden door that secured the cell. A lack of air movement, plus the high temperature, created an oppressive atmosphere. Since being placed in the cell the three had been fed only twice—plain boiled rice in a single wooden bowl. Water had been offered in plastic bottles, a well-known global brand. The sealed contents were tepid, but none of them complained. They drank sparingly, wanting to make the ration last.

This was their second day in the cell.

In turn each of them had been taken to the cell down the passage and subjected to beating by the cane-wielding Taliban, who still could not get any kind of response from the Phoenix Force commandos.

Apart from when their meager food and water were delivered, the trio had not seen or heard from their captors for half a day.

"You think we're going to be ransomed?" Hawkins said. "That's why all this waiting."

"Doubtful," McCarter said. "They don't know anything about us. Don't know our names. Who we work for. "

"If that's the case, guys, I guess we're screwed."

"They must want something," Manning volunteered. "If we don't have any value they would have simply shot us."

"Cheerful sod, isn't he?" McCarter said.

"Man *is* right though."

"I know." McCarter pushed himself to his feet and worked his arms and legs to ease the stiffness. "I'll be bloody mad if I find out Cal and Rafe are enjoying themselves somewhere."

"Holed up back in a hotel," Manning said.

"With cool drinks and fried chicken," Hawkins said. "Greens and gravy with a side order of hot biscuits."

"Give us a break, T.J., this is bloody Pakistan. Not downtown Dallas." He glanced at the grinning younger man. "Food all you can think of right now?"

"Hell, no, boss, but you don't want me to describe what I'm really fantasizing about."

Manning chuckled. "We're back to that blue-eyed blonde again."

"You calm down there, young 'un," McCarter said. "Forget the girl. I don't need you getting all hot and bothered. We don't have that much room and you're too close for comfort already."

THE TALIBAN GUARD at the far end of the stone passage glanced up, not sure what he was hearing. Then it came to him that the ragged sounds coming from the cell were hoots of laughter. He listened, trying to understand why the three men were laughing when their condition was so serious, and could only surmise they were crazy.

Perhaps, he thought, the stories he had heard about

Westerners were true. These men were rabid simpletons, sent from America to bring their madness to infect all true believers.

CHAPTER THIRTEEN

Jabir Rahman understood only too well how Americans worked. They wormed their way into favor by stealth and deceit, promising much during the courtship to those with the gullibility to believe. It was so easy to be blinded by the guile employed. With the Americans it was, in the end, always a matter of money. They purchased favors by first pretending to have the willing victims believe it was from a generosity of spirit and understanding. Money weakened resolve. Gifts were lavished on the unsuspecting, while behind the smiles and feigned sympathy, the horned devil waited for the opportunity to pounce. American guile masqueraded in many forms. Political. Military. Any and all kinds of aid to cushion the inevitable treachery. America was all-powerful. A behemoth rich beyond all human imagining. It cajoled and persuaded anyone who stood in its path.

"The Americans insult us by their presence. By their very existence in this world," he would inform his gathered brethren. "The air they breathe becomes poisoned and we are tainted by their breath. These vermin must be put in their place, and that place is the dirt beneath our feet.

"They are a godless race. Unclean and without honor. If we are to create a paradise on Allah's world we must first rid it of these soulless monsters.

"There are those who associate with these Americans. Who sully the image of Pakistan by colluding with our enemy. They plot and conspire to hurt our friends, so they must be cleansed, as their American friends will be attacked. They must be made to see the path they walk is the wrong path. Our strike against both the U.S. homeland and the American military based on our soil will show we refuse to stand for this blasphemy."

"Fazeel is still hard at work," Radesh said, interrupting Rahman's thoughts. "He insists on perfecting his expertise with the Barracuda."

"We chose well, my friend," Rahman said. "Now come inside and sit with me."

When they'd settled themselves, a white-garbed member of Rahman's staff served them green tea, a favorite Pakistani drink. Rahman spoke quietly with the man, who gave a brief bow of his head as he withdrew.

"To your health, Luba," Rahman said as they drank. "And to our success."

Radesh smiled. "Of that I have little doubt. Everything is working out as we planned." He paused. "Correction, of course. There are the matters of the affair in London and the unfortunate loss of the weapons and drugs in the Swat Valley area."

"The death of Winch in London is to be regretted, but the man failed to act in a sensible manner," Rahman said. "He did not make sure the policeman he shot was dead, and so was exposed as an informant. His stupidity left Prem and Hussein open to investigation." Rahman took more tea. "As to the destruction of the ordnance and the heroin, yes, I will admit that was regrettable. Naj Hajik will not be pleased at the loss. However, those items are replaceable, though it will take time and a great deal of trouble. I regret more the deaths of our Taliban brothers. Too many good men died during that engagement. But at least we now have a number of the men responsible confined."

Radesh was openly surprised by the revelation. He had not heard about the capture. "This is true? You caught them?"

"There were six in the group. Three escaped, but the report I received informed me that they most likely perished in a rockslide when they took shelter in a cave. There was a mortar hit and they were buried.

"The others were taken alive. The Taliban wanted to kill them on the spot, but I ordered them transported to the old fort at Pradesh Qatar, where they could be interrogated.

"It is quite obvious these men are on Pakistani soil illegally. They have not been fully identified yet, but I am sure they are the same individuals who were in London. They could be working for the Americans or the British. We will find out. Capturing them could be a coup for us and an embarrassment for whoever sent them. It may help to divert attention from our operation."

"Of course there will be full denial. No one will admit who these men work for," Radesh stated.

"No doubt, but we still have them, and can obtain some measure of information from them. Our Taliban brothers can be extremely persuasive when it comes to extracting details. For now we can make their lives uncomfortable."

Food arrived then, with a procession of servants bringing in various dishes they placed on the long, low table. Curried beef, lamb, chicken. Rice and fresh vegetables. Naan breads. Pickles made from mangoes, carrots and lemon. Cool, refreshing yogurt. In the traditional Pakistani manner, Radesh and Rahman ate using their right hands only, scooping up the spicy food with chunks of bread.

"Will your people get these men to talk?"

Rahman smiled. "In time, I am sure," he said. "There are three of them, so the odds are on our side. The Taliban are experts in many forms of persuasion."

"How much do you think these trespassers know? Is there a possibility they may have sent information back to their American masters?"

"All in good time, my friend. Don't forget we have much to do. Get the nuclear rods into America. Have the drone missiles worked on by our technicians. Now, try this chicken tikka. It is my chef's specialty. Delicious."

"WELL?" Calvin James asked.

Encizo ducked back into cover. He glanced across at Nasir Hanafi. "I think you were right. Small setup. I counted five guys outside. All Taliban. All carrying. They have an old Land Rover. No way of knowing if there are any inside or how many."

"I was unable to gain complete information," Hanafi said, "but I do know that both Rahman and the Taliban have used this place before to contain prisoners they wish to isolate."

"And as far as that goes, they don't have any other detainees at the moment?" James asked.

Hanafi shook his head. "I am not a great believer in coincidence, but your friends were captured within the last two days and no other incidents have been reported since."

"So it's looking to be a safe bet our guys are in there," Encizo said.

"Works for me," James said.

"Time to roll the dice and hope for boxcars." James said.

"What does he say?" Hanafi was frowning.

James smiled. "Craps is an American dice game. Numbered dice are thrown. If you come up with both dice showing six, you've made a lucky throw. 'Boxcars' is slang for a pair of sixes. Sometimes it's called midnight. Two sixes. Twelve. Midnight."

Hanafi shook his head. "It can be a strange language sometimes."

"Hey, I'm from Cuba," Encizo said. "How do you think I get on?"

James finished checking his AK-47. He turned to his holstered autopistol. Encizo and Hanafi did the same.

"I wish I could have brought you more weapons," Hanafi said. "These were all I was able to lay my hands on in the time I had."

Encizo touched his shoulder. "No worries, Nasir. You did okay."

"No point in waiting," James said. "Longer we leave it the more the chance of reinforcements showing up. Let's get close. Then we hit them head-on."

"If there are more inside," Encizo said, "and they hear shooting, they might decide to execute any captives. You two give me cover. Let me go straight inside. Once you've handled the outside group, follow me in."

James nodded. "You sure?"

"I'm sure."

THE HARD CRACKLE of an AK-47 on full auto shattered the quiet. James and Hanafi broke cover and stormed in the direction of the stone building. Two of the robed Taliban went down from the first assault, bodies bloodily ravaged by the impact of 7.62 mm slugs from the Russian weapons.

Encizo was already on his way inside the building.

The remaining three Taliban reacted swiftly, turning their weapons on the attackers, who were weaving across open ground, firing as they moved.

The heavy racket made by the combined AK-47s split the air around the building. Slugs blew chunks of crumbling stone from the front wall. Others kicked up dusty spouts of earth.

Encizo tracked in on the guy closest to the open door, pumping the Taliban with a long burst that threw the man backward into the solid wall. The fatally hit man bounced forward, and Encizo's second burst struck his face full on, tearing through flesh and muscle. The guard's features disintegrated in a bloody flash as he flopped to the ground. Seeing his opportunity, Encizo angled away from the other Taliban and charged for the door, going in without a moment's pause, regardless of the reckless move he was making. His thoughts were on the possibility that his Phoenix Force teammates might be inside and under imminent threat....

HANAFI, DUCKING INTO a combat crouch, raised his AK-47 and triggered a short burst that clipped his target's shoulder. The shock of the 7.62 mm slugs tearing into his flesh held the guy back for a second and allowed Hanafi to fire again. He squeezed his trigger and stitched the Taliban from waist to neck, slugs hitting the assault rifle the man was holding. The wooden stock shattered, driving splinters of wood into the opened wounds, kicking the guy off his feet and leaving him jerking in the dust. There was no hesitation in Hanafi's movements as he stepped up close and hit the downed man with a burst to the head.

James had already engaged the final Taliban, letting out a sharp gasp as something hot burned across his left side. He stumbled, regained his balance and settled his own weapon on the bearded and scowling Taliban who was resighting his rifle. The black Phoenix Force commando fired on reflex, finger easing back on his trigger, feeling the AK-47 jerk as it fired. His tight burst ripped into the target's left arm, tearing the elbow joint apart. The useless limb flopped at his side, hanging by shredded sinew, blood starting to pump from the ragged flesh. James adjusted his aim and jacked out another burst that was aimed at the chest. The powerful 7.62 mm slugs cored in, breaking ribs before they tore apart the guy's heart and dropped him to the blood-spattered earth.

James and Hanafi spread, checking out the area in case there were other hostiles they might have overlooked. They each replenished their weapons with fresh magazines.

"You okay?" James asked.

Hanafi nodded. He saw the bloody patch showing on James's combat shirt. "You are hit?"

"Feels like it."

"We should check it," Hanafi said.

James might have agreed, but the sudden clatter of autofire reached their ears, and it was coming from inside the building....

ENCIZO RECOGNIZED living quarters as he went in through the door. There was an untidy spread of clothing, weapons and food. The air was tinged with smoke from a smoldering fire in a stone hearth on one wall. Across from him a door led deeper into the building, and the Cuban went directly for it.

He picked up voices, the slap of feet on the stone flooring, the rattle of weaponry. Someone was coming in his direction. As soon as Encizo went through he flattened himself against the rough stone wall, his Kalashnikov held ready. The light was low but he could see the passage ahead of him, doors leading off right and left. The place stank of dust and sweat.

A robed figure burst from one of the doors, weapon up and opening fire when Encizo's shadowed form came into view. In that instant before full recognition, Encizo dropped to a crouch. The fired burst tore into the soft stone over his head. Ignoring the rain of fragments that showered him, he returned fire. A man screamed as hot steel slugs ripped into his torso, spinning him around so that Encizo's second burst hit the back of his skull and pitched him face-down on the flagged floor.

A couple more figures, robes flapping like huge bat wings, crowded the passage. Encizo fired the moment they were exposed. His withering spray caught the Taliban on the move, the 7.62 mm slugs penetrating flesh and pulverizing internal organs. The men went down in a flurry of arms and legs, crashing hard on the stone floor.

Encizo waited only seconds before he pushed to his feet, ejecting his nearly exhausted magazine and snapping in a fresh one. He prowled the passage, collecting weapons from the dead before he moved on.

James's voice reached him. "Are we clear?"

"Clear," Encizo called back.

He heard the others moving in behind him.

"Anything?" James asked.

They checked the few rooms and found them empty. Farther on was a short flight of stone steps leading to a lower level, a short passage with wooden doors on either side. Each door had a barred grille. The whole are had a fetid odor, the air hot and rank.

"If they are here this would be the place," Hanafi said.

"You here, guys?" James called. "Room service on its way."

The reply came from a familiar voice.

"About bloody time, you lazy buggers."

They reached the barred door the voice had come from. It was secured by heavy iron bolts top and bottom. As the door swung open and the cramped cell was exposed, McCarter, Manning and Hawkins stumbled out. They were grubby, sweating and barely able to move without falling.

James took a look into the filthy space where his friends

had been held. "That's what you get for booking into a utility hotel."

Manning gave a ragged chuckle. "Didn't even have cable."

When they emerged into daylight the bright sunlight hurt their eyes, and the three shielded their faces as they adjusted.

Hanafi ducked back inside the building, searching the living quarters. He located a supply of bottled water and dragged the plastic-wrapped bundle outside. James passed bottles to his friends. Hanafi located the packs McCarter, Manning and Hawkins had been carrying. AK-47 rifles were gathered, as well as extra magazines. James picked up a couple of LAWs from the small ordnance supply and handed out a few spare fragmentation grenades.

"Take it easy with that water," James said to McCarter. "Small sips at first. Don't drink too much at once."

McCarter used part of his first bottle to sluice his unshaved face. With the dirt washed away his bruised flesh was exposed. Manning and Hawkins showed similar bruising.

"You upset them?" James asked.

"I guess we shouldn't have complained about the lack of room service," Hawkins replied.

"Here," Hanafi said, holding out a crumpled pack of cigarettes to McCarter. "I found these." He handed the Briton a plastic throwaway lighter.

"I didn't think the Taliban smoked," Encizo said.

"Makes you hope they can't be all that bad, then," McCarter said, a crooked grin on his bruised lips. He lit one of the thin cigarettes, coughing violently as he drew in the smoke. "Bloody hell, what do they make these things out of, old shredded socks?"

Hanafi laughed at the Briton's woeful expression.

"Local cigarettes," he said. "Probably the scrapings off the floor of the opium factory."

McCarter took a few puffs, then tossed the cigarette aside. "I'll wait until I can get my hands on a pack of Players."

"You should tend your wound," Hanafi said to James.

"I forgot," he answered. Then pulled his medi kit from his pack and cleaned the bullet tear.

HANAFI COLLECTED every piece of ordnance he could lay his hands on, and loaded it into the Land Rover. There was a determination in his actions that told Phoenix Force he had the intention of making certain nothing was left behind that might give the Taliban any advantage. The pack of bottled water was also loaded onto the vehicle. Then Hanafi climbed into the vehicle and fired up the engine.

"You feel better now?" McCarter asked. "No desire to level the building?"

Hanafi frowned at the Phoenix Force leader for a moment, then gave a wide grin. "No, my friend, I think the Taliban will get the message well enough."

They drove for almost six hours. It was fully dark when Hanafi braked the Land Rover and cut the engine. They were stopped outside a large stone-and-timber house that showed no sign of habitation.

"Where are we?" McCarter asked.

"This place used to belong to my uncle. When he died he left it to me. I haven't been here for some time. It will provide for us tonight."

They climbed out of the Land Rover and Hanafi led them inside the house. There was no electricity, he informed them as he went around lighting a number of oil lamps. The soft glow revealed the large, main room to be roughly furnished, with a floor of stone slabs. In the center was a large wooden table flanked by benches.

Backpacks were dumped on the table, opened and gone through to assess what they had in the way of food.

"I am sorry there is no other sustenance available," Hanafi apologized. "When I came here before I always brought food with me."

"Hey, don't fret," Encizo said. "We all love field rations."

"WHERE HAVE YOU GUYS been?" Barbara Price asked, recognizing McCarter's voice. "Why no checking in the last couple of days?"

"I guess you could say some of us have been experiencing Taliban hospitality," McCarter said.

"Are you all okay?"

"More or less. Some cuts and bruises. Nothing a hot shower, clean clothes and food won't cure. Any developments on that UAV?"

"Intel we picked up indicates it's been used."

"Doesn't sound as if I'm going to like this."

"A consignment of irradiated uranium rods being moved from the Kanupp nuclear facility was hijacked. There were three vehicles in the convoy—two escorts carrying armed security personnel and the truck carrying the rods. Both escort vehicles were taken out and the truck with the rods was driven away. A Pakistani goat herder reported seeing streaks of fire in the sky before the trucks were hit. No sighting of any aircraft."

"Missiles from the UAV. Flies high. No one can see or hear it. Pinpoint targeting via the control center. Take out the escort vehicles, leave the rods alone and unprotected. Bloody great," McCarter said. "Just bloody great. Not the result we came here for."

"Well, knowing you guys, this is just going to make you more determined to find those rods."

"Thanks, love, but that doesn't make me feel even a little bit better."

"Listen, David, we might have a connection here. Aaron and the team have been checking the cell phones having anything to do with Rahman and his associates. They're still piecing the data together but we have found one link. A guy named Luba Radesh. Serbian Muslim. He's known as a radical but up until recently he's never been allied to anyone."

"Now he is?"

"He was sighted by British intelligence in Belgium, in conversation with Umer Qazi some time back. We only found this out a while ago. Rumor has it that Qazi, among other things, is a recruiter for extreme Muslims. He has ties with the Taliban and contacts in al Qaeda. And more to the point is his association with Colonel Jabir Rahman."

"The plot thickens."

"Radesh has been doing some recruiting of his own, it seems. Pulling together a small team of his old Serbian Muslim brothers, our intel informs us. Now, our Mr. Radesh is a little casual with his cell phones. Bear and the team have pinned down a few texts he sent over the last few weeks to various people. They all seem a little pally, so to speak. Called each other by name, so Aaron got a Janos and a Miko Sevisko. Going on that, a little more digging came up with Janos Lasko. Lasko and Sevisko were fliers in the war. Part of a Serbian commando team led by Radesh. Nothing could be proved, but the UN investigators working after the conflict had Radesh's group linked to some nasty work against non-Muslims. They vanished before anything could be pinned to them."

"Same old story," McCarter said. "In other words they

were allowed to get away. Aaron dig up anything on their recent activities?"

"He tracked Radesh and his team to the U.K. They were there around the time the UAV was hijacked, then vanished off the radar until one of them used a cell to call Khalil Amir's number."

"Our Boston connection."

"The conversation was brief. Just a text to confirm that an order had been filled and was on its way. They replied yes and the call was finished."

"Any location for the incoming call?"

"Sorry, David. Aaron still has the team trying to get a trace."

"Okay. I'll take a guess and say it originated in Pakistan. Right where we are now. I'll bet they were talking about the UAV on its way here."

"Any thoughts on Radesh's pilots?"

"We came into this on the basis of some plot against the U.S. and Pakistan. Now we have this bunch of crazies holding a crate of nuclear rods. How does this sound—they split the cargo. Half for use on home ground, the other destined for America. Quickest way would be to ship it on a plane, right into the hands of Rahman's local chapter."

"You can't just fly a nuclear package into the States, David. It isn't that easy." Price considered her comment, then added, "Not legally, anyhow."

"Exactly, love. Where these blokes come from legal doesn't come into it. And on or off the books, nobody mentioned easy, but these people are not what you'd call rational. Plus think about the amount of air traffic flying into the U.S. every damn day. If Rahman has been planning this for a long time, he'll have every base covered. The guy has unlimited finances. The Taliban. Al Qaeda. God knows who else. Money can buy anything you want if you hand it to the right people. Flight plans on the sly. Grease a few palms to get him safe passage so his plane can be refueled at sympathetic airstrips. There are a lot of people out there ready and willing to help brothers of the faith. A strike against the unbelievers. And there *are* sympathizers in America, love. We both know that. No use pretending otherwise."

"So he gets his plane on U.S. soil. What about customs clearance? No way he's going to get his nukes through there."

"Enough determination and planning can achieve all kinds of things. Bloody hell, Barbara, these buggers orchestrated the theft of a consignment of nuclear rods. Stole a UAV to open the way, and went and did it. Tells me we're not up against a bunch of wannabes. Rahman is playing a serious game."

"If he's that serious why not land his plane in some isolated spot? Out of the public eye where he can unload it and no one is the wiser?"

"Fair point," McCarter said, "but any tracked aircraft of significant size showing up on radar and landing in the boonies would be viewed as suspicious. If they did do that, they would still have to transport it to its final destination. Shipping nuclear rods by road would be a risky exercise. Landing it close to where they want it would make more sense."

"Well, maybe, but they still have to get it out of the airport."

"If I was doing it I'd plan some kind of diversion when the plane lands."

"You know, David, a phone conversation with you is always a challenge."

THE DISCUSSION CENTERED around what Rahman would do with the nuclear rods now they were in his possession.

"He needs to work on them if he intends shaping them into explosive devices," Encizo said.

"That means he has to have a place where he's out of sight and not likely to be disturbed." Manning glanced at Hanafi. "Nasir, you know Rahman and you know how he works. Where would he hide the rods?"

"Nowhere in a city or town," Hanafi said. "Too many chances to be discovered. He will take them somewhere isolated where he can control things."

"You say he controls areas along the border country. Maybe an abandoned village?"

Hanafi shook his head. He sat forward, his voice rising with excitement as he spoke. "Denupra," he said. "The military base at Denupra. Within Rahman's military authority. It used to be a helicopter station many, many years ago but was closed through lack of finance. There is a large hangar. Smaller buildings that used to house men and equipment. Not many remember it, but I once noticed a circle drawn around it on a map in Rahman's office. I wondered at the time why he would mark such a place. I did not ask why it was circled in case my interest aroused suspicion."

Manning produced a map from his pack and spread it across the table. "This help?"

"Yes. Yes." Hanafi pored over the chart, tracing a line with his finger. He stabbed at a spot. "There. Denupra. You see where it lies. Far from anywhere. Remote. It would be ideal for Rahman's purpose. With his own people to man it. No disturbance."

"Well, except maybe from us," McCarter said. "Can you guide us there, Nasir?"

Hanafi nodded. "Yes. From here it will take us at least half a day. On foot, because there are no real roads in the area until you get close to Denupra. Then there is a bad road that takes you to the border. A wide swing around and it will bring you close to where you were originally dropped." He used his finger to trace the route. "Hard country with roving Taliban who do not welcome strangers—especially Westerners."

McCarter grinned. "Don't forget we already had a taste of Taliban hospitality."

"Yes, sorry, I forgot. If we are to go we should sleep now so we can start early."

McCarter rested a hand on Hanafi's shoulder. "If Rahman learns you're with us, he isn't going to be pleased. He'll realize you've been working undercover. Trying to get the goods on him."

Hanafi shrugged. "Things have been getting harder for me recently. Maintaining my cover while I learned about his business was bound to end in tears. But with what we have now discovered I can expose him, so breaking away is really the best thing for me."

"As long as you're sure."

"It is not a problem, my friends. Both our presidents will be able to use the information we have gained. And this madness Rahman is preparing to unleash is more important than worrying about our safety. Yes?"

"Nasir, welcome to the club," James said.

CHAPTER FOURTEEN

They took as little in their packs as possible. They loaded up as much ammunition as they could handle and a plentiful supply of the bottled water. James carried the pair of LAWs he had taken charge of. They ate a meager cold breakfast, pulled on their packs and moved out at first light. Hanafi strode ahead, confident in his line of travel, with Phoenix Force strung out behind him.

The terrain was uncompromising. Rocks and dust, little vegetation. In every direction the view was the same—ridge upon ridge, the distant horizon showing where the land rose in higher elevations.

They all carried their AK-47s in readiness, aware of the hostile inhabitants in a punishing environment. The Phoenix Force team understood they were deliberately placing themselves in harm's way, but that was how it was every time they undertook a new mission. They always took on tough opposition, faced enemies who were posing hard threats against the U.S.A. The SOG mandate was to recognize and fight the factions that threatened America and her allies. The truism held fast—Stony Man was a frontline organization, ultrasecret, that took on what no one else could. They confronted the enemy without fear or favor, fought him on his terms, pushing aside the rules and dispatching the opposition any way possible. Evil had to be dealt with on its own level.

Which was what they were attempting to do now as they

tramped across the dusty Pakistani back country, understanding that at the end they were going to be facing Rahman's breakaway force. The men who followed the colonel through the conviction of their religious beliefs thought that anyone who came from the West was so much dirt beneath their boots. The evil, Satan-loving degenerates needed to be subjugated and brought under the heel of an Islamic regime. In the jaundiced eye of Colonel Jabir Rahman, that was sufficient justification to detonate a nuclear device on American soil in pursuit of his campaign. And as a diversion he was willing to contaminate Pakistani soil by exploding a similar device to destroy an American military presence in his own country, ignoring the fact that it would kill Pakistani citizens.

Midmorning they took time for a break. Hanafi had located a relatively shaded spot. They drank sparingly, the bottled water already warmed in the heat. No one complained. They were all seasoned combat veterans. At least they had water.

McCarter sluiced his unshaved face, washing away some of the dust. He was still bruised from his time in Taliban custody, and the heat of the day did little to ease the discomfort.

"I swear, next time they send us out, it's got to be somewhere cool."

"Maybe they'll ship us off to Alaska," Encizo said.

"Some contrast," Hawkins said.

"My country has cool places," Hanafi said. "It is not all like this."

"Problem is, Nasir, bad guys never set up shop in those kind of places," James said. "They like to hide out in dusty, hot backwaters like this. Nice spots don't have the same appeal."

Hanafi smiled. "Listen to me, my friends, you are doing

very well. We have made good time. We should reach Denupra within the next couple of hours."

"That's about the best news we'll hear today," Hawkins said.

"You see, a good sign," Hanafi said, pushing to his feet in readiness to move out.

The two shots came fast, from close by.

Hanafi grunted under the impact as the 7.62 mm Kalashnikov rounds hit his right side, just below his ribs. The impact spun him around and he slammed to the ground.

"Son of a bitch," McCarter said, his own AK-47 coming on line.

"There," Encizo yelled, his autorifle already on target. He triggered in the direction of the three dark-clad, bearded shooters emerging from the rocks ahead, weapons up and spitting fire.

Taliban. A scouting party, most likely.

Handing out violence to the strangers in their territory.

The response from Phoenix Force was fast and deadly. Five AK-47s erupted in the hands of seasoned warriors. The hard cracks from the Soviet combat rifles rattled across the emptiness. The Taliban, who had not expected such retaliation, were caught in the relentless stream of copper-jacketed slugs. They fell back, bodies riddled, flesh punctured and burned by the volley. Hawkins and Manning ran over to where the men lay, delivering final killing shots, then spread apart to check out the surrounding terrain.

James was already kneeling beside Hanafi. The Pakistani was barely conscious, his clothing soaked. James pulled open his shirt to expose the bruised entry holes. He gently rolled Hanafi on his side to see if the slugs had exited. They had not. If they had he would had seen ugly holes in the man's flesh. James laid him on his back and took out his medical kit.

McCarter bent over, his hand on James's shoulder. He didn't need to ask the question.

"Not good," Cal said quietly. "Two slugs inside. No way I can tell what damage they've done. All I can do is clean up the holes and try to stop the bleeding. If the penetration dragged in any dirt, infection could start pretty quick."

"What bloody bad luck," McCarter said.

"Who for?" James asked as he got to work with his limited equipment.

"For Nasir," McCarter muttered. "Bloody hell, Cal, it isn't too good for us, either. There, I said it. Feel better now?"

"Not really, and I wasn't being cynical. I like the guy, too. But this could put a crimp in our chances."

Hanafi groaned as James kept working on him. He opened his eyes and stared up at the two Phoenix Force men.

"That really wasn't cricket," he said. "Not giving the other man a chance."

"You keep making bad jokes like that and I'll figure you're not so badly hurt, after all," McCarter said.

Hanafi looked at James. "Just make sure that bandage is on good and tight. I don't want to delay you."

"You figure on going somewhere?"

"I can't stay here. You need to get to Denupra. I need to show you how. What else is there?"

"Nasir, you have two bullets in you. Undue movement isn't going to help. You should be—"

"Waiting for a rescue helicopter? I agree, but it isn't going to happen. Let us not play games, my friends. I'm not trying to be a hero, but what you are doing is important. So help me get on my feet and we can go."

James completed his basic first aid, using sterile pads

and rolls of bandages to bind the wounds tightly. His skilled hands moved gently over Hanafi's body, but it was obvious to the Phoenix Force medic that the Pakistani was in severe pain. Sweat shone on his face and he clamped his teeth together to stifle any sounds. When James fastened Hanafi's shirt they helped him stand. Encizo and Hawkins moved in without being told and supported him.

"Just tell us where to go," McCarter said. He picked up Hanafi's pack and AK-47 and led the way forward.

Hanafi's two hours stretched to over three. There were no complaints about the slow travel or the frequent breaks they took so Hanafi could rest. It didn't help that the terrain was becoming increasingly difficult to cross. There were times when Hanafi could have directed them to an easier path. He didn't, putting up with the rougher patches because it got them closer to Denupra by the quickest route.

James and Manning took over, relieving Hawkins and Encizo. They were still with Hanafi when he raised his head and told them to stop.

"Over that ridge," he said. His voice was reduced to a whisper. As they lowered him to the hard ground, resting his head on his own pack, James saw that fresh blood had soaked through the man's shirt. He reached out to check it, but Hanafi shook his head. "We both know you have nothing left in your medi kit. You have done all that can be done. Now it is time to concentrate on why you are here."

McCarter crawled to the top of the ridge, peered over, and found himself looking down a slope. Where it flattened out, their objective spread in front of them.

Denupra.

"NASIR, I'D SAY YOU GOT this right on the button," McCarter said. "Take a look."

Hanafi had been moved to the top of the ridge. Mc-

Carter passed him the binoculars from his pack. The Pakistani scanned the area, concentrating on the large hangar that dominated the center of the base.

"It is there," he said, excitement in his voice. "The drone. Just inside the doors. I can see it. Wait, they are working on it. Around the hard points where the missiles are fitted." He handed the glasses back to McCarter. "What are they doing?"

"At a guess I'd say installing some kind of device to carry the rods to the target," McCarter said. "Fly that bloody drone to the spot they want to hit, and detonate it so the rods fracture and spread radiation."

Hanafi leaned back against the slope again. His face was ashen, his skin beaded with sweat. It was obvious his wounds were weakening him. The efforts of the past hours had taken their toll. McCarter saw more blood seeping through his shirt.

"Jack, we must stop them," he said. "This must end here. Rahman is a madman. My country has suffered enough already. He must be stopped…."

"We didn't come all this way just to admire the scenery," James said. "Now you lie back and rest." He took water from his pack to give to Hanafi. "I might have some painkillers. Let me find them for you."

While James tended to Hanafi, the rest of Phoenix Force went into a huddle.

"We won't get a better chance at stopping Rahman's little game. We need to hit hard and fast. Main priority is disabling that bloody UAV. Whatever else, we have to cripple that thing so it can't deliver its payload," McCarter concluded.

"We'll need to get in close," Manning said. "If they have already installed those rods, we can't risk any action that might shatter the casing. Don't know about you guys, but getting exposed to radioactivity is not on my wish list."

"He's right," Encizo said. "We have to put the drone down but keep the rods intact."

"Sounds like a fun deal," Hawkins agreed. "I've been doing a head count. We've got around fourteen, maybe fifteen armed guys walking around the area. No way of knowing how many there are inside the hangar. I've seen four working around the drone. Techs, most likely. Can't see too far inside."

"Okay," McCarter said. "There are two manned machine gun nests. Two choppers with side-mounted .50 calibers. Vehicle pool to the east side of the hangar. Let's do a weapons check. See what we have."

In addition to their sidearms and the AK-47s, the Phoenix Force team had two LAWs and a number of fragmentation grenades.

"Not exactly an endless supply," Manning said.

"Hey, guys, MacGyver would have managed with a stick of gum and two rubber bands," Hawkins said.

"So call him up on your sat phone," Manning said.

McCarter had been studying the layout below them. His eyes settled on the helicopters as he worked out how to launch Phoenix Force's assault.

"We can take out both choppers using the LAWs. When they go up it's bound to cause a distraction. As soon as the choppers blow we hit from positions we've already moved to."

"Autofire should cripple the drone," Manning said. "Chop up the fuselage, the wings. Anything to stop the thing getting off the ground."

"So who gets to play with the LAWs?" Encizo asked. "I vote Landis. He did pretty good back at the village."

McCarter glanced across at James. "You okay with that?"

The black Phoenix warrior nodded. "I'm cool."

"Constantine, you're with me," McCarter said to Encizo. "Allen teams with Rankin." He made a crude diagram in the dust. "I'll cover the north end of the hangar with Constantine. Allen, you and Rankin take a position where you can take out the machine gun crews. If you can gain control of the guns, use them on the roving troops. Hit the buggers hard. I'm not looking for prisoners here. The name of the game is extreme prejudice." McCarter glanced at Hanafi. "Sorry, Nasir. No time for niceties."

Hanafi said, "These men are planning to detonate a nuclear device in their own country. You think they deserve special treatment?"

They geared up for the move. The fragmentation grenades worked out at three each except for James. They final checked AKs and handguns, sheathed knifes. James slung the LAWs by their carrying straps. Hanafi insisted on being given his AK-47 and a couple spare magazines.

"I can at least give you covering fire if needed," he said. "Let me be useful."

"Nasir, you've already been that and more," McCarter said. "No wild downhill charges. I don't want you getting excited."

"I promise," Hanafi said. His voice was becoming strained.

"Let's get this done, girls," McCarter said. "Check your watches. We'll give ourselves thirty-five minutes to get in position. Anybody late has to buy dinner. Signal to go is when Landis hits the first chopper."

Hanafi was eased into position close to the top of the ridge, given his AK-47 and extra magazines.

"Go with God," he said.

"Stay safe," Hawkins replied.

Phoenix Force moved out, offering brief nods to each other before they split and started the long trek to reach their individual attack positions.

Every man understood the risks he was taking and the possibility that this might be the last strike any one of them might be making. They were aware of their individual frailties. Each of them faced his own demons. Realization that the kind of combat they were moving toward left them open to harm, maybe sudden death. It did nothing to slow them down or implant fear that could impair their fighting skills.

Nasir Hanafi watched the group disperse, using available natural cover to conceal their approach to the hangar. He imagined he would be able to follow their movements easily from his vantage point, but was surprised to find after a few minutes that they had all vanished. He searched for any sign of Phoenix Force movement that might betray their passage. There was nothing. No sight or sound. Not even a drift of pale dust to show where they might be.

Hanafi shook his head in admiration for those men. Their skill was second to none. He had listened to the casual banter they indulged in, and noted their easy manner with each other. Now, moving in on their targets, they were proving just how experienced and capable they were, and Hanafi saw that Rahman's people could well be in line for a sudden and deadly shock when the moment came.

He felt a surge of agony from the wounds in his side. Sharp pain drew a gasp from his lips. He shifted position, hoping that might ease his discomfort, but it helped only a little and he was forced to lie completely still, his breathing restricted.

Hanafi was aware his wounds were serious enough to be draining away his reserves of strength. Being a realist, he refused to pretend his condition would improve if he remained unmoving. Bullets caused serious harm to the human body. It was not designed to be violated in a such a way, and damage that could not be seen resulted from such attacks. The slugs were lodged deep in his flesh and the trauma they caused contributed to the increasing possibility of fatal wounds. He decided that for now all he could do was rest, conserving his strength for the fight that would surely come. When his friends started their attack, he would return to his position and add his contribution to the battle.

When he opened his eyes again, not realizing he had drifted, Hanafi glanced at his watch and saw that more than thirty minutes had gone by.

Thirty.

Close to the deadline Coyle had allowed for his team to get into position.

Hanafi rolled over and began the slow, painful crawl to position himself in a suitable firing spot. It seemed to take an eternity and he was drenched in sweat by the time he reached it. Below the slope nothing had changed.

Rahman's men were still moving around the area. The sentries manned their positions. There was no disturbance. No sign of—

One of the helicopters blew up in a flash of fire that expanded as the machine came apart. The fireball rose skyward; smoke and the shattering boom of the explosion followed. Debris and burning fuel were scattered across the landing pad. A few moments later the second chopper was hit, and the landing pad turned into a blazing mass. The crackle of exploding ammunition from the boxes attached to the .50-caliber machine guns added to the noise. Hanafi could hear the slugs whining and zipping viciously as they were blown clear of the wrecked choppers.

As the heavy detonations of the LAWs faded, Hanafi heard the distant rattle of autofire, and knew the battle had been joined.

DEBRIS FROM THE EXPLOSIONS rained down on the hangar roof. Crouched in the dry weeds at the rear of the building, McCarter and Manning felt the ground tremble as shock waves expanded out from the helicopter pad.

"Let's do this," McCarter said.

He pushed to his feet and stepped up to the inset door. The Briton slammed his boot against the dry wood. The door splintered, swinging open. McCarter followed, breaking right, with Manning on his heels and taking the left. They dropped to low crouches, letting their eyes adjust to the dimmer light inside the hangar.

Their end of the place was piled high with the detritus of years; old packing cases, dented fuel drums, abandoned equipment. The air stank of oil and diesel. The cracked concrete floor was thick with dust and covered with dark stains.

"Wouldn't want to fly with this airline," Manning commented as he and McCarter edged their way through the trash.

Alerted by the explosions outside, armed figures were moving back and forth farther down the length of the hangar. Someone with keen eyes spotted the recently opened door behind McCarter and Manning. The guy raised a shout. More figures turned and followed him.

"So much for a quiet entrance," McCarter said. He raised his AK-47 and triggered a short burst that took out the guy who had called the alarm. The man went down in a flurry of arms and legs, hitting the floor with a thump.

Return fire splintered wood and clanged against steel drums.

The Phoenix Force pair went in opposite directions, staying low and using the crates and drums for cover.

Autofire increased. McCarter felt a couple close misses where slugs penetrated steel. He could hear the opposition advancing through the wide formation of containers.

He took a fragmentation grenade and yanked out the pin. Making a swift mental calculation based on the effective range, he realized the distance to the front section of the hangar would prevent any blast from the grenade falling anywhere near the UAV being prepared for flight. He was concerned that the nuclear rods might already be in place.

"Grenade," McCarter yelled in Manning's direction, warning the Canadian to stay low.

He tossed the explosive in the direction of the advancing combatants, ducking down behind the cluster of empty drums.

There were shouts of alarm from the oncoming men. Then the grenade detonated, the sound of the blast magnified within the confines of the hangar. Shouts became agonized screams and groans as the white-hot grenade fragments found human flesh and bone. Fuel drums were tossed aside, grenade slivers piercing the metal. McCarter and Manning waited out the blast, then moved forward, weapons up and firing at the scattered opposition.

McCarter tracked in on a pair of Rahman rebels, triggering the AK-47, punching 7.62 mm slugs into the men. They twisted under the hits, bodies reacting to the powerful impact of the slugs, tumbling to the floor in bloody heaps.

Only yards away, Gary Manning raised his head following the grenade burst, and saw a trio of armed rebels swinging away from the blast site, moving at an angle that would bring them directly to where he was concealed. The

Canadian raised his shoulders and brought the AK-47 on line, making his target acquisition quickly. He triggered the Russian assault rifle, pulling the muzzle from man to man, and saw the three combatants go down in a misty haze of red as the 7.62 mm slugs cored through their upper bodies.

"Go," McCarter yelled.

The Phoenix Force pair made a swift forward move, eyes fixed on the armed figures converging from the front of the hangar, while they picked up the distant crackle of autofire from outside the building.

THE DESTRUCTION OF THE helicopters was the signal for Encizo and Hawkins to make their move on the machine gun posts situated at the front of the hangar. They had used the advance time to work their way to within thirty feet, using the cover provided by scattered vehicles and abandoned machinery and equipment. They had been forced to change their angle of approach on more than one occasion due to the movement of Rahman's armed protection squad, so reached their current positions with little more than a couple minutes to spare. Now they were able to see the machine gun posts clearly. Sandbags had been used to construct the half-circle barricades, behind which two-man teams tended the L1A1, 12.7 mm Heavy Machine Guns.

"I'll take the right side," Encizo said. "You handle the other team. Soon as Cal drops those LAWs on the choppers, we hit them. Take out the teams, then we move in and man one of the machine guns. Field of fire will let us cover the main area. You okay with that?"

Hawkins nodded. "No problem."

The LAWs struck less than a minute later, filling the area with noise and smoke and flying debris.

Encizo and Hawkins went into action without further discussion, AK-47s set for single shots. Each man fired two rounds, the 7.62 mm slugs hitting their targets with deadly force, sending the machine gunners sprawling. As the teams went down, Encizo and Hawkins broke cover and sprinted for the closest emplacements, rolling over the top of the sandbags. They pulled aside the dead rebels and took command of the machine gun. While Encizo made sure the weapon was cocked and ready, Hawkins took up his position with the ammunition feed, checking the belt and the ammo boxes.

The Phoenix Force maneuver had been seen by the roving rebels and armed figures started to move in their direction. Swinging the machine gun on its tripod, Encizo tripped the trigger and the powerful weapon began to spit out its awesome loads. The thunder of the weapon blotted out every sound close to the Phoenix Force warriors. Encizo swept the fire left to right, the large-caliber slugs chewing flesh and bone, reducing men to bloody wrecks, bodies twisting and jerking as they were driven off their feet. Muscle, skin and bone were pulverized in the aftermath of the autofire. Blood spurted as the bodies were reduced to so much glistening pulp.

As Encizo panned back and forth, the continuing fire from the L1A1 impacted against parked vehicles, puncturing tires and bodywork. Glass shattered. Encizo's fire found fuel tanks, leaving ragged holes spurting raw gasoline across the concrete. A medium-size fuel bowser took the full brunt of Encizo's fire, sending more liquid gushing free.

In a brief lull Hawkins pulled the pin on one of his grenades. He hurled the projectile across the concrete, where its forward momentum rolled it closer to the stand of vehicles. When it detonated the flash of the explosion ignited the fuel that was pooling across the ground. The flames spread rapidly, fed by the gasoline still spilling from tanks and bowser. The sudden surge of fire engulfed vehicles, rising rapidly. A single dull explosion was followed by a succession as tanks blew, adding to the noise and confusion. Heavy smoke blew across the area, swirling and dipping as the dry wind caught it.

HANAFI WATCHED THE SCENE unfold from the moment the pair of helicopters erupted. He picked up the crackle of autofire, the detonation of a grenade inside the hangar. He saw the machine gun posts attacked and the resultant hostile fire when the men he knew as Constantine and Rankin took over and used one of the big guns to take down Rahman's thugs. The rebels who survived the deadly effects scattered and sought cover at the extreme edges of the area. Which brought a number of them within range of Hanafi's AK-47.

The Pakistani pulled himself to the firing line and laid his rifle in front of him. That simple effort left him in more pain, but he was determined to offer his help to the group below. He set the selector for single shot and chose his first target. The Kalashnikov sent a 7.62 mm slug into the chest of a moving rebel. The man stumbled, dropping his own weapons, and clutched at his ravaged torso as he collapsed. As he went down, Hanafi moved the rifle and laid down his second shot. The fatally hit rebel fell with a slug in his side. Hanafi's third shot cored in through the top of the guy's skull, emerging below his jaw in a welter of lacerated flesh.

Hanafi's intervention drew aggressive retaliation from the rebels. The slope immediately below him was struck by hostile fire, sending grit and dirt spraying the area, and forcing Hanafi away from the top of the slope. He realized it was covering fire to allow the rebels to climb to his position. He dragged himself a couple of yards to the left, fighting the lethargy his severe wounds were inflicting on him. He was leaving a trail of blood as he moved, but he ignored it.

His ears picked up the sound of booted feet as the rebels scrambled up the slope. Hanafi pulled his AK-47 close as he raised his head and shoulders over the ridge to find three rebels nearing the top. He flicked the rifle's selector back to auto. One of the men spotted him as he pulled back on the AK's trigger. The harsh, loud crackle of autofire filled the area as Hanafi laid down his burst. The 7.62 mm slugs tore into the rebels, stitching them from waist to chest. Bodies twitched and squirmed under the impact of the close-range fire. The rebels had no chance to respond. They were kicked back down the slope in a trail of dust, their flesh torn and bloody.

Hanafi heard the rifle click on empty. He ejected the magazine and replaced it with one of his spares. With the AK-47 reloaded he scanned the slope and the area below.

The machine gun was still hammering out bursts that wreaked damage on men and vehicles.

He saw the lanky figure of the black commando, Landis, working his way in the direction of the hangar's main entrance. He was engaging any rebel who came within range of his Kalashnikov.

CALVIN JAMES SAW two rebels go down, their bodies sliding along the concrete from the hard impact of shots from his AK-47 on full auto. His long legs took him forward at a reckless speed, weaving him toward the hangar in a zigzag pattern.

The rebels were having a hard time gathering themselves following the suddenness of the attack. From the moment the LAW rockets had destroyed Rahman's prized helicopters, Phoenix Force had pushed forward with ruthless efficiency. Losing the machine gun posts and then having one of the weapons turned on themselves had been a further shock for the Pakistani and Taliban fighters. As their companions fell around them the Rahman soldiers tried to regroup and offer a collective response. There had been added insult when three of their comrades had been gunned down on the slope bounding the edge of the area as they tried to find safe cover. The attackers seemed to have blocked all avenues of escape and were reducing the defending force with deadly precision.

This was not what Rahman had envisioned for them. The isolated hangar on this forgotten airstrip, a remnant of a previous administration, had seemed the ideal place for him to secrete and prepare the UAV for the flight that would deliver the dirty bomb to its target. Suddenly the peace and security had vanished, and the group was under attack, and losing the fight.

Being cut down where they stood weakened their resolve. Death and destruction had exploded around them. Fire and smoke drifted across the area. Gunfire echoed from every direction. The rebels remaining on their feet fought on, but their resistance was waning with each trigger pull.

CHAPTER FIFTEEN

Colonel Jabir Rahman pressed the sat phone to his ear and heard the crackle of autofire in the background. There were shouts and cries.

"What is happening?" he demanded.

"We are under attack, Colonel."

"Under attack? By who, Ahmed?" Rahman had recognized the man's voice. "Tell me what is going on."

"They came out of nowhere," Ahmed said. "They are killing everyone in sight. Many are dead. The helicopters have been destroyed. Vehicles, too."

Rahman tried to keep himself under control. "Tell me the drone is safe. The rods. Have the rods been damaged?"

"Safe at the moment."

"Fazeel? Has he been protected? His safety is paramount. The drone cannot be launched without his guidance."

"Shiran is at his side. He will protect Fazeel with his life."

Ahmed's voice faded as a concentrated burst of autofire overwhelmed it. All Rahman could do was listen to the sounds of combat. His frustration was compounded because of his helplessness. He was too far away to be of help, and his fear was increased as he realized his operation to launch the drone could be compromised by this attack on his isolated site. He could scarcely believe what was happening after all his planning and execution. The theft of the nuclear rods and the delivery to the mountain site had all gone to plan.

But now?

"*Ahmed.* Ahmed? I order you to speak."

"I am here, Colonel." The man's voice was shaky.

"Have you identified the attackers? Are they government troops? Security operatives?"

"Neither, Colonel. I believe they are the Americans we have already encountered."

Rahman's voice rose an octave. "Five men? And they are overrunning you? Ahmed, I cannot believe what you telling me. With all the weapons and men you have, five foreigners are—"

"If you were here you would understand." Ahmed shouted an order. "Stop them. Protect the drone. Watch over Fazeel. You must—"

Before Rahman could speak there was a sustained burst of autofire and the dull explosion of a grenade. Then the phone connection was terminated.

Luba Radesh watched the expression on Rahman's face change. For a fleeting second the colonel showed defeat, his eyes growing blank as he stared at the dead phone in his hand. His lips compressed into a thin line. As Radesh studied the man, Rahman sucked in a long, slow breath, held it for long seconds before releasing it. His eyes moved until he had Radesh in his sights.

"We may have lost the drone."

"Did I hear right? The site is under attack?"

"Ahmed believes it is those damn Americans. The ones who destroyed the drugs and weapons cache. They escaped from Hajik's Taliban and now they are—"

"We could be there in a couple of hours. I can assemble a team quickly."

Rahman waved a dismissive hand. "To do what, Luba?

What if these Americans destroy the drone? What then? Repair it with glue and sticky tape? Without the drone we cannot deliver the device to its target as we planned. And if these men capture the drone it is certain they will retrieve the rods."

"Are we certain the Americans have actually defeated our force? Maybe Ahmed's team have been able to reverse the situation, and we are still in possession of the rods and the drone. I will have someone try to raise the site. Use the radio link."

Rahman nodded. He ran both hands over his face as if to wipe away his doubts. "Yes, you are right, Luba. Let me know how you get on."

He waited until the man had left the room, then picked up the sat phone and hit a speed dial number. He considered what Radesh had said. Perhaps he had been too swift to accept defeat. If that was the case, Rahman allowed, he must be letting the pressure of the operation get to him. Matters had crowded him recently. With everything coming together so quickly, Rahman had moments of self-doubt—which he kept to himself—and the responsibility was making him concerned over every detail. The setbacks they had suffered in the U.K., followed by the resistance from the covert group of specialists, undoubtedly from America, had created chinks in his armor.

He heard the connection sound and a moment later Umer Qazi spoke. "Colonel?"

"We may have a problem here," Rahman said. "I have just been informed that a strike force has hit the site, possibly disabling the drone. We are in the process of verifying as I speak."

"Do we proceed here?"

"Most certainly. Just one change in the plan. Forget the original date. Go ahead as soon as the device is ready. If we have been compromised, we have to assume it could happen there. So step up the time and do it as soon as humanly possible."

"I understand. It will be done, Colonel."

"I will wait to hear from you. May Allah be with you."

JABIR RAHMAN STEPPED OUT into the courtyard. The warm air brushed away the fever clouding his thoughts. The paved courtyard was a mass of color from the many flowers and exotic plants growing in heavy pots. Rahman was aware of their scents filling the air. He moved slowly through the garden, enjoying the quiet. He spent as much time as he could here, especially when he had problems to work out.

He was aware of the great task he had undertaken. It had taken a long time to set up. And a great deal of money to organize the various operations. Both the Taliban and al Qaeda had bankrolled the venture. Rahman was well aware of that. As much as they were motivated by religious fervor, both organizations demanded results when they laid out as much money as they had. They were neither casual backers nor naive believers. If the operation went completely to the wall, Rahman could expect recriminations. And when it came to payback, the Taliban and al Qaeda were past masters at the art.

He turned and snapped his fingers. One of his house servants came running.

"Bring me a drink," Rahman said. "A *real* drink."

The man left, understanding what his master meant.

WITH MANNING CLOSE on his six, McCarter snapped in a fresh 30-round magazine for the Kalashnikov. He angled across the hangar, his attention on the UAV and its attendant technicians. To the left of the drone was the electronic guidance setup. The console glowed with digital readouts and monitor screens. A lone operator sat there, swiveling his chair as McCarter appeared. The young Pakistani held a chunky autopistol in one hand, but from the expression on his face he was no weapons man.

That made little difference to the Phoenix Force leader. Rahman's rebels intended to launch the drone and its deadly payload onto an unsuspecting target. People would be killed and many others would suffer the agony of radiation poisoning. These men intended to bring this horror to their victims, disregarding any moral wrongdoing. They had chosen their path, and that put them outside any kind of consideration.

"I got the drone," Manning yelled as he barreled past the Briton, his AK-47 up and abruptly firing.

The Canadian's response was fast and on target. He stitched the men working on the drone, slamming them to the concrete floor in a haze of bloody spray. The techs were dying even as Manning turned his weapon on the drone, loosing a long autoburst that shredded the flimsy fuselage of the UAV. The ferocious power of the AK-47 on full auto cut the drone in two, ending any chance of flight.

AT HIS CONSOLE, Anwar Fazeel saw the destruction of the drone, and his world fell apart. He had been on a high since the successful flight that had led to the destruction of the convoy and the theft of the nuclear rods. He had found it hard to ignore the excitement of the moment when he guided the armed drone along its path, setting the coordinates and instructing the machine to deliver its payload. Watching the missiles streak away and wipe out the convoy's trucks had given him a feeling of power he could never have imagined. In his newborn fanaticism, urged on by Rahman and his aides, Fazeel was ready for the second phase of the operation. The sudden, unwarranted attack on the site had thrown confusion into the mix, and Fazeel, shocked by the death and horror he saw around him, did not know what to do. All his recent feelings were driven away as he saw men die next to him. This was no long-distance death, viewed via a monitor screen. This was real and bloody and noisy. It was unlike anything Fazeel had experienced before. He wished he was far away, safe and back home.

He had seen Ahmed talking frantically into his sat phone. The man seemed as confused as Fazeel. He had been standing out in the open, still in conversation, when he had been hit by autofire. Fazeel had seen the look on the man's face, the bloody wounds that appeared in his body as he dropped to the concrete. Fazeel had picked up the pistol he had been given and shown how to fire, but the weapon felt alien and awkward in his hand. He felt a strange calm wash over him, then anger at the men who were denying him his promised victory. He turned his chair and raised the pistol in the direction of the tall infidel running toward him.

Fazeel didn't take notice of the hard, hammering sound of shots. All he felt was the brutal impact of the storm of 7.62 mm jacketed slugs as they cored through his body. He was pushed off his chair and fell back against the console. More slugs hammered the instrumentation, shattering the monitor screens and wrecking the control panels.

McCarter held the trigger of his AK-47 and swept the muzzle back and forth, the concentrated power of the assault rifle tearing the Barracuda's control center apart. The shredded body of the operator slid off the blood-streaked console and dropped heavily to the floor.

Beyond the open doors of the hangar the heavy rattle of the machine gun eased off, then ceased. The last of the shell casings bounced off the concrete apron and an odd silence fell.

McCarter reloaded. He saw Manning doing exactly the same.

They crossed to the drone. McCarter prodded the broken fuselage with the toe of his boot.

"Look what you did," he said in a shocked tone. "You do realize how much one of these things costs."

Manning shook his head. "No," he said, "but I'm sure you'll be reminding me all the way home. And by the way, the rods are not here."

The rest of Phoenix Force moved into view from different directions. They all still carried their weapons ready to use.

James surveyed the interior of the hangar, homing in on the drone. "Man, that thing ain't ever going to fly again." He grinned when McCarter surreptitiously waggled a finger in Manning's direction. "Hey, Gary, you figure out how much one of these babies costs?"

Manning's reply was succinct and to the point.

"Encizo, go see how Hanafi is," McCarter said. "And scout around for visitors. Cal, check for casualties. Do what you can if there are any survivors."

"You got it."

"T.J., go clear any loose weapons. Let's not risk some jihad hothead trying for a last-minute ticket to paradise. Gary, let's go find those nuclear rods."

Manning was already at the front of the drone, examining the missile pods where the technicians had been working. He shook his head when McCarter joined him.

"They were getting close," he said. He pointed to the assemblies mounted to the brackets that would have held the missiles. "Looks like they were going to fix the tubes holding the rods here. No need for launching connections because the rods would be staying in place. Explosive charges would be fixed to blow the protective tube covers and disperse the radioactive element."

"How would they do that?" McCarter asked. "From the control console?"

"Integrated system used to launch the missiles. All the techs had to do was divert to the explosive charges so that when the drone landed they could be detonated."

"Like a bloody electronic suicide bomber," McCarter said.

"This Rahman is a cold-blooded bastard."

"Show me a terrorist who isn't. It's the way the buggers work."

They moved across the hangar to where equipment and stores were stacked. It didn't take Manning long to find what he was looking for.

A mid-size, secured box stood on a low table isolated from everything else. Manning grasped one of the handles and tried to lift it. The box was too heavy.

"It'll be lead lined inside the metal shell," he said.

"So how do we get it out of here?" McCarter answered his own question by turning about and walking out of the hangar, searching the area until he spotted a couple vehicles that stood well away from the hangar and had survived the firefight. He made his way to them, his eye already on a big military spec 4x4 with a long wheelbase and an open cargo section behind the passenger cab. McCarter opened the driver's door and slid behind the wheel. He hit the start button and the powerful diesel engine rumbled to life. Checking the fuel gauge, he saw that the tank was full. McCarter put the 4x4 into gear and drove it up to the hangar.

"That should do nicely," Manning said.

"We'll load up and get out of here," McCarter said.

"Grab as much ammo as we can. Some extra AKs. In the back along with the rods and—" He paused as he saw Encizo returning from looking for Hanafi. The expression on the Cuban's face answered any question he might have been ready to ask.

"A brave man," Encizo said. "He shot four of them as they tried to escape over the rise. Even in his condition he managed to take them on and kill them before he died."

"Sorry to hear that," Manning said.

"So let's make sure he didn't die for nothing," McCarter stated. "We need to get to the pickup point and get those bloody rods out of Pakistan. Let's move it, guys."

He pulled out his sat phone and made contact with Stony Man. Barbara Price came on the line and McCarter gave her a rundown on what had happened.

"Isn't over yet," the Briton said. "We're still in Rahman's backyard with his nuclear rods. Sooner we get out of here the better. I need you to give the heads-up to our extraction unit. They need to be ready when we hit the border. Have them on standby."

"Do you have an arrival time yet?"

"Too early to say. I'm figuring at least four hours. But that will depend on how Rahman acts when he finds out we took his rods away. He could very well come after us. In fact I *know* he'll come after us. That bloke isn't about to quit."

"David, we ran a satellite scan of the terrain around you. Isn't looking too good. They had bad floods a few months back. Lost a number of bridges, and some roads, which were already pretty bad, were washed away. The water may have subsided, but rebuilding some of those isolated roads is going to take a long time."

"We've commandeered a military 4x4. Should take a

hammering if we hit rough roads. Best we can do under the circumstances."

"I'll liaise with a pickup team," Price said. "Ask if they can fly in closer once you near the border. They have to watch in case they overfly the line. The Pakistanis are pretty touchy about U.S. infringement of their territory."

"Well, bloody hell, we wouldn't want to start a war, now, would we," McCarter said drily. "Just do what you can for us. We'll handle this end."

"THIS IS NOT THE RESULT we were hoping for, brother," Rahman's al Qaeda contact said.

"A setback I am endeavoring to rectify," Rahman said, feeling his throat drying even as he spoke.

The calm, modulated voice carried on as if Rahman had not spoken. "We have expended a great deal of money for your project, Jabir Rahman. A very great deal. As the Americans would say, we expect a significant return on our investment. Where is that return going to come from now you have lost your weapon of destruction?"

"My people are searching for it as we speak. Once we locate the ones who attacked my site and stole the rods, we will take them back."

"You sound nervous, Jabir Rahman." The voice on the phone paused, then said, "And so you should. You, as much as anyone, should know we do not tolerate failure. We are in a war and defeat is not something we accept."

"I offer no excuses for the mistakes. All I can do—"

"You can attempt to bring matters back on line, Rahman. The reports we have received show a catalog of blunders going all the way back to London. We have lost Samman Prem. Also our operator from within the counter-terrorism unit, and a great deal of harm has been done to our U.K. network. Now these strikes in Pakistan that have cost us lives and a valuable cache of weapons and drugs. How else should we view all this except as abject failure on your part?"

Rahman didn't dare answer. There was nothing he could say to excuse what had happened. At the end of the day he was responsible. As the man in charge he shouldered the responsibility. So he remained silent and waited for the chilling voice on the other end of the phone to speak.

"If I call again, Jabir Rahman, you should hope it will be to congratulate you on a successful mission in America. Pray to Allah this is how it will be. If you fail to put things right, God will not be able to save you. He may be merciful. We are not."

The line went dead and Rahman felt a chill envelop him. He was not foolish enough to believe that what he had just heard was a simple warning. Al Qaeda did not issue simple warnings. These people, like the Taliban, were serious in every word and gesture. Their view of the world was in simple black-and-white. You were with them or against them. There was no wavering. No possible variation. If you were on their side the rules were strict and unchangeable. If you were their enemy… Rahman refused to even consider that option.

"Colonel, Radesh is on the radio. Calling from the helicopter."

Rahman followed his soldier through to the comm room. He took the headset the operator handed him, adjusting the microphone.

"Luba, report," he said.

Radesh's voice was sharp and to the point. "The site has been disabled. No survivors. Both helicopters are wrecked and so are most of the vehicles. The UAV has been destroyed beyond repair, and the case containing the rods has gone."

Rahman sighed. “As we expected,” he said. “Those damn Americans. Luba, see if you can track them. We have to stop them from crossing the border. Keep me informed of your position. I am going to contact our Taliban friends in the area and get them to intercept if possible.”

“Good. Just one thing, Colonel. I found Nasir Hanafi’s body among the dead. From what I could read of his position, it appears he was fighting *against* your people. There were dead facing him on a slope away, from the main combat zone.”

“That could explain a number of things,” Rahman said. “His behavior recently. The reports I had about him asking unusual questions. He tricked me. I believed he was one of us. Too late now. Luba, did you see any tracks leading away from the site?”

“Yes. Tire marks from a single vehicle heading toward the border. Only a few hours old.”

“Find them, Luba, and we might still be able to salvage something from this mess.”

“We found fuel drums. The chopper is being topped up now. I’ll be in the air shortly.”

“Good.” Rahman signed off. “Get me Hajik quickly,” he ordered the operator.

“At once, Colonel.”

Naj Hajik was the driving force behind the local Taliban group that controlled the border area. It had been Hajik’s weapons and drugs the Americans had destroyed, so Rahman had little doubt the man would be eager to get his hands on the Westerners. If anyone knew the border area as intimately as Hajik, Rahman had never met him.

“Colonel, I have Naj Hajik.”

Rahman clicked on his headset again.

“Brother Hajik, good to speak with you.”

"What do you want?" Hajik possessed little grace. He was a man of few words and had no time for niceties.

Using the man's title was the closest to a compliment Hajik would respond to. "The Americans who destroyed your drugs and weapons are still in the area. I am sure you would enjoy the opportunity to get your hands on them." Rahman refrained from saying *again*. Reminding Hajik he had allowed the men to escape from his clutches would not be a wise move.

"You know where they are?"

"I have a helicopter tracking them right now. As soon as my man spots them I will instruct him to contact you. They are on the road to the border, using a military vehicle they stole from one of my units."

"Roads in the area are still in poor condition since the monsoon floods. Travel by vehicle is restricted. But I can make good time on foot."

"They are carrying something valuable that must not be destroyed," Rahman said. "A weapon that will benefit us all."

Hajik's laugh was a deep rumble. "I know what you stole, Jabir Rahman. Have you forgotten it was my fighters who took the truck it was stored in, and killed the driver? And also what you intend to do with it. If we catch these Western unbelievers and they have your weapon, I will return it. My men are not versed in such technology. *I* understand the dangers of such material—they do not. My orders will be that they do not touch it."

"May Allah guide your footsteps, Naj Hajik."

"I will find these dogs and they will be reminded it is not wise to take from me."

THE CHOPPER PILOT BANKED the aircraft, dropping the nose so he could show what he had seen.

"There," the pilot said. "The vehicle we have been looking for. Yes?"

"Take us lower," Radesh ordered.

The helicopter swooped in toward the 4x4, painted in military livery.

"Has to be the one." Radesh keyed his headset and made contact with the base operator. "Let me speak to the colonel." He picked up a pair of powerful binoculars and focused in on the moving vehicle. "Colonel, you want to check this vehicle number," he said when Rahman came on the line. He read off the white stenciled letters on the 4x4's rear panel.

"We can run it through the computer," Rahman said, giving instructions to one of his soldiers.

It took only a couple minutes before Rahman came back, confirming the vehicle had been assigned to his command and had been at the site.

"When we finish," he said, "change to the frequency I am going to give you. Speak to Naj Hajik. He and his men can reach that truck before anyone. On foot they will cover more ground than any wheeled vehicle. Give Hajik the location."

"Okay, Colonel. I'll keep a watch over the truck, too."

"Luba, be courteous to Hajik. He may be only a local warlord, but treat him with respect. He's a little touchy about his status."

"Understood, Colonel. We'll get the bastards."

Ending the call, Rahman returned to his office, closing the door.

We'll get the bastards.

I hope so, Luba, Rahman thought. My life may depend on that. As much as I have dedicated myself to Allah, I am not yet ready to meet him.

CHAPTER SIXTEEN

"Chopper is still there," Hawkins said. "That mother is tracking us. It's like a damn burr that won't come unstuck."

"Shame we don't have any more LAWs," Encizo said. "With Cal on a roll with them he could bring it down easy."

"If he comes low enough we can rattle him with some AK fire," Manning said. "We've got plenty of ammunition."

Before Phoenix Force had departed the hangar site they had loaded up the rear of the truck with 7.62 mm magazines and boxes of 9 mm cartridges. They had found cases of fragmentation grenades and had taken those. Manning had located bottles of water and field rations.

The lead-lined container holding the nuclear rods was placed in the open rear, secured with webbing straps to the metal cargo loops fixed to the inside of the body.

"Like a Sunday family day out," McCarter said.

"The Sunday from hell," Manning commented.

"Cheer up, Gary," James said. "If things get busy you can throw lots of grenades. You know how you like to make explosions."

Manning scowled at him for a moment, then said, "That's true."

The helicopter had picked them up hours earlier as they traveled along a badly rutted, hard-packed road. Progress was slow due to much of the route having been washed away during the floods caused by the monsoon rainstorms weeks earlier. The road wound its way through the low, barren hills, appearing to go on for miles. McCarter, who was driving, had to maneuver past deep potholes and work his way around sections that had collapsed completely. It was only the 4x4's military design, with high ground clearance and excellent suspension, that allowed it to cross the severely damaged patches. McCarter's arms were aching after hours of wrestling with the steering wheel. This was a military vehicle and didn't have the sophistication of power steering. Hauling the wheel back and forth did little to ease the Briton's mood, and the names he called the 4x4 were becoming increasingly colorful as time passed.

"David, take a break," Encizo said. "Let me drive for a while, hombre."

McCarter rolled the truck to a stop and changed places with the Cuban. He sank back in the passenger seat, flexing his aching arms. Hawkins passed him a bottle of water. McCarter took it and unsealed the cap as Encizo dropped the 4x4 into gear and they rolled on again.

Then the Phoenix Force leader sat upright, dropping his bottle of water and snatching up the AK-47 propped at his side. "Incoming," he yelled. He swung the weapon out the open window and fired off a burst at the bearded, dark-clad figure wielding a similar weapon. The Taliban's autoburst clanged viciously against the heavy-gauge steel side panel of the 4x4. McCarter's return fire kicked up splinters of stone and gravel inches from the Taliban's feet, causing the man to step back. McCarter fired again, this time with greater accuracy, and the attacker was knocked off his feet as 7.62 mm slugs slammed into his chest.

Encizo hit the gas pedal, the powerful engine roaring as the truck drove forward, dust billowing up from beneath the heavy treaded tires.

The rest of Phoenix Force had their weapons on line

now and were targeting the figures breaking cover and firing at them. They traded shots with the Taliban, who were visible on both sides of the rutted road.

"You know a favorite weapon for these guys is an RPG," Manning pointed out.

"Thanks very much for that piece of information," McCarter said.

"So why haven't they dropped one on us?" James asked.

"Good question," McCarter said.

Encizo rolled the truck back and forth across the road, making it as difficult a target as he could for the Taliban.

Above the continuous rattle of fire from the team's AK-47s, Manning raised his voice to a shout.

"I think they know what we have in that box. Rahman put them on us but warned them what we're carrying. He wants his rods back, and doesn't want to risk having his Taliban buddies vaporize them by hitting us with a missile." The Canadian held up a grenade, pulling the pin, and wound down his window. "But I don't have any worries on that score."

He threw the grenade from the 4x4, angling it in the direction of several moving figures. The blast scattered the Taliban. Manning continued to lob grenade after grenade, his powerful throws resulting in a series of explosions that forced the armed attackers to fall back. Autofire continued, slugs hitting the truck.

With the continual bullet hits and the uneven, potholed road, Encizo was having to concentrate fully on his driving. The truck swayed and bounced across the treacherous terrain, and the Cuban's arm muscles strained as he fought to keep the vehicle on course. Slugs had shattered most of the windows, showering Phoenix Force with glass.

Manning passed grenades from his plentiful supply, and

the rest of the team alternated autofire with throwing the hand-launched missiles.

The Taliban were proving to hard to dispel. On foot, they were able to keep up the pressure, moving from cover to cover while maintaining constant streams of autofire. Only because they needed to keep on the move were their shots less than accurate; firing on the run reduced the ability to pinpoint a target. The 4x4 took the erratic fire and resisted it, and this might have continued until the truck ran out of the range of Taliban rifles.

But then a stray shot came in through the driver's window and lodged in Encizo's right arm, high up. The Cuban gasped at the sudden impact, his grip on the wheel slackening long enough for the truck to veer off the road onto even rougher ground. Encizo summoned all his remaining strength to get the vehicle back under control, and might have succeeded if a deep, rocky fissure had not appeared directly before them. Encizo hauled on the heavy steering wheel, hoping to avoid the drop, but the truck's speed took it in a broadside slide and the right wheels bounced over the edge. The Cuban yelled a warning to his teammates seconds before impact. The 4x4 slid into the fissure at an angle, dropping with a sickening crunch of metal against stone, and came to a sudden stop.

Aware of time running out, Phoenix Force exited the truck, using it for temporary cover as they swept the area for the trailing Taliban. Manning dragged out ammunition boxes.

McCarter hit the transmit button on his sat phone and sent out the pickup signal to the Marine base across the border in Afghanistan. The GPS locater would transmit Phoenix Force's position. It was all McCarter could do. Until the U.S. rescue chopper locked in on the signal, the Stony Man team was going to have to hold off the enemy force. Once he had sent the message, McCarter turned his rifle on the Taliban as they made their presence known.

James had dragged Encizo from the truck, pulling him to cover in the fissure. The feisty Cuban refused to lie still, using his good hand to keep his AK-47 in firing position while James did what he could to deal with his wound. The slug had stayed in the muscle of Encizo's arm, causing a lot of bleeding and leaving the Cuban in pain. That pain only succeeded in increasing Encizo's determination to fight on.

Manning and Hawkins had hauled out a box of grenades. They dumped it on the ground between them and started to prime and throw grenades in every direction the Taliban showed.

The spot where the truck had stopped was an uneven, open stretch of ground, so the Taliban had no cover as they approached. Phoenix Force had the stalled truck, which at least gave them a small tactical advantage, and the wide, deep fissure provided further protection.

Slugs pounded the terrain around them, chipping away at the flinty stone. The Phoenix Force veterans kept their heads down as much as possible, aware the Taliban would have experienced snipers among their number. Allied forces had learned the hard way that the extremists used skilled, long-distance shooters to strike at unwary soldiers. Taliban tacticians utilized all kinds of expertise in their hostile attacks.

Leaving Hawkins to keep up the grenade assault, Manning locked in a fresh 30-round magazine, cocked his AK-47 and positioned himself for some return fire. The Canadian was no slouch himself when it came to sniper skills. He chose his first target and made his play. The Kalashnikov snapped out a single shot. The distant Taliban, showing above a soft hummock, jerked back as Manning's 7.62 mm slug cored into the side of his skull and blew out the far side, taking a wedge of bone and flesh with it. Manning delivered two more of the rebels to whatever paradise they believed in before the rest of the group realized their error and withdrew to more substantial cover.

"COMMANDER, WE ARE LOSING too many of our men," the Taliban fighter said. "We should blow that damn truck out of the way, and the blast will kill those Americans."

"You have my orders," Naj Hajik said. "Just carry them out."

"It is foolishness. I see my brothers dying, for we cannot fight the way we should."

Hajik turned on the man, his rage exploding in a roar. "The truck will not be destroyed. It carries something we need to recover intact. All of you listen. I command this group. My word is law. Anyone who does not think so can face me now and we will settle the matter. If not, then face the enemy and fight like men, not whining women."

His words struck fear into the Taliban around him. They also spurred them on to fight. As Hajik had said, they *were* Taliban, fighting warriors who had a fearsome reputation, and reputation was a powerful stimulant to the insurgents. If word got around to the other camps that Naj Hajik's warriors had been defeated by a mere five American infiltrators there would be much mocking laughter, and the story would be embellished as it was passed from group to group.

Hajik himself would never be allowed to live down the shame. There was no doubt in any of their minds that if such a thing happened, Hajik would see to it that his men suffered the humiliation.

So they doubled their attack and hurled themselves at the stranded and isolated American dogs.

Hajik heard the beat of rotors again as the helicopter

sent by Rahman swept overhead, bearing down on the combat area. The Taliban commander heard his headset crackle, then he picked up the voice of Luba Radesh.

"Commander Hajik, is there a problem down there?"

"Colonel Rahman's instructions were that the truck must not be damaged because of its cargo. While the Americans have it as cover my men are unable to move in close enough to overcome the enemy. And the Americans appear to have a plentiful supply of ammunition and even hand grenades."

"You are aware of what that cargo is?"

"Yes."

"Then we must regain control. I have a machine gun on board. I will have my pilot go around the far side and see if we can lay down covering fire. A distraction may allow your men to move in."

"Do it. I will order my warriors to make their move as soon as you open fire."

"IT'S GONE A LITTLE TOO quiet," James said. "Those guys having a union meeting or what?"

"Something's brewing," Manning said.

They scanned the area. No Taliban were in sight.

"Maybe we scared them off," Hawkins observed.

"Hardly." James was checking out the surrounding terrain.

"Heads up, ladies. I hear a familiar sound," McCarter said. "Chopper, but not our ride. Too light for a military freighter."

They scanned the sky. It was Encizo who spotted the incoming helicopter.

"Three o'clock," he said.

Heads turned and Phoenix Force watched the aircraft vectoring in on their position. They eyed it for some seconds as it dropped lower, angling in on a sideways approach.

"Son of a bitch has an HMG in that open doorway," Hawkins said.

McCarter grunted in acknowledgment. He had turned back to check the Taliban firing line, and saw a few turbaned heads showing as the insurgents began to gather.

"Crafty buggers," he said. Raising his voice, he warned, "That bird is going to lay down machine gun fire to keep us busy so those sods can rush us soon as."

"Stuck between a rock and a hard place," Hawkins said.

The Phoenix Force pros loaded their AKs with fresh magazines. Manning dragged a full box of grenades to where everyone could reach them.

"Try not to get hit," McCarter said. "Pay gets docked if you do."

"Hey, I already took mine," Encizo commented. "It doesn't count."

Manning said, "Coming in."

The heavy pounding of the door-mounted machine gun reached their ears as the helicopter traversed the length of the fissure. A line of .50-caliber shells slammed across the lip, showering Phoenix Force with debris. A couple shells hammered the underside of the truck. A fluid line was shredded and oil began to leak from the tear.

"Face front," McCarter yelled above the machine gun fusillade.

As the Phoenix Force commandos turned about they saw the grouped Taliban breaking from cover, charging across the open ground, weapons firing as they came.

"Grenades," Manning said.

Every man snatched one up, yanked out the pin and threw the sphere from his concealed position beneath the truck. The grenades landed, bounced and rolled directly into the path of the charging Taliban, detonating within microseconds of each other. They fragmented and hurled their deadly loads into the Taliban. It was a scene of utter devastation as the five blasts merged, producing flame and smoke and white-hot death. Skin and bone were shredded. Macerated flesh showed bloody red as the stricken targets were blown off their feet by the concussion and left writhing and screaming in confusion.

"Keep it going," McCarter ordered, and the AK-47s crackled, 7.62 mm slugs finding targets as the backup Taliban, watching their comrades go down, thrust themselves forward.

There was little nobility or heroic action as the opposing groups fought for superiority. It was men against men in a bloody engagement that did little to express human advancement.

It was far from the hushed solemnity of war expressed in reminiscences.

It was, pure and simple, killing to survive.

ENCIZO WAS THE FIRST to hear the heavier rotor sound of a larger machine. He turned and saw the U.S. Marine Corps CH-46 as it loomed into view, its own onboard weapons thundering as it bore down on Luba Radesh's weaker bird.

Ragged holes appeared in the fuselage of the smaller machine. The heavy fire from the U.S. craft ravaged the helicopter, which yawed to one side, a sudden trail of smoke billowing out from beneath the engine cover. As the chopper faltered more gunfire drove into the rotor housing, blowing apart the spinning main shaft. The whirring rotors shuddered as flying debris slammed into them. The stricken helicopter began a slow dive that ended when it hit the rocky ground and came apart, fire adding to the horror.

There was a final, grumbling roar and then a ball of flame as the aircraft blew apart.

With the destruction of the chopper, the CH-46 swung around and the door-mounted .50-caliber machine gun spit out a deadly stream of cannon fire, traversing the Taliban line, shredding bodies like cut-down wheat. After a few moments of defiant resistance the insurgents fell back and scattered, their spirit broken, knowing there was no way they could do battle with the heavily armed American machine.

THE CH-46 TOUCHED DOWN yards from the scene as Phoenix Force dragged themselves from the fissure, a dusty, bedraggled bunch. They were all bearing bloody scrapes and minor wounds. Encizo was the worst hit, but the first thing they did was free the tethered box from the truck and haul it between them to the waiting chopper.

"Snap it up, guys," the door gunner said. "We are three miles inside Pakistani territory here, so haul your sorry asses inside and let's go."

"That's *arses* to you, sonny," McCarter said, grinning from ear to ear.

The heavy box was pushed on board, followed by Encizo, then the rest of Phoenix Force climbed in. The moment their collective feet touch the deck plates the gunner spoke into his throat mike and the Marine helicopter powered up and rose into the air.

ON THE GROUND, Commander Naj Hajik stood with the few surviving Taliban and watched the helicopter depart. Below where he was standing the downed helicopter sent thick clouds of dense smoke into the air. Hajik shook his head. As much as he hated the Americans, he had to acknowledge that today the five men he had pursued had acquitted themselves well. There was no shame in defeat against good fighters.

He called his radio operator and instructed him to contact Rahman. As he waited, Hajik tried to imagine the colonel's disappointment when he heard his precious cargo had finally been removed from his grasp. He would not be a happy man.

Nor, Hajik thought, would the al Qaeda backers who had provided a greater part of the funding for Jabir Rahman's grand operation.

They would not be happy at all.

The handset was passed to Hajik. He held the instrument for a moment before he pressed the transmit button.

"Jabir, since your man is spread across the hillside along with his helicopter, I thought I should be the one to tell you your missing cargo is no longer our concern. We fought and lost today. I would guess by now it is across the border and in Afghanistan, under the protection of the U.S. Military…."

INSIDE THE CH-46 the noise was deafening. Phoenix Force lay strewn across the deck, still clutching their weapons, faces heavy with fatigue.

McCarter managed to get through to Stony Man on his sat phone. The connection was shaky, but it was good enough for the Phoenix Force commander to get his message through to Hal Brognola.

"We're okay. A little bloody and battered. Rafe took a slug in the arm but he'll be all right. What…? Oh, yeah, calm down, mate. The *package* is with us. Safe and sound. All you have to worry about now is Able Team cracking their bit…."

CHAPTER SEVENTEEN

Boston

Thirty-three years old, Ajmal Pirzada was ready and willing to carry out his part in Colonel Jabir Rahman's operation. The Pakistani national had been in the United States for almost three years and worked in the accountancy business in a company owned by an uncle who had come to America fifteen years earlier. Pirzada's work was dull and repetitive, but while he outwardly walked his way through his daily routines, he watched and listened and learned, adding to his not inconsiderable skills. He had spent two years on an intensive course in nuclear physics before leaving Pakistan, learning a number of intricate procedures. He also was tutored in the handling of explosives, detonators and timers. Those skills would be called upon one day, he had been told, but until then Pirzada kept a low profile, did nothing to arouse any suspicions as to the real reason he was in America. Since his arrival, he had made no moves that would arouse curiosity.

Pirzada was one of Rahman's front line agents simply waiting for the day when the call would come through and his waiting would be over. Until then he remained an ordinary inhabitant of the city of Boston. He lived in a small apartment his uncle, who had no idea of his nephew's real intent, had provided for him. He drove a three-year-old Ford and indulged his only vice—chess—on weekends at

Harvard Square, where chess tables were set up when the weather permitted, and enthusiasts challenged each other as the busy crowds came and went. The renowned square, in fact a triangle shape, brought in the shoppers and the connoisseurs of the cafés and restaurants. If the weather changed and chess had to be abandoned, Pirzada would retire to the Au Bon Pain café and sit drinking coffee and eating a sandwich while he observed the Beaners at play.

Pirzada was an accomplished game player. He had the mind-set and the patience for chess. He never gave anything away, kept his moves inside his head, without even the betrayal of a flickering eyelid. Among the regulars he was considered a worthy opponent. He was dignified in victory and respectful in defeat.

None of the people he played against, none of the people at his work, knew of his double life, or the animosity he held for them. Pirzada existed day to day, under no illusion, simply waiting for the call.

It came one Saturday. A warm, pleasant weekend. Pirzada had finished a game, which he incidentally won, against one of his longtime opponents—an eighty-year-old with the sharp mental reflexes of a teenager. For want of something else to do Pirzada retired to the café, then took his coffee and sandwich to a table outside. He had been seated only a few minutes when he became aware of someone standing by his table. When he glanced up he found Umer Qazi looking down at him, a smile of recognition on his face.

"Yes, it is you, my good friend. How wonderful to see you here." Qazi reached out and shook his hand.

It took Pirzada a moment to get over his surprise, but he responded quickly. Behind the pleasantries was the certain truth that Qazi was here in Boston for one reason only.

Pirzada had to calm his excitement as the man sat across from him.

He looked the same as he had the last time they had spoken, the day Pirzada left for America. If he were pressed on the matter Pirzada would have sworn Qazi was wearing the same clothes.

A waitress Pirzada knew passed by and he signaled her. "Would you bring fresh drinks for us, please? Another coffee for me." He looked at Qazi. "For you?"

"Coffee, please. Black."

The girl nodded and moved away.

"When did you arrive?" Pirzada asked.

"A couple of hours ago. I checked into my hotel, made phone calls, then came to find you."

"I am always here at the weekend."

"Yes, I know. You appear very comfortable, Ajmal. This city is good for you?"

"Only as long as it serves my purpose which is what you have come to discuss. Why else would you come here?"

Qazi smiled. "Why indeed, Ajmal Pirzada."

They waited until their drinks arrived. Pirzada's elderly chess opponent passed by, pausing at the table.

"Next time I will beat you," he said, smiling. "Now I have learned your secret. I understand your strategy."

Ajmal nodded. "Then I must be on my guard." He indicated Qazi. "This is an old friend. We have not seen each other for some time, so we are catching up."

"A pleasure to meet you," Qazi said. "Is Ajmal still a good chess player?"

The old man leaned on his silver-topped cane. "Indeed," he said. "This young man hides his skills well. There is a lot going on inside that head."

They watched him as he moved across the square.

"If only he knew," Qazi said.

They drank coffee and enjoyed the busy scene around them until Pirzada was no longer able to contain his curiosity. "Is this the time I have been waiting for?"

"Yes." Qazi passed him a folded sheet of paper. "On there is a cell number. Call it tonight. Eight o'clock. You will be given instructions. From now be extra cautious. Do not do anything that might raise suspicion. Everything will be explained. There will be a great deal to do over the next few weeks."

"All right. Umer, is this important? A big strike?"

Qazi drank his coffee. "Be patient, brother. All will be explained tonight. Rest assured you will have a vital role in this. What you learned back home will be of great use."

"I knew this time would come. When I moved here Rahman told me to have patience. That I would be of great use one day."

"True, my friend. Your day is fast approaching. What we do here will be something the Americans will never forget."

"Then my prayers have been answered. God *is* great."

"Calm yourself. Show nothing that might arouse suspicion." Qazi stood, shaking his hand once more. "I will see you tonight."

He turned and strolled casually across the square. Pirzada watched until he could no longer see the man. He forced himself to stay focused, to maintain his composure, though inside he was shaking with excitement.

He tried to imagine what plan Rahman had devised. The way the colonel thought suggested something powerful, something that would shake the Americans. Pirzada could not think what it might be.

When he returned to his apartment later, letting himself in, he was still agitated. He sat down and stared across the room at the bare wall, making himself calm. If he showed up in such an agitated state whoever was there might decide he was too excitable to carry on with any mission. That, he decided, was not going to happen. He needed to present a professional, stable temperament.

Pirzada glanced at his watch. It was still many hours before he could make his phone call. He closed his eyes and relaxed. A little later he moved from the chair to pray. When he had finished he returned to the chair and sat, relaxed and at ease within himself.

He stayed in the armchair until seven-thirty. Then he pushed to his feet, went into the small kitchen and switched on the kettle. As the water boiled he spooned instant coffee into a china mug. When he had made his drink he sat down again, checking his watch.

Twenty minutes to eight.

Then fourteen.

Pirzada drank his coffee as it cooled slightly.

Eleven minutes.

On impulse he took out his phone and checked the power level. It was high.

He found it hard to realize he had been in America for nearly three years. Years of waiting, wondering if the day would come.

Now it had and Pirzada admitted to himself that he was scared. Until he made his call and followed his instructions he had no idea at all what he was going to be asked.

He took out the slip of paper Qazi had given him and read the number, then checked the time.

Six minutes to go.

Should he call early, in anticipation, or wait until the moment? Something flashed in his mind. A remembrance of Colonel Rahman's rigid adherence to doing everything right. Of appearing at the right moment. Always on time.

The military mind-set. Follow orders. Be punctual. Allow no deviation.

Pirzada tapped in the numbers and waited to send.

He saw the hand on his watch reach the hour, and pressed the key. Heard the connection and the ring tone. The call was answered after the third ring.

"Yes?"

"Ajmal Pirzada."

"It is good to hear your voice, brother. Look out your window in a moment and you will see a black SUV waiting for you. Hang up now."

The line went dead. Pirzada pulled on a jacket as he crossed the room and looked from his window. He saw the SUV come to a stop outside the building. Dropping his phone in his pocket, he hurried from the apartment and down the stairs. The rear door of the vehicle opened for him and he climbed in, pulling the door shut.

Besides the driver, there was another man in the car, sitting on the rear seat. Pirzada barely had time to acknowledge him before the man leaned forward and slipped a silky black hood over his head.

"Please do not fight it," he said. "This is just a precaution until we can be certain."

Pirzada felt sweat break out on his face. The hood was stifling, a black void.

"Certain of what?"

"That you are with us, Ajmal Pirzada. Now sit back. The journey will take a while. If you relax it will be a lot more comfortable."

PIRZADA FELT THE SUV SLOW. It made a left turn and rolled to a stop. A hand on his arm guided him from the vehicle and led him across a hard, even surface. He heard a door open and he was taken inside a building. The door closed behind him. The hood was pulled off and Pirzada blinked in the light.

"Ajmal, welcome, welcome."

It was Qazi. He stepped forward to grasp Pirzada's hand and introduce him to the group of men standing before them.

Pirzada counted five. He knew none of them, but Qazi introduced each in turn.

"Haidor Rana and Talib Ahmed brought you in the car. Here is Zahid Usami, Syed Alam and Zarin Haruni." Qazi patted Pirzada on the shoulder. "Brothers, this is Ajmal Pirzada. He is going to be an important member of our group."

"Easily said," Ahmed pointed out. "But can he do what is needed?"

Pirzada confronted the bearded, solid-looking man. "If someone will tell me what I am expected to do, then maybe I can answer that question."

Syed Alam, a slender man wearing heavy spectacles, smiled. "A fair question."

"Of course," Qazi said. "Colonel Rahman, as we speak, is in possession of a consignment of used uranium nuclear rods. These are highly irradiated. If the operation goes as planned, the consignment will be divided into two sets. One to be kept in Pakistan, the other brought here to the U.S. Both will be deployed as nuclear devices, to be detonated with low-powered conventional explosives. This will fracture the nuclear rods and allow the radioactive elements to be freed, creating what are sometimes called dirty bombs. Do you understand the term, Ajmal?"

Pirzada nodded. "I studied the concept during my training in Pakistan."

"When the cargo arrives in the U.S. it will be brought here, and your part of the operation will be to build the explosive device for attachment to the rods. As you have training involving nuclear materials, it will be your responsibility to maintain safety protocols, work out how powerful the explosives need to be, and ensure they will correctly fracture the rod casings."

Pirzada became aware of the close watch the other men had placed on him. The seriousness of the situation weighed heavily on his shoulders. He realized the importance of his position in the operation, what he would be expected to do.

He also knew with certainty that if he failed to respond in a positive way, his life might be forfeit. That knowledge came to him abruptly when he saw Talib Ahmed, who was standing slightly apart from the others, move slightly. Ahmed's right hand was at his side, partly concealed by the folds of his long topcoat. As he moved the cloth swayed briefly and exposed the dark, squat shape of a handgun he was holding.

Pirzada looked around. They were inside what seemed to be some kind of barn. A generous space with strip lighting. There were some boxed items and a couple workbenches. At the midsection of the barn was a metal construction. It was new. Thick Perspex windows were installed in the solid-looking door.

"The rods will be brought here?" Pirzada asked.

Qazi nodded. "Still in the shielded container. This is why we have constructed the chamber," he said, indicating the metal structure. "It has been made so that no radiation will leak out. And there are haz-mat suits and integrated breathing masks to be worn. It has its own power and air supply."

"You make it sound so real."

"Because it *is* real, brother," Ahmed said.

"You can put away your gun," Pirzada told him. "My

years in America have not weakened my resolve. When Colonel Rahman sent me here he said one day we would strike a terrible blow against this godless place, against those who weaken Pakistan by siding with the Great Satan. I am ready to do whatever is needed so we can succeed. *Anything*."

"Talib, I believe you have your answer," Qazi said. "Now we are really ready to start our work."

CHAPTER EIGHTEEN

They made four stops to refuel. The arrangements had been worked out well in advance. Money was paid each time the regular and the extra fuel tanks were replenished. All transactions were in cash, American dollars. The large amounts, in used notes, were carried in heavy zippered bags. Money was not a problem for Rahman. He had access to unlimited funds via his al Qaeda and Taliban connections, and there was the cross-border smuggling to add to his cash flow. Religious fervor was well and good, but money was always needed to bring schemes to fruition.

Just the two of them were on board the JetStar, an airliner from a now defunct Pakistani airline company, bought through Rahman's agents.

Intricate negotiations had taken place to procure authentic flight plans for the aircraft's passage from Pakistan, across Saudi Arabia, Egypt and Libya, angling across Algeria and into Moroccan airspace, where it made its final refueling stop before the flight to Boston.

Assistance from the Muslim brotherhood in various countries was vital in smoothing the way, with involvement from al Qaeda. Vast amounts of money changed hands as a number of useful individuals, already groomed and vetted, became extremely wealthy when they accepted the untraceable cash offers. Each bribed official was left contemplating what would, most definitely, befall him if any betrayal occurred. It was made clear they were under obligation to al Qaeda, and there was no escape from the long reach of bin Laden's vengeance.

The Lockheed JetStar would land at a freight distribution air terminal in the Boston area, its cargo manifest showing it was carrying hand-carved furniture. The Pakistan-based exporter was in reality little more than a shell company created to explain the cargo.

The aircraft's crew were from Luba Radesh's team. They had been pilots during the Kosovo conflict, operating under Radesh's command. They took turns flying the aircraft. Both were aware of the risk. Neither of them was concerned over his own safety, or anyone else's, to be truthful. They considered the flight to be an act of faith, something they were doing not just for Rahman, but for their one true god. No sacrifice for him was too great.

Until they were on the final leg of their flight, out across the Atlantic, they had been unable to fully relax. Now, with nothing between them and America except the gray, choppy sea, a sense of well-being came over them. They knew their ordeal was far from ended. Perhaps the greatest test would come once they began to sight the U.S. coastline. Until then they set the autopilot and helped themselves to the food and flasks of coffee they had been supplied with at the final refueling.

There was no radio contact with Radesh. They would wait until they were over American soil. Then a simple call would be placed. It had been decided that too much contact could be risky, just in case a message was overheard. Some small phrase could be picked up by electronic listening devices that were on permanent standby. These fragments of conversation could be recorded, flagged and passed to security agencies. It was not fanciful thinking. The systems existed and it was simply not worth taking the risk of being picked up. So the crew flew the plane, talked to each other, ate the spiced Moroccan food and drank the rich local coffee that had been given them.

It was unfortunate that for one of them, Miko Sevisko, something in the food he ate was not as fresh as it should have been. An hour after he had completed his meal he fell ill. His body reacted violently and he began to sweat, his stomach churning as it prepared to get rid of what was poisoning him.

His partner, Janos Lasko, realized his friend was in pain. He reached across to help him from his seat.

"Go," he said. "To the toilet, quickly, Miko."

Sevisko struggled out of his copilot's seat, clutching his stomach as its contents surged.

"Go," Lasko urged.

Sevisko lurched almost drunkenly and fell forward across the controls, hands thrown out to steady himself. He felt Lasko haul him upright.

Without warning the plane yawed violently to starboard, then back again. Both Lasko and Sevisko were thrown across the cockpit, slamming into the bulkhead. By the time Lasko pulled himself to his feet the plane was swinging back and forth, out of control, and he realized that during his tumble Sevisko had disengaged the autopilot. The jet was in free fall.

"Miko, get out of here before you vomit all over the fucking instruments."

As Lasko pulled himself into his seat, reaching for the controls, the last thing he saw was his partner disappearing into the main compartment. Sevisko dragged the door shut behind him.

Lasko regained control of the aircraft easily. Even so, his face was sheened with sweat and he was silently cursing Sevisko for being so clumsy. He brought the plane back on course, reset and switched on the autopilot. Then he leaned back, taking a breath and offering a quick prayer for his deliverance from what might have been a lot worse scenario.

He realized Sevisko had been gone a long time.

Too long.

He reached for the internal phone and keyed the transmit button.

"Hey, Miko, pick up, my brother. Are you still ill? Talk to me."

Nothing happened immediately. Then contact was made and Lasko heard a raspy exhalation of breath.

"Miko? What is wrong?"

Again only breathing.

A flicker of alarm registered. "Miko, I am coming to find you."

This time there was a response.

"No." The word was shouted. Panic in the voice. "Do not open the door, Janos. Stay where you are, brother."

Now Lasko was concerned.

He forced himself to remain calm, because something had emerged from the deep recesses of his mind. Something he did not want to even consider.

"Tell me what is wrong, Miko."

"The container broke from its straps. It sprang its catches and came open. One of the bundles came partway out. I had to put it back and fasten the catches again."

"You touched the rods?"

"There was no other choice. If it had been left, radiation could have spread through the plane. Now it is sealed away again."

"But if it came out perhaps radiation leaked out already." Lasko paused, because the realization came to him with a rush. *"Miko, you touched the rods?"*

"Yes."

"With your bare hands?"

"It was the only way to get the bundle back in the container so I could secure it." Sevisko cleared his throat. "I know what you are saying. I was exposed. I handled the rods, but it had to be done. It is our mission to deliver them safely. That is why you must keep the door closed. You must stay safe and land the plane, Janos. We *must* follow the plan."

The line went dead as Sevisko cut the connection, leaving Lasko alone in the cockpit, his mind racing as he tried to work out what he should do.

Turn back?

To where?

There had been no contingencies built into the plan to cover this kind of development, no arrangements for an emergency landing. With an illegal nuclear cargo on board no one was going to welcome them with open arms.

Of course, Lasko realized, he could ditch the plane here and now, in the Atlantic.

But everything would be lost. Colonel Rahman's strike against the enemies of Islam would fade and be forgotten, and he had no intention of allowing that to occur.

He stared out through the windshield until his mind reached the only decision it could under the circumstances. Lasko reached for the sat phone resting on top of the control panel and switched it on. He decided that it would be the lesser of two evils to use the phone rather than the radio. At that moment he had no choice, and the possibility that the sat phone might also be listened to never occurred to him. Regardless of the break in orders, he made the call, because the problem of radiation exposure had to be addressed.

LUBA RADESH COULD HEAR the soft whine of the aircraft engines in the background. He knew who it was before Lasko spoke.

"We have a problem."

"What is it?"

The muscles in Radesh's stomach pulled tight. If Lasko was calling it had to be important.

"The container was breached. An accident. But rods fell out and Miko had to push them back inside so he could lock it again."

"He was exposed?"

"He must have been. Yes. But he stayed in the rear compartment. The door to the cockpit was not opened."

"*Damn.* Are you well?"

"No signs of anything yet."

"Miko?"

"He terminated all communication with me. I don't know if he is still alive. Luba, what do we do?"

There was a pause before Radesh replied.

"Unless you are told different, carry on. We will arrange alternate procedures and let you know. When you reach America it will be Qazi who will direct you. Take care, brother. Now switch off the phone."

The sat phone went dead as Lasko ended the call.

RADESH STARED AT THE blank wall, his thoughts spinning as he tried to gather them. A last-minute setback was unacceptable. Too much had gone into the planning for it all to go wrong now. As his mind settled on the matter at hand Radesh felt himself calming down, reviewing the situation. He knew his first action must be to let Rahman know what had happened. The colonel would be even more furious if he was not informed.

He found the man speaking over a radio connection, discussing preparations in the operation center where the Barracuda was being worked on.

The moment Rahman saw the expression on Radesh's face he realized trouble was walking his way.

"What has happened? Tell me, Luba."

Radesh drew him aside and detailed his conversation with Lasko. Rahman accepted the information with quiet resolve. He stood, his hands clasped behind his back, his gaze turned in the direction of the waiting UAV and the technicians working on it.

"Lasko is still in control of the plane?"

"Yes, Colonel."

"And everything is ready at the Boston airfield?"

"The diversion will be activated the moment the plane is down on the runway."

"We still have time, then," Rahman said.

"According to Lasko the container has been resealed and locked again," Radesh said. "So the transfer from the plane to the vehicle could still go ahead." He paused. "However, there is now the problem of lingering radiation."

Rahman paced back and forth for a while, muttering to himself. The man was improvising, Radesh guessed. Working out someway to overcome this possible setback and salvage the operation. He would not allow the plan to be destroyed.

Rahman stopped and turned, wagging one finger in the air. "We *can* make this work," he said. "The ambulance that is already waiting to join the airfield rescue team will continue as planned. The only difference is that the men who go into the aircraft must wear the radiation suits we already have on site for handling the rods when they reach Boston. The unloading proceeds as scheduled and the team will take Sevisko and Lasko with them."

"Of course," Radesh said. "I had forgotten about the radiation containment at the airfield warehouse. This should work, Colonel."

"It must work, Luba. If we do not get the rods, then our American operation will not happen. I refuse to allow us to fail. This has been too long in preparation."

"I am not questioning your judgment, Colonel. You know I have faith in your vision and what you intend to achieve. Perhaps my strength is not as powerful as yours."

"Your input is welcome, Luba. I appreciate your calming voice. I must admit my enthusiasm sometimes gets in the way of thinking logically. Whatever happens, continue to be my alternative voice."

"But you are right, sir. We have the means to stabilize this setback. With the diversion, we may well yet bring a satisfactory conclusion to the matter. Qazi will be told to contact Lasko once he is in over U.S. soil. I will let him know what has happened, and inform him of the way we want to handle this."

"I have faith in Lasko's abilities. I know he will come through, and he will receive his reward from Allah himself."

CHAPTER NINETEEN

Umer Qazi's voice was calm and deliberate as he spoke over the sat phone to Lasko.

"When you touch down, turn off the main runway at J7. It will be on your left. Simply taxi along it and stop at hangar 7. Your arrival there will be the signal for our people to activate the diversion. There will be an explosion. Much fire and smoke. There will be confusion. Injury possibly. That will be to our advantage. The Americans will not be expecting such a thing to happen. Shock will delay a rapid reaction. Everything is in place for when you land."

"I am starting my descent now. Touchdown in five minutes."

"Good. Are you feeling all right?"

"Yes. Let's just hope this goes to plan. It's one hell of a gamble."

"But worth it if it succeeds."

"Making my final approach."

"God will protect you, brother."

The sat phone went dead.

LASKO HEARD THE CALM, unhurried voice of the air traffic controller giving him the runway number and approach vectors. It wasn't as if Lasko actually needed the instructions. He and Sevisko had made landings under some of the worst conditions imaginable, with no guidance from below, air bursts following them down, their aircraft shuddering and swaying around them. That had been war. The world they lived in day to day. Avoiding missiles and streams of cannon fire. In rain and snow. Flying through swirling clouds of smoke.

On reflection, he realized he was embarking on a new war. There might be hostiles shooting at him under terrible conditions, but this strike against America and Pakistan was the beginning of a new campaign for Islam, and he, Janos Lasko, was a soldier in the struggle that was bound to follow. However this plan of Colonel Rahman worked out, there would be conflict. Blood would follow, as it always did. His commitment was absolute. As he had promised the colonel it would be.

He saw the blur of the gray runway below, coming closer with each second. There was no turning away. Once the wheels of the plane made contact he would be in enemy territory, an enemy combatant. No matter what happened Janos Lasko would give his best, as he always had. He glanced at the weapons on the rack at his side. If he had to use them he would make sure that he took down as many Americans as possible. His fight was for Allah, the one and true God, and he would not fail.

Lasko felt the wheels brush the strip. He smiled at the smoothness of his landing. He allowed his pilot's responses to take over, making the necessary adjustment as he reversed the thrust of the engines and began to ease down on the brakes, correcting any drift. The roar of the engines filled the cabin. Lasko watched the freight terminal buildings emerge in the distance, take form and color. The voice of the air traffic controller filled his headset, advising him he was now able to cruise along the feeder strips to his termination location. Lasko thanked the control tower and signed off.

He counted down the lanes as he rolled smoothly along, noting the bay numbers.

Five.

Six.

Seven.

He eased the nose of the jet around, taking it onto the last stretch. Ahead he could see the wide hangar with the number emblazoned on the huge doors: 7.

He knew that once he ended his run and the plane was motionless, a customs vehicle could make its way across the apron and he would—

Though he had been expecting something dramatic, the explosion caught Lasko by surprise. He slammed both feet down on the brakes and the jet came to a hard stop. His hands moved over the controls and cut the engines. To his right was a rising wall of raw flame that appeared to have engulfed the whole area. He felt the plane rock under the pressure wave caused by the explosion. Debris slammed against the fuselage. Something struck one of the side windows of the flight cabin, cracking the Perspex. Lasko could feel the heat as the inferno outside increased in ferocity.

Qazi had told him there would be a diversion. He had not lied, but to Lasko it was like being back in a war zone. A second explosion rumbled. More flame. And thick smoke rising near the plane.

Lasko unbuckled himself, snatched up his SMG and clipped the belt holster in place, checking the SIG autopistol.

He heard distant sirens almost drowned out by the roar of the flames.

Emergency vehicles?

Out of the writhing clouds of smoke he saw a red-and-white ambulance come rolling up to the jet, rear doors swinging open and three haz-mat suited figures jumping out. They began to throw metal canisters across the concrete apron. The canisters erupted with clouds of thick smoke that added to the already substantial flame and smoke from the explosions. The ambulance turned, reversing up to the plane's rear door. Lasko kept losing sight of the vehicle as the thick smoke billowed and swelled.

Glancing forward, he saw the raging flames still forming a dramatic barrier between the jet and the airfield. Now more sirens could be heard, a raucous wail on the far side of the flames.

Someone banged on the cabin door.

Lasko unlocked and opened it.

A figure in a haz-mat suit stood there.

"Let's go, Lasko. No time to hang about now."

"What about the—?"

"Just move. Fast. You'll be okay. Now go."

Lasko ran the length of the cabin to the open exit door. An aluminum ladder had been propped there. He climbed down fast, peering through the smoke as he hit the concrete. A gloved hand emerged from the haze and guided him to the open rear of the ambulance. Lasko went up the step and inside. Suited figures followed him in. The doors slammed shut and the ambulance lurched into motion, sirens on full volume, emergency lights strobing.

"Fifteen seconds," someone yelled at the driver.

"To what?" Lasko asked.

"To the device I left in the plane going boom," the man in the suit said.

"Your plane is going to be turned into scrap metal," someone else told him. "A little extra for the firefighters to have to deal with. More confusion for the stupid Americans."

The blast behind them turned the jet into another fireball, the JetStar disintegrating from the high-explosive detonation. The ambulance swayed on its suspension.

"It worked," someone said.

The ambulance slowed as it reached the gated side exit. The driver leaned out and yelled to the gatemen.

"Let's go, let's go. Two badly burned patients inside. Another with an arm and leg missing."

"What happened?"

"Don't know yet, but it's bad. Bodies all over."

"Where you takin' 'em?"

"Trauma at Mercy Hospital. Now let's go, guys."

As the ambulance sped through the opened gate, rocking as it made the turn onto the highway, Lasko remembered two things.

First Miko.

He turned and saw his partner on a stretcher fixed to the side of the ambulance. He was inside a transparent, zippered body bag. Miko was still, his face flushed and glistening with sweat.

"Is he alive?"

One of the men shrugged, his own face impassive behind the visor. He handed Lasko a haz-mat suit.

"Put it on. Just in case."

"The rods?"

On the other side of the ambulance, fixed to the floor, was a large, heavy-looking metal box, the top pulled down tight and held in place by metal screw clamps.

"Inside," the man said. "Lined with solid lead. It's where we were going to keep the rods once we had them on site. Lucky we already had it built."

Sweating inside the thick haz-mat suit, breathing air from the cylinder that pumped it around, Lasko slumped against the side of the ambulance and tried to clear his head. The rapid chain of events from the moment he'd heard the first explosion had left him a little confused. His head was starting to ache and he felt a degree of nausea, which he attributed to the hectic minutes of his arrival in America.

He realized the ambulance siren had been turned off and the vehicle was not driving so fast now.

He glanced at the three men sitting across from him, gloved hands resting on their knees, heads pressed back against the side of the ambulance. They were not very talkative. Maybe he was imagining it, because he couldn't see their faces clearly through the plastic visors, but it felt as if they were all staring at him.

Watching.

Lasko smiled at his own thoughts.

He was tired after the long flight and the rushed exit from the plane.

He needed to clean up, eat and then sleep.

He wondered if it was the cool air circulating around his mask that made his eyes water. Or was it the headache that seemed to be getting worse rather than easing off? And if he could have removed the thick gloves that came as part of the haz-mat suit, he would have scratched at the itchy sensation creeping across his hands.

"THE BLAST MUST BE powerful enough to fracture the outer casing of the rods so that the cores will be exposed. The uranium pellets came from a working reactor. They are extremely irradiated. The term is *hot.* This is why they are so dangerous. We are all aware of how Miko was exposed and poisoned, even though he was in contact with the rods for only a short time. The designed explosion then must split the rods, but not damage them too much or the effect may be lost."

"So this is not just a case of attaching explosive and detonating it?" Usami asked.

Pirzada shook his head. "Yes and no. A safe explosion, but not one that would neutralize the power of the pellets. Which is why I need such information as the thickness of the rod sheathing, its tensile strength and how much pressure the blast must generate."

"Is this the reason you also need to be in contact with Fazeel?"

"The technicians in Pakistan are working under the same constraints," Pirzada said. "Fazeel is my counterpart. We both need to be constantly checking each other's calculations. In the end, our results must be the same."

"Good luck with that," Usami said.

"Yes, we must leave you to your work, Ajmal," Qazi said. "Allow you peace and quiet." He added, "The list you gave is being filled at the moment. We have to be careful, but we will get what you need. We have contacts who can bring it to us."

"Soon, I hope."

"Work your calculations, Ajmal, and let us do the worrying."

"The containment chamber is working well," Pirzada said. "Your people have done a wonderful job."

ALAM TOOK QAZI ASIDE. It was obvious he had something on his mind and it didn't need any stretch of the imagination to figure out what.

"You are worried about Lasko."

"Not just me. This radiation poisoning has everyone nervous. No one expected something like this to happen. It has been two days now. He will not get any better. He will die just as Sevisko died."

"Which is why I have quarantined him in a separate room in the farmhouse."

"But is that enough?"

Alam could see in Qazi's expression the man did not have a satisfactory answer.

"I do not believe the radiation will spread."

"We should move him," Alam said. "It is for the good of the group. We know he is going to die. As long as he remains here there will be unrest, and unrest is something we cannot have at this time. Our brothers need to be focused on what we came to do. You must understand that, Umer."

Alam's logic could not be denied—or ignored.

"Arrange for him to be taken to Khalib Mustaph's apartment. If I recall, there is a basement area. If Lasko is placed there the chance of him infecting anyone is small. Make sure the team who transport him wear their protective suits, but take care not to be seen. At least he will be with his friend Miko again."

"Tonight," Alam said. "We can keep a team there to look after him. They can stay in the house, away from the basement."

Qazi nodded. "Until the operation is complete we must not let Lasko's condition alert the American police. If he was discovered, there would be a wide alert and more chance of our presence being exposed. We cannot risk that. There is still much activity in the area since the incident at the airfield. The authorities are extremely agitated."

"I will organize everything."

Qazi was secretly glad that the problem of Janos Lasko would soon be off his hands. There was too much riding on the success of the operation. The discovery of one sick man, as unfortunate as it was for Lasko, could have torn the whole plan to shreds before they had a chance to trigger the nuclear device.

Lasko's sacrifice had to be accepted. In conflict there were always casualties. Never planned for, but to be absorbed and spoken of in thought and prayer.

Qazi immersed himself in other business, so he failed to see Alam speaking quietly to the brothers who were to be assigned the task of removing Lasko from the farm. He did not hear what was said, including the agreement that Lasko should be taken far away to be disposed of. Alam made it clear to the team that it was too risky to take a second sick man into the city at this time. They would drive him somewhere secluded, make certain he was dead, and hide the body. By the time he was discovered the device would have been deployed and the Americans would be far too busy with the effects of the dirty bomb to worry about Janos Lasko.

CHAPTER TWENTY

"Nice rooms," Blancanales said as he joined his partners in Lyons's suite.

Able Team had arrived in Boston just over an hour ago, picking up their rental at the airport and heading directly for the prebooked hotel. As soon as Lyons reached his room he'd made direct contact with Stony Man via his encrypted sat phone. He was in a conversation with Price when Schwarz opened the door to admit Blancanales.

Schwarz brought his partner up to speed.

"There's been a development since we left home," he said. "You heard about the aircraft incident at a local airport a couple of days ago?" They had picked up the news reports and the TV coverage while in transit. "The place handles freight and business aircraft. When it landed and taxied, there were explosions. Hell of a lot of confusion. The plane blew, as well. While all this was going on, apparently an emergency ambulance exited the field, the driver claiming he had badly injured people on board and was bound for a local hospital. Only no ambulance showed up at the designated hospital, or any others…."

HUNTINGTON WETHERS EASED his chair back from his monitor. He stood and crossed to where Aaron Kurtzman was staring at his own screen display. Even Kurtzman was starting to flag after the long hours the cyber team had been manning their stations. At that present moment he and Wethers were the only ones working. Carmen Delahunt and Akira Tokaido had been relieved from duty to catch up on much needed sleep. The team had been running nonstop trawls of every security agency database they could. Utilizing the programs Kurtzman and Tokaido had developed, Stony Man was able to take sneak-peeks into the most sophisticated systems that existed. Aaron Kurtzman had no qualms when it came to obtaining the information he needed for the Stony Man teams. Firewall protocols and encrypted files were simply challenges he faced every day. Despite the ease with which he broke into sensitive areas, Kurtzman never contemplated misusing his skills. Once he gained needed information he left the particular database as he found it. Even he admitted he worked on twisted logic, but when the need arose he pushed it aside.

Barbara Price was on speaker with Carl Lyons. It allowed a multiple conversation with the rest of the cyber team.

"The plane was blown up at the airfield outside Boston," Wethers said. "I found something interesting in a restricted file from the FBI investigation. Restricted in the sense the Bureau kept it buried deep."

"Don't keep me in suspense," Lyons said.

"They found an explosive device had been detonated inside the plane. Deliberately to destroy it, their investigators decided. The same criteria applies to the explosions that caused the fires. Devices had been rigged to a couple of fuel tankers. When the FBI finalized their investigations it was concluded that the explosive used on the plane and the fuel tankers was the same. They also located detonator fragments, and when they pieced them together they all matched."

"The fire was a diversion to draw attention away from that aircraft?"

Wethers nodded. "That's my assumption. They wanted something off that plane and needed to conceal it. I think I know what it was."

"I hate to ask what," Lyons said.

"Being the FBI, they ran every test they could. Including a radiation check. And they found trace evidence of uranium contamination."

"Uranium as in the nuclear rods hijacked in Pakistan," Kurtzman said. "So it's looking more than likely the rods have already been brought into the country."

"That first ambulance out of the airfield claimed to be carrying victims of the explosions," Kurtzman said. "Nobody at the time realized it had moved too quickly from the scene to be legit. It must have been kept out of sight, ready to go when the explosion was set off."

"Anything on that?" Lyons asked.

"Security camera overlooking the gate recorded footage," Wethers said. "When the FBI checked they found the ambulance plates were false. And there was no visit to Mercy Hospital. No patients admitted."

"Because all that ambulance had on board was a container holding those nuclear rods," Lyons concluded. "And possibly the flight crew off the plane."

"There were no bodies in the plane wreckage. A lot of planning went into that operation," Wethers said. "It was smart. Risky, but it paid off."

"There's always a downside," Kurtzman said. "Some little thing they overlooked. Somewhere, they left us something we could work on. And Akira found it."

Price had already updated Lyons on Stony Man's collective data. "Akira came up with an ID for the ambulance driver," she said. "I'll download it to your laptop."

Lyons had fired up his computer. "The way you're talking, it sounds like we have an exclusive," he said.

"We do, so you can move on it any way you want if it gets us closer to the bad guys."

"How come the FBI didn't get it?" Lyons asked.

Price shrugged. "Feds," she said in an exaggerated mocking tone. "It was Akira who spotted it. Hell of a fluke but the kid did it. You know how he loves playing around with images. Well, he thought he saw something in the driver's exterior mirror. Some misty blur on the glass. He isolated it and ran it through one of those weird programs he and Aaron keep creating. Has something to do with digital imaging and enhancement. He kept working at the detail he spotted and it turned out it was the driver's face. Took him half the night before he worked it up into a recognizable picture. Then he captured it and ran it through facial-recognition databases. There's a ninety-nine percent chance the guy is one Khalib Mustaph. A naturalized Pakistani, he's been in the U.S. for seven years, but get this, his sheet has him on a watch list. Seems Mustaph has been photographed in the company of Khalil Amir. No hard evidence, but the guy sounds a little iffy."

"Him driving that ambulance makes it a whole lot iffy," Lyons said. "We got an address?"

"Of course," Price said. "You think this is a cheapskate outfit we have here? Everything you need will be on the download."

Able Team gathered around the laptop as the open connection to Stony Man downloaded Mustaph's image. There was also text data on the man.

"We checked out Mustaph's phone records," Kurtzman said. "He makes lots of calls, so we sourced his contact list. Seems he's made a bunch of calls to a number that turned out to be Khalil Amir's export business. We're still collating other calls and we'll let you know if anything interesting comes up."

"What does Mr. Mustaph do for a living when he isn't driving suspect ambulances?" Lyons asked.

"You'll love this," Price said. "He runs a vehicle customizing shop. Location is in with the data."

"Thanks, Barbara. Give Akira a pat on the head for me."

"FOR A BUNCH who pulled off that airport trick," Blancanales said, "they let themselves down when it comes to telephone calls."

"Surprising how many people aren't aware their calls can be back traced," Schwarz said.

"Up to us to take advantage of their stupidity," Lyons said. "Gear up and let's go. Clock is ticking on this. We need to move fast."

THE CUSTOMIZING SHOP owned by Khalib Mustaph was situated down a wide side street that seemed to have a number of similar enterprises—repair shops, parts suppliers, vehicle electrical repairs. Most parking spaces along the street were taken up by cars and trucks waiting for work to be carried out.

Schwarz drove on by the shop that bore the sign identifying it as belonging to Mustaph. He parked at an open spot.

"Go on, take Pol with you," he said to Lyons. "I'll cover your backs in case the locals get restless."

Lyons and Blancanales stepped out of the rental, loosening their jackets to allow easy access to the holstered handguns.

The shop had a wide entrance that allowed access to a generous work area. Tube lights threw a stark glow over the interior. Around the walls were body parts, metal panels, steel wheel rims. The acrid smell of auto paint and solvent tainted the warm air. At the far end of the shop double doors were open, showing the inside of a paint bay. The heavy sound of a rap CD was coming from a dusty player jammed at the back of a littered workbench. There were three parked vehicles in various stages of repair work.

As Lyons walked inside, his keen gaze immediately spotted three men in stained coveralls. Blancanales stayed a few steps behind and to the side, covering Lyons's back.

"What do you want?" The question came from a heavy-set man clutching a steel pry bar. He wore a stained ball cap, peak backward, which irritated Lyons straight off.

"Maybe I want a custom paint job," Lyons said. "Your crappy attitude isn't going to help me make up my mind."

Ball-cap grunted and spit on the concrete floor. "And maybe I got enough fuckin' work so I don't need to be polite."

Lyons glanced in Blancanales's direction, slowly raising his eyes.

"You the boss?" he asked Ball-cap. "Or maybe you're the guy who forgot to go to customer-relations class."

"Look, you son of a bitch," the guy said. "You know something. I smell cop."

Over the big man's beefy shoulder Lyons focused in on one of the other men. The guy was inching away, eyes searching for a way out. He was dressed like the other men in stained coveralls, holding a can of paint in one hand. Lyons recognized him without difficulty.

Khalib Mustaph.

"You see him?" Lyons asked his partner.

"I got him," Blancanales said.

He began to edge away from Lyons, concentrating on Mustaph.

"You should go," Ball-cap said.

Lyons remained motionless as the big guy stepped up

to within a few feet of him, his right hand flexing the steel pry bar.

"You should go," he repeated.

"Slow echo in here," Lyons said.

Ball-cap let out a hard grunt and swung the bar at him. But Lyons wasn't there any longer. He had dropped to the concrete floor and, sweeping his muscular leg around, took Ball-cap's feet from under him. The big man slammed down on the floor, breath bursting from his lips as he hit hard. The back of his skull rapped against the concrete. He lost his grip on the pry bar and it bounced across the floor.

Lyons rolled, pushing to his feet, sweeping aside his jacket to reach for the Colt Python, snapping it from the shoulder rig and pulling the barrel around as he spotted the third man producing a Glock 19 from inside his coverall.

Lyons didn't hesitate. He leveled the big revolver and burned off two fast shots. The .357 Magnum slugs plowed into his target's chest, kicking him backward. One burned its way clear through his body, blowing out between his shoulders in a messy spray. The guy hit the closest solid object, the wall, and hung for a moment before he slid to the floor.

As the racket of the shots filled the workshop, Mustaph broke into a dead run for the door, flinging aside the can he was holding and ignoring the fact that Blancanales was in his way. As he closed in he lowered his head and slammed into the Able Team hardman. The impact pushed Blancanales back a few feet before he braced himself and snapped his left arm around Mustaph's thick neck. The guy grunted, encircling Blancanales's waist and trying to lift him off the floor.

"Oh, hell," Blancanales said.

He reached down to pull his Beretta, slamming the solid steel barrel across the back of Mustaph's skull. Flesh split, bleeding, but the man hung on, pummeling him with his clenched fists. Blancanales hit him a few more times before Mustaph groaned and slid to his knees. He slumped to the concrete, blood pouring from his head as Blancanales stepped back, staring at the bloody pistol in his hand.

Schwarz appeared in the doorway, weapon ready. He took in the scene, shaking his head.

"Let you two out on your own," he said disapprovingly.

The approaching wail of police sirens told them the shooting had been reported. Boston PD cruisers slid to a stop outside the shop. Armed cops swarmed inside. For the next minute the customary shouting and orders to lie on the floor rang out. The Able Team members placed their weapons down, hands held clear of their bodies, but resolutely refused to spread themselves on the dirty concrete.

"You want to shoot me, go ahead," Blancanales said. "No way I'm getting down there."

One burly uniform reached out to restrain him. "You do as you're damn well told," he bellowed.

"Hey," Lyons yelled. "Don't." The authority in his voice made the cop hesitate. "I'm reaching inside my jacket with my left hand. I need to show you something." Every gun in the shop was trained on Lyons as he slowly extracted the leather ID wallet and passed it to the closest officer. "Just read it."

The cop scanned the ID card, then passed it to one of his buddies. "Justice?" he said.

"Working out of Washington. Looking for the perps who worked the airfield crash," Lyons explained. "We identified him—" he pointed to the inert figure of Mustaph "—as the ambulance driver. And it's looking like the fake ambulance was built here, too. We came to check this place out. Guy over there drew down on me and I had to defend myself. Call the number on the ID and you can confirm what I've said with our superior."

THEY WERE STILL AT the location an hour later, along with more cops, most of the new ones suits. Following telephone conversations with Brognola, tension had eased for Able Team, the Boston cops placated by the fact they had one of the airfield incident's perpetrators in custody.

The burly cop who had yelled at Blancanales spread his hands. "Hey, what do I say. For all I knew you guys might have started shooting."

"No sweat, Cassidy," Lyons said, reading the cop's name off his uniform tag. "Doing your job. Never gets any easier, huh? When I was in L.A. I had to call it in English and Spanish."

"You wore the uniform?"

"Yeah."

"Looks like you came a long way since then."

Lyons shrugged. "Cassidy, you'll never know."

"So what is this all about?" the cop asked.

"Right now all I can say is terrorist plot. No more details. Sorry."

Cassidy shrugged his broad shoulders. "Ain't nothing we haven't been told before. Ground troops get the shit, the suits get the sugar."

Lyons grinned. "Not this time, Cassidy. Even your bosses only have the line I gave you. It stays that way until we know more ourselves."

"Local PD is going over the scene to see what they can pick up," Blancanales was telling Brognola. "I don't think they'll find anything here, but I'm staying around. Carl and Hermann are going to check Mustaph's home address."

"Okay. Keep me in the loop."

KHALIB MUSTAPH LIVED in a quiet residential district. In recent years many of the houses had been upgraded and turned into apartments. The street was quiet this close to midday. A few cars were lined up at the curbs. Somewhere a dog was barking, the sound distant and mournful.

Schwarz eased the SUV to a stop and cut the engine.

"How do we do this?" he asked. "Nice and polite or gangbusters?"

"Considering what these sons of bitches are planning," Lyons said, "I can't cough up much sympathy for them."

Schwarz glanced across at him. Lyons shrugged in a noncommittal way.

"What? We into sign language now?" Schwarz asked.

"These perps are planning to set off a nuke in the city. We agreed on that?"

"Yeah."

"So any human rights these bums might have had go out the window for me."

"Fine." Schwarz said. "Why didn't you say so?"

"I like to see you working things out."

They exited the SUV. Schwarz used the remote to lock it. "That won't stop anyone stealing it," Lyons said. "Probably have their own tow truck."

"Magic word," Schwarz said. *"Rental."*

They were crossing the street.

"You want me around back?" Schwarz asked.

Lyons nodded and Schwarz moved across the uncut lawn and vanished around the side of the building.

Lyons went inside. He checked out the entrance hall.

The pleasant surroundings and peaceful atmosphere clashed with the reason why Able Team was visiting the building.

He reached the door of Mustaph's apartment. Lyons leaned in close to the door. No sound. He reached out to try the handle. It gave easily, the door cracking open when he pushed.

Lyons eased the door open.

A hall stretched the length of the apartment. To his immediate left was a single door, with a light switch set in the wall next to it. Lyons guessed it was for a basement.

Impatience, long ago diagnosed as something Carl Lyons failed to possess, pushed him along the hallway. He reached the next door, ready to check the room. The door cracked open, then was jerked wide, and an armed figure confronted him. The muzzle of a Glock was thrust into Lyons's face.

"You don't walk as quiet as you think," the man said. "Inside."

The moment Lyons was in the room the door was slammed shut. He saw that the gunman was not alone. There were two more, both armed with holstered autopistols. They were all dark skinned, with black hair.

"This one of them?"

The question was aimed at the guy holding the gun. He nodded. "He was at Mustaph's place. Him and two others. There were cops all over the place. Almost walked into them myself." He was patting Lyons down as he spoke. His face split into a toothy smile when he located the Colt Python. He yanked it out and held it up. "Look at this piece of artillery." He dropped the Colt on the floor and slid it aside.

"Thinks he's Dirty Harry," one man said.

"He was a wuss. You need to know that," Lyons said. If the trio had known Lyons at all, they would have realized he was not joking. "Maybe you sissies are his brothers."

His remark had the effect he wanted. The guy with the gun gave a whispered curse and swiped the barrel of his Glock at Lyons's head. The Able Team leader leaned back as the pistol came at him, then reached up and caught hold of the guy's wrist with his left hand, yanking him around. His right closed over the Glock. Lyons pulled the guy in close, planting himself behind him. He slipped his finger inside the trigger guard of the Glock, angled the guy's arm and squeezed on the trigger. The Glock fired, the slug hitting the farthest man in the chest. He fell back with a stunned grunt, knees buckling.

The third guy went for his own holstered weapon, but Lyons, his left arm now snaked around his captive's throat in a savage choke hold, swept the Glock around and fired again. And another time. His aim was high and both slugs cored through the target's face. The guy's nose vanished in a splurge of blood. The next slug ripped away his lower jaw on the left side of his face. The man went down screaming, slamming to the floor, where he lay wriggling in pain.

Lyons's captive struggled to free himself from the arm encircling his neck. It was a futile attempt. Carl Lyons always took exception to being held at gunpoint. And he reacted with unrepentant violence. He applied even more pressure, his taut muscles straining as he squeezed the life out of his captive. With his air cut off, the guy had nowhere to go. His frantic thrashing only used up what little air he had left, and Lyons felt the man's struggles weakening, then ceasing altogether. He pulled the Glock from the limp hand and let the guy slip to the floor. He retrieved his Python and holstered it, keeping the Glock in his right hand.

He took a final look around the room. At the bodies on the floor.

"Told you," he said.

Pounding footsteps beyond the door told Lyons his partner was on his way. Schwarz burst through the door, weapon up and searching. He took one look at the three bodies, then glanced at Lyons. The Able Team leader gave him a questioning look.

"What?" he said.

"I could have stayed in the damn car."

"We need to check the place out," Lyons said.

"Check the place out," Schwarz muttered.

"Before anyone calls the cops."

"Boston PD is going to love us being around," Schwarz said.

They moved through the apartment, finding nothing out of the ordinary. Lyons was not satisfied.

"Three guys. All armed. Pretty uptight," he said. "Why?"

"We've looked the place over. Found nothing."

"Not the basement," Lyons said.

"Basement?"

"Yeah." Lyons led the way to the door at the end of the hallway. He indicated the light switch set in the wall. "Switch *outside* a room?"

He flicked it and opened the door. They both saw the wooden steps, and Lyons started down them. He made it only halfway when he called, "Stay back, Hermann."

"What is it?"

"We've got a body. By the look of him he's been exposed to some kind of radiation. In a bad way. We need to call Hal. He should get a haz-mat team in here and get this place closed off and the apartments cleared."

They retreated from the basement, Lyons closing the door.

"If that guy has been exposed, it means they already have the rods in the country," Schwarz said to no one in particular.

Lyons already had his sat phone in his hand, tapping in the speed dial number that would connect him to Stony Man.

"Barb, initiate a haz-mat team response to our location.

Khalib Mustaph's home address. We have a dead guy who could have been exposed to some kind of radiation. No, I don't think we're in trouble, but we'll stay around to get checked out. Is Hal there?"

"Standing next to me."

"Put him on."

Brognola listened as Lyons explained the situation. "Barbara is calling in a haz-mat team," he said. "You sure you guys are okay?"

"Pretty much," Lyons said. "We didn't stay close once we realized what was happening. Hal, we also have perps who decided it was better to try shooting it out instead of quitting. Better let the Boston PD know there's been another incident."

"I'll do that. We'll have to keep a blanket over this. If word gets out about radiation it could get tricky. We could end up with multiple agencies on the scene. FBI. Homeland Security. I'll try and get the haz-mat people on site first. Let them check you guys out."

Lyons ended the call. "Get some images of those guys and send them through to Kurtzman. They can run them through facial-recognition systems. We might be lucky and get a hit. Tie them up to Rahman's organization."

Lyons went back and rechecked the apartment. His previous life as a cop left him with the instincts of an investigator. An empty room could be as informative as a live witness if you knew where to look.

"What are we looking for, Carl?" Schwarz asked.

"Something that's going to tell us about Mustaph. Who his friends were. Kind of car he drove. Anything."

They circled the apartment, searching silently, until Schwarz spoke up.

"Cell phone."

He lifted the instrument he had located on a bookshelf,

between a couple of volumes. From its position, it may have been set down on a book and fallen. Schwarz activated the phone. It showed a three-quarter-full battery. He negotiated the memory and ran through recent calls received and sent. There was a significant number.

"Our boy was busy," Schwarz said. "All these calls are within the last few days. Before that there were only a few."

"The busy list starts around the day of the airport incident," Lyons said, peering over his partner's shoulder.

"We need to get Kurtzman onto this," Schwarz said. He took out his sat phone and made contact with Stony Man. "Hey, Barb, patch me through to the Bear.... Hey, Aaron, I'm going to give you a cell number and the service provider. I need you to pull up Khalib Mustaph's call list. Check out names and link to addresses."

"You found him then?"

"Yeah. Local law enforcement officers have him in custody."

"Anything you can dig out could be useful."

"Get back to you," Kurtzman said after Schwarz passed along the data he needed.

Lyons and Schwarz continued looking around the apartment.

"Gun," Lyons said, holding up a 9 mm Beretta autopistol he had found beneath a pile of underwear. He unloaded the weapon and threw it and the magazine onto the bed.

Schwarz was prowling around the apartment, eyes searching. In one of the bedrooms he located a plastic bag beneath the unmade bed. Inside was a crumpled coverall with Paramedic stenciled across the back.

"Sloppy guy," he said. "He should have disposed of this."

Lyons found a wastebasket with crumpled sheets of

paper stuffed in the bottom. He took them out and rifled through them.

"Somebody printed off the airport layout," he said. "Shows entrance and exit gates." He checked the print-out date and the origin of the diagram. "Printed a month back. Came off the airport's official website. Don't these idiots ever learn? They might just as well have an entrance marked Come Inside and Attack Us. Everything you need to know for a successful strike."

"Ownership papers here," Blancanales said. "Mustaph's car." He checked the details, then made his way outside to search for the vehicle. "Not around," he said when he returned.

"Lent it to someone?" Lyons wondered. He used his sat phone again and relayed the vehicle details to Stony Man. "Run a check on it," he told Hunt Wethers. "See if you can locate it. It's fairly new…eight months old. Might have a manufacture's LoJack system built in. Worth a look."

The haz-mat truck pulled up to the curb, the suited team coming inside. Lyons identified himself and explained what they had found. Before anything else happened the Able Team duo were checked over and pronounced clean. The apartment was also checked. No radiation traces were found.

The basement was designated off-limits after the haz-mat team inspected the body. The squad commander gave Lyons and Schwarz the details.

"Exposure to uranium radiation. Looks like he's been dead a couple of days." The man glanced at Lyons. "This anything to do with what happened at the airport after that plane blew apart?"

"Could be," Lyons said.

The commander smiled. "Okay, I get the message. We need to keep this under the radar. One sniff of the word *ra-*

diation and Boston will be in meltdown. Maybe that wasn't the most appropriate description, but you understand what I mean."

Lyons nodded. "Cops will be here any minute," he said. "You'll put them in the picture?"

"No problem."

"We clear to move on?" Schwarz asked.

"Yeah. Take it easy, guys."

Police cruisers were closing off the street as Lyons and Schwarz left the apartment building. The first uniformed cop they saw was Cassidy. He was unable to repress an broad grin.

"This going to become a regular thing?" he asked.

Lyons patted him on the shoulder. "Think of it as keeping Boston PD in a job."

Schwarz was calling Blancanales on his phone. "See you back at the hotel," he said after telling his teammate what had happened.

"WHAT DO WE REALLY HAVE?" Lyons asked. *"Nada."*

Blancanales glanced up from pouring coffee from the jug delivered to Lyons room. "When you say it like that, I guess so," he said.

"Our main drawback is we don't have any damn idea when this operation goes down. Could be a week away. Or it might be on its countdown right now. Whichever way you cut it the clock is ticking."

"The man has a point," Schwarz said.

"I know. That's the trouble," Blancanales said. "And how come you're agreeing with him all the time? There something I should know about you two?"

Lyons's ringing phone cut short taking the conversation any further.

"Bear? Tell me you have something for us."

"We locked on to Mustaph's car. That LoJack tip is working. I'm watching the car on the move as we speak. I can give you its current position and relay any changes to you over your cell. Once you have a visual you can take over."

"Do it," Lyons said. "We'll be mobile in five."

"Carl, it could be the car was stolen and all we'll have will be a bunch of kids."

"I get it. I promise I won't shoot until I see their IDs." Lyons was about to give the order to move. When he turned, Blancanales and Schwarz were already heading for the door.

CHAPTER TWENTY-ONE

Janos Lasko opened another plastic bottle, swallowing the chilled water without pause. He felt it slide down his swollen throat, bringing brief relief. The problem would come later, he knew, after it had settled in his stomach. His body would start to reject the water, as it was doing with anything he ate or drank, and Lasko simply took the signs as confirmation he had the same radiation poisoning that had affected his partner, Miko Sevisko. He had managed to keep the knowledge—he hoped to have kept the knowledge—from the rest of the group. It had been two days since Miko had been spirited away from the base during the hours of darkness and taken to a location Janos had not been told about. The last he had seen of Miko, he was being carried out by men dressed in protective suits.

It hurt Lasko to see his friend go this way. They had been professional partners for a long time, had come through a war and had survived countless combat situations. They had answered when Radesh had called, proud to be part of an operation that had been gestating for a long time. Since the Kosovo war and the aftermath, there had been rising discontent with the West for its interference, an interference that continued to this very day.

Colonel Rahman's intended double strike would bring shock and terror to the United States and Pakistan, making them realize they were not going to be allowed to continue meddling and plotting in the affairs of others.

The cleverly orchestrated diversion at the airfield, intended to draw attention away from the plane carrying the consignment of nuclear rods, had worked brilliantly. Workers planted at the airfield weeks before had detonated the explosive devices that had obliterated the pair of fuel tankers driven into position only minutes before Lasko had rolled the jet up to hangar 7. The massive explosion had destroyed buildings and killed a number of airfield service personnel. An added bonus, Rahman had called it. While the out-of-control flames had blocked off access to the plane, added smoke canisters had created a further blanket of confusion. The fake ambulance, already outfitted with the solid-steel, lead-lined container, had been loaded with the box holding the rods. Miko Sevisko had been transferred, as well, sealed in a body bag. Lasko had followed, donning a protective hazard suit, and the ambulance, lights flashing and sirens screaming, had been waved from the airfield. An explosive device left on the plane had destroyed the jet, simply adding more chaos and confusion for the airfield authorities.

Since the incident, local and national radio and television networks had been awash with reports, and as usual, a great deal of hysterical speculation. Investigations into the fires and the explosions were ongoing. The authorizes were saying very little, refusing to be drawn out.

Among Lasko's group there was agreement that by now the Americans would have retrieved evidence of explosive devices. They would be considering the possibility of a deliberate attack. The debate at the moment would be whether it was the work of some domestic organization or a terrorist act.

"As long as they can't make up their minds," Qazi said, "it will slow them down in their investigations."

Lasko wasn't so sure. His dislike of the Americans did

not blind him to the fact they were not fools. They had excellent investigators, people with experience and knowledge based on years of work in the area. They would find remains of the explosive devices used to trigger the detonations. With the backing of their technical laboratories they would pin down the type of explosive, triggers and detonators. And when they found out that the bomb placed inside the aircraft had been made using the same materials, it would kick-start a deeper investigation. They would want to know where the plane had come from and why it had been necessary to destroy it. There would be connections made. When it was learned the badly injured men being transported to Mercy Hospital had not arrived, and didn't fit any list of airfield employees, the searches would widen. Piece by piece a picture would form. A check through employee files would pinpoint personnel recently hired, who would have their backgrounds looked into. Somewhere along the line evidence would link someone to a known individual. Maybe on a list. Perhaps exposing a false identity. Small things that, when looked at under a microscope, might point the finger and lead to something more substantial.

Lasko had time to dwell on these things. He had little else to do. Within the group he was not given any specific task. His part had been the flight from Pakistan to America. That was over, and he had been told to rest for the next few days. So he lounged in his room in the farmhouse, watching TV, trying to fill his mind with inconsequential things. He found it difficult. He had never been content to sit around. But thoughts filtered through the constant headaches that seemed to have become part of his life. He took tablets, but they did nothing to help. So he went over the recent events, because at the back of his mind a small, nagging matter kept trying to make him listen to it. The problem was every time he thought he had it, the query slipped away. Lasko was convinced it had importance.

His other concern was the way the others in the group had started to avoid him—in subtle ways he failed to spot initially. But as time went by he realized he was being kept at arm's length. He didn't understand at first. His headaches. The nausea. The skin irritation. These demanded attention. It was only on the third day, when he caught a glimpse of himself in a mirror, that Lasko understood.

He looked ill. His skin pale, sallow. Dark patches under his eyes. Cheeks starting to show hollows. When he raised his hands to touch his face he saw the protuberance of his knuckles.

Lasko understood what was happening. Realization registered with a sudden, jolting shock.

Radiation sickness.

He had been poisoned, after all, and now the effects were making themselves visible. It was why the others were stepping around him. Keeping him at arm's length.

He was disappointed at their attitude, yet at the same time he understood. He may have been part of the team, but now he could become a viable threat. There was too much at stake. Anything that could possibly affect the outcome of the operation must not be allowed to happen.

It would seem that Lasko had become a liability.

It was only when he saw Alam in close discussion with Qazi, turning aside when they spotted him, that his fears, irrational or not, began to tell him what he should do.

He was aware of what they had done with Miko. How they had taken him away to…to where? And was he still alive? Lasko understood they would not have taken him to a hospital. A patient suffering from radiation poisoning would have raised the alarm, and the city would have been locked down. So Qazi had ordered Miko to be hidden away while preparations for the bomb strike went ahead. Now Lasko was showing symptoms. He would have to be dealt with in the same way.

Like it or not Lasko would become a disposable asset. The thought startled him.

And angered him.

He would not be taken away to some dark corner so he could die quietly and without upsetting the others. They were supposed to be brothers to the end, looking out for each other even in difficult situations. That seemed to have been pushed aside.

Alam moved away from Qazi, beckoning to a number of his companions. They stood in a tight huddle. Lasko caught a glimpse of a clumsily covered autopistol being adjusted in one man's jacket.

He backed away, intending to distance himself, and heard Alam's voice. "Janos, wait. We need to talk, brother."

Lasko kept moving, feeling the hostility in his words.

"Janos." This time it was a harsh command. "Do not go."

Lasko saw the side door, pushed it open and stepped outside. Rain sluiced down out of a clouded sky. He hurried along the length of the building and saw the parked vehicles. Without further thought he broke to the right and reached the first car, which he recognized as belonging to Khalib Mustaph, the driver of the ambulance. Lasko yanked open the door, leaned inside, and saw the keys in the ignition. As he went to climb in he felt a heavy hand on the door frame, turned and saw Syed Alam. The man's face was taut with anger.

"You will not leave."

The request allowed no resistance. Over Alam's shoulder Lasko could see the others hurrying to reach him, weapons out. He reacted as any soldier would in a desperate situation. Lasko turned to Alam, his right hand sweeping up in a powerful blow that struck him full in the face. The man stepped back, gasping in shock from the sudden surge of pain from his shattered nose, from the blood squirting in scarlet streams. As Alam stumbled away Lasko threw himself inside the car, one hand reaching for the key, the other dragging the door shut. He heard the engine fire up and dropped the stick in Drive, slamming his foot down on the gas pedal. The car lurched forward, slipping on the wet ground until the tires bit.

Lasko hung on to the wheel, feeling the car pick up speed, water and mud spraying up from the rear wheels as it sped forward. He glanced in the mirror and saw the armed figures shrinking behind him as he aimed the car for the dirt road ahead. He barely cleared the fence as the vehicle bumped through the open gate, then he was speeding recklessly down the rutted track.

Lasko knew with a sickening certainty that Usami and his men would follow. They would not let him drive away, and leave it at that. Lasko knew too much. The location of the base and what they were planning. Right now he wasn't sure what he might achieve by breaking free, but one thing was certain. He had no intention of letting his former companions dictate how he would live or die. Not after the way they had disposed of his good friend Miko Sevisko.

Miko had deserved better.

So do did Janos Lasko.

His destiny lay in his own hands now. However long he had left, only *he* would make that decision.

When he reached the main highway he deliberated for a few moments before swinging the car to the east, heading away from the base.

FOLLOWING KURTZMAN'S directions over the cell, Blancanales swung the SUV out of the hotel parking lot and onto the street. He pushed the big SUV as fast as he could. As he drove, Lyons calmly guided him, relaying the information he was getting from Stony Man.

"Car is about twenty miles ahead of you. We have your locator on screen now. Got you on the satellite feed," Kurtzman said. "You'll need to do some hard driving to cut the gap. Car is moving away from town. Just stay on your current heading."

The midday sky had darkened as they left the hotel. More clouds were rolling in. Minutes later the rain started falling, changing quickly from a light sprinkle to a heavy downpour. Blancanales switched on the wipers. Silver spray flashed up from vehicles ahead of them. He saw the freeway ahead and took the first on ramp he came to, his foot hard on the gas.

"Where the hell is that car going?" Blancanales asked.

"Stay on your route," Kurtzman said, his voice coming through the phone's speaker as Lyons activated it. "He's still directly ahead."

Long minutes later Lyons asked, "How we doing, Aaron? We've got heavy rain here. Don't want to lose this car."

Kurtzman relayed more information. Blancanales followed the directions to switch lanes and take the next off ramp, curving down the slope to pick up another stretch of highway.

"He's just made a right onto a feeder road for an industrial park. It's coming up."

Blancanales made the turn. The road ahead, lined with industrial warehouses and workshops, was clear of vehicles.

"There it is," Lyons called. "Mustaph's car."

Blancanales slammed his foot to the floor, sending the heavy SUV surging forward at breakneck speed. The wipers were having difficulty clearing the rain from the windshield now. The low cloud was blanketing the area in a gloom.

"I don't think this guy is going anywhere," Schwarz said. "His driving is all over the place."

Blancanales had to grin. "Who does that remind you of?"

"You want me to take over?" Lyons growled.

"Only a passing comment," Blancanales said.

"He turned into a warehouse area ahead," Kurtzman said over the phone.

"We saw," Lyons said. "Breaking off now, Aaron."

"Go easy, guys," Kurtzman advised.

Blancanales eased off the gas, letting the SUV slow. "Where?"

"Right," Lyons said. "There."

They were coming up to a block of abandoned industrial units, large, deserted workshops and storage facilities. A sagging chain-link fence ran parallel to the street. Signs on the fence indicated the site was up for sale. Blancanales pulled through an open gate and brought the SUV to a stop.

"You see him?"

The expanse of concrete, sprouting weeds and industrial debris was empty, with no vehicle in sight.

Blancanales studied the area. "Over to the right," he said. "Beyond that pile of metal scrap. Exhaust smoke showing."

Blancanales let the SUV roll forward. Beside him, Lyons slid the Colt Python from its holster and placed it on the seat.

"Expecting trouble?" Schwarz asked.

"Always," Lyons answered.

LASKO PARKED on one side of the warehouse and sat listening to the rain drumming on the roof of the car. It had a soothing effect on him. He was grateful for that. The last few days had gone by in a jumble of mixed emotions. It had started with Miko getting poisoned by the nuclear rods. That had been an unavoidable accident. Miko had been acting with good intentions, wanting to preserve the rods for the upcoming attack, but in doing so he had exposed himself to the deadly radiation. Even then he had done everything he could to make sure Lasko was safe, by locking himself in the cargo bay. Now he was dead, his body ravaged by the effects of his exposure, and Lasko had been helpless to save him.

They had been together for a long time. Fighting the war in Kosovo, then after, when they had been forced to move on. Despite their risky alliance, Lasko and Sevisko had looked out for each other through good and bad times. Sharing life. Sharing danger. Money. Women. It had all been the same for the pair.

Now Miko was gone, and Lasko was on his own for the first time in more years than he cared to recall. He felt the downpour increase, the rain slanting in across the deserted yard. The bleakness of the afternoon only added to his loneliness. Here he was, in America, alone. Illegally. Almost a fugitive. Not the situation he would have chosen for himself. As he shifted in his seat he felt the heavy handgun nestling under his arm. He had always experienced carrying a weapon to be comforting—something he could use to defend himself against potential enemies. Right now his gun did little to increase his sense of safety. In the vast continent of America he was a man without friends. Certainly no Americans. And he had the same feelings about his own people now.

Alam had set them against him; Lasko knew that for certain. If he had not run they would have removed him.

Locked him down so that he could die without affecting any of them. Qazi had obviously agreed, sealing Lasko's fate.

He leaned against the headrest, closing his eyes. He couldn't make sense of it all. He knew what was happening to him—the radiation poisoning leeching through his body. The problem was the tiredness that kept sweeping over him. A deep weariness. It was a sensation he had never experienced before. Oh, he had been tired after long hours of combat. The same from flying. But this was worse. Being so tired that it was taking him over. And the recurring headaches, too. He had not been a man who suffered much from headaches. Even the day after a prolonged drinking bout. Sevisko had always joked with him about that, telling him he was indestructible. Lasko was feeling far from indestructible right now. In fact, he felt like a ninety-year-old man.

No energy.

Weary to the bone.

His head pounding.

And now a nosebleed.

He could feel it snaking from his left nostril, over his lips so he could taste the coppery…

Lasko sat upright, staring into the rearview mirror in front of him. He had a shock when he saw his reflection.

The blotchy skin.

The blood on his upper lip. He rubbed at the thick trickle with the sleeve of his coat, smearing it across his cheek.

A cold sensation gripped his gut. He raised his hands in front of his face and stared at them. Saw the discolored traces at the base of his fingernails, the trembling. When he flexed his fingers he felt the ache in his joints.

There were aches in his lower body, too. The base of his spine. In his groin. His symptoms were increasing with more speed now.

"No. Please, no," he muttered, and even his voice sounded heavy and drawn. When he swallowed he felt the harsh restriction in his throat, far worse than it had been earlier.

Lasko fumbled with the handle, pushed the door open. Cold rain drifted into the car, wetting the edge of the seat as he dragged himself outside. When his feet touched the ground his legs almost gave under his weight. He gripped the edge of the door frame, pulling himself upright. The rain soaked him quickly, but for a few moments the coolness felt good, because his temperature had risen. He leaned against the side of the car, turning his face to the heavy rain. It penetrated his clothing, wet his body. The weakness seemed to overwhelm him now. His legs collapsed and he sank down onto the rain-soaked ground, staring out at…at nothing…because he had no idea what he needed to do. His mind was reluctantly assimilating what was happening to him….

Miko had tried to save him from the radiation by keeping the cargo bay door closed, preventing Lasko from coming to see what had happened. Lasko had believed that gesture had saved him, but it now appeared they had both been wrong.

The radiation had been weakened by the barrier of the closed door, but not blocked completely. Lasko had been irradiated, but at a lower level, so that the effects had taken longer to show. The symptoms he was now exhibiting had simply taken time to manifest themselves.

The small matter that had been nagging at him, then drifting away, irritating him by its elusiveness, came to him at that moment. He had been trying to recall what it was, because it had seemed important and he had wanted to tell the others. He was glad it came back now, if only for his own satisfaction. The others would have to realize it for themselves. If they didn't, it could betray them. Make the Americans even more determined to track the group down.

Even though the plane had been destroyed by the bomb planted inside it, there might still be traces of radiation from the rods being exposed. If the FBI found those traces, they would realize what had been on board the plane and what had been smuggled from the airport during the diversion.

There would be a massive hunt for the people involved. It would put even more pressure on Rahman's group. Possibly panic them into making a strike before they were fully ready. That could be a mistake.

Lasko felt no concern over the matter. He was already paying the price. The ultimate price. Even of he had wanted to there was little he could offer his former colleagues. They would have to work out their own destiny now.

He felt more blood leaking from his nose, but couldn't be bothered to wipe it away.

Janos Lasko knew he was dying. Knew his life was winding down. No fault to lay at anyone's door. The rolling dice had delivered him a losing hand this time.

He felt a constriction in his already sore throat. Muscles convulsed and he began to cough. The powerful reflex action made him arch his body forward, head down. The cough became a continuous action that wouldn't stop. Hot fluid forced its way up from his stomach and scalding bile filled his mouth until he was forced to spit it out. He retched violently, the semifluid discharge surging from him. Lasko leaned to one side, gagging and spitting, and even in the relentless retching that watered his eyes he recognized the dark streaks of blood within the discharge. His gut hurt, the pain rising until he was forced to cry out, and almost fainted. When he recovered some semblance of feeling, he flopped back against the side of the car, staring vacantly around. Something had caught his attention.

A dark-colored SUV had appeared and was parked across from where he sat on the sodden ground. Lasko saw three men emerge from the vehicle, weapons in their hands as they approached. They stopped yards away, eyeing him. One of them, a powerful-looking blond-haired man, raised a hand to stop the others from coming closer.

Lasko watched all this as if it were happening to someone else. He felt a strange detachment from his surroundings. Though his discomfort was increasing, he found some inner core of strength to begin a litany of prayer. He realized his suffering could end very soon, and Janos Lasko wanted to face his God prepared. In death he would stand before Allah in humility.

His part in Jabir Rahman's plan would still go ahead. The nuclear cargo he and Sevisko had delivered onto American soil would be used to deliver a deadly blow to the country. The U.S.A. had brought this upon themselves by their craven acts and their godless treatment of Islam. This strike would cause America suffering and pain and humiliation. It would be a just punishment, a way to bring the Great Satan to its knees. Janos Lasko felt pride in what he had helped bring about. He knew now he could die a true believer, a disciple of Islam who had sacrificed all to the glory of the one true God.

As darkness began to shadow his vision, Lasko allowed himself to fall into the hands of death, where a heavenly paradise of unconfined joy and peace was already prepared for his arrival.

In his final moments he felt the warmth envelop him. The brilliant light of Allah's presence.

"Allahu Akbar."

God is Great.

Lasko's words were spoken in a soft tone that only he could hear.

THEY SPOTTED THE CAR and saw Janos Lasko on the ground, slumped against the open door.

Lyons picked up his revolver and pushed his door open. Blancanales and Schwarz followed, their own autopistols in their hands. Lyons waved them back. He had seen the blood that had spilled from the man's slack mouth.

"What?" Schwarz asked.

"I think he might be sick. Like the other guy we found."

"You mean radiation poisoning?"

"Could be. He was Sevisko's partner."

"Call it in?"

Lyons nodded.

The squeal of tires on concrete alerted Able Team to company. They turned as one and saw the dark BMW 7 Series come to a stop, doors swinging open and disgorging armed figures.

Gunfire crackled. Slugs whined off the concrete as Able Team dispersed, weapons up and returning fire.

As Lyons took cover behind the SUV he saw one guy moving around to widen his field of fire. The man carried a squat SMG and he was triggering short bursts with little effect. Lyons raised the Python, gripped two-handed, and triggered a single shot that hammered the target just above his left eye. The shooter fell back, a big chunk of his rear skull missing. He slammed onto the concrete, blood spurting in bright splashes.

Blancanales and Schwarz, crouching, hit back at the other three shooters, their Berettas sending 9 mm slugs both at human targets and at the BMW. The gleaming bodywork was punctured and window glass blown out. The overall effect was to unnerve the three. One guy went to his knees, clutching a bloody shoulder, his SMG sagging in his hands. Lyons caught him in his sights and placed a .357 round in the guy's skull, pitching him on his back.

"Do it," Lyons yelled, sweeping his left arm around.

As the surviving shooters moved to reset themselves, shrugging glass fragments off their clothing, Able Team opened fire in a concerted effort, their weapons thundering in unison, catching the two men in a withering volley. They both went down, bodies shuddering under the impact of 9 mm and .357 slugs. They hit the ground together, clothing bloody and shredded.

Blancanales and Schwarz moved in quickly, clearing weapons from the bodies and checking for life signs.

"Dead," Blancanales confirmed.

Lyons glanced up from reloading his Colt. "Good," he said. "Now get the hell away from them in case they have radiation poisoning, as well."

"Thanks for the warning," Schwarz drily.

"What are friends for," Lyons said, pulling his phone out to contact Stony Man.

JANOS LASKO WAS DEAD long before the haz-mat team arrived, lights flashing and sirens wailing. When the inspection team, clad in protective suits, checked his body, their equipment confirmed that Janos Lasko had indeed died from radiation poisoning.

The four shooters were inspected and cleared of any radiation. They were simply dead.

Able Team, standing by, received the news with little pleasure. Carl Lyons had been hoping the man might be able to provide them with information that could lead them to the group responsible for importing the nuclear rods.

With Janos Lasko dead there was no way they were going to get anything from him.

Blancanales used his cell to take photos of the BMW. Then he took face shots of the dead shooters. He sent the images to Stony Man with a request for them all to be checked out.

"I'll check with the department of motor vehicles. The mug shots can go through the facial-recognition database," Akira Tokaido said.

"Make that a global check," Blancanales said. "I got a feeling these guys are not domestic."

"You got it."

"Contact Ironman on his sat phone if you get anything," Blancanales told Tokaido.

By this time Carl "Ironman" Lyons was talking to local law enforcement. A number of Boston PD cruisers had shown up. He used his Stony Man-provided Justice ID. The cops were more than curious because of the haz-mat unit being present. Lyons, always comfortable in the presence of uniformed police, talked to them in a language they understood.

Schwarz checked out the shooter team and came up with a couple cell phones. The dead men carried little else but phones for contact. There was no identifying material in their pockets.

"They don't even have cab fare home," he said when he joined Lyons.

"Sounds like a hit squad."

The haz-mat team placed Lasko in a protective body bag and carried him to their vehicle. A couple then checked Lasko's vehicle.

"Some trace radiation," the lead technician told Lyons. "Where the guy sat. We'll have it picked up and taken away. Have your people contact us in a couple of days if they want to look the vehicle over."

"Thanks, guys," Lyons said.

The technician spoke to the local cops and arranged for them to leave a car behind to watch over the suspect vehicle until their recovery unit arrived.

Schwarz and Blancanales checked over the BMW. There was nothing in the car to offer any information. It was so tidy inside it had to have come straight out of a dealer's showroom.

"You don't think the shooters stole it, do you?" Blancanales asked.

"Right now I'm ready to believe anything," Lyons said. He glanced at his partners, shaking his head. "Why are we standing around discussing this in the damn rain?"

They were in their SUV when Blancanales cell rang. It was Kurtzman. He asked for Lyons.

"Makes it harder to track because there's no background," Kurtzman said. "A burn phone is usually for a one-off contact. Make your call and throw it away. Doesn't leave a trail worth a damn. Kind of thing a terrorist cell would use. From what Akira managed to track on the cell you sent in, it was from a consignment stolen from a retail store in Brooklyn six months ago. Perps broke in one night and took a box of the things. Akira used the phone's serial number and found it was from the hijacked lot. If your guy was part of Rahman's group, it looks like they use 'em and lose 'em."

"Nothing in the memory?" Lyons asked, impatience edging his tone.

"Nothing."

"Goddammit, Bear, those bastards are going to set off a bomb. Give us a break. Something. Anything."

"We did luck out on the BMW license. Not a rental. It

belongs to Khalil Amir. We're running his profile on databases right now. Only other thing is we did get a hit on one of the shooters. Name of Marko Sebrinka. Serbian Muslim. Been in the country for just over three years. That something?"

"Better than a kick in the head," Lyons said.

"I'll download anything we get to your laptop."

"Okay."

"Good hunting, guys."

Lyons put away his phone. "Stony Man thinks they may be able to get us some background information on these guys."

"Maybe even a lead?" Schwarz said hopefully.

Lyons nodded. "Could be. Let's head back to the hotel. Get cleaned up before we go chasing these mothers. I need a hot shower and a change of clothing."

"Food, too," Schwarz said. "I can't perform my best when I don't eat."

Blancanales glanced at him. "You must miss a lot of meals, then."

Lyons shoulders raised briefly, then he laughed. "He got you there, Gadgets."

"Very funny," Schwarz said.

BACK AT THEIR HOTEL Able Team went to their individual rooms. After showering and changing into clean, dry clothes they joined up again in Lyons's room, ordering meals from room service.

As soon as he'd arrived Lyons had powered up his laptop using the room's wireless internet connection. There was nothing from Stony Man yet. The teammates were enjoying their food when the incoming-mail alert attracted their attention. Lyons crossed to check it out and found there was a message for him, with attachments.

"What we've been waiting for?" Blancanales asked. "Or an invitation to join someone's Facebook?"

Blancanales and Schwarz joined Lyons and peered at the screen as he opened the attachments and scrolled down the photographs and accompanying text.

The data Stony Man had sent them identified the dead shooters.

Marko Sebrinka, the one already spotted, had a rap sheet that started in Europe, where he had been tagged as an arms dealer and had a fringe association with human trafficking. His war record in Kosovo linked him with Luba Radesh, which also associated him with the other men from the shootout. Criminal activities appeared to be their common ground.

"How are these people getting into the country?" Blancanales asked. "What's Immigration playing at?"

"You can have all the departments you want," Schwarz said, "but they can't stop everyone getting in. These bastards will work their way around the laws."

"These jerks all had the skills Rahman needed," Lyons pointed out. "He hires Radesh, who scouts around for his old military buddies. They're all freelance now. Lasko and Sevisko were wartime pilots. Marko Sebrinka and the others were guns for hire. Rahman plants them here in readiness for his operation, and pushes the button to activate them when his cargo is flown in."

Schwarz pointed at the screen. "Check out the old IDs. We've got their Serbian rap sheets on the international database, their fake names and data on the U.S. system. Somebody slipped up and didn't delete the original information."

Lyons carried on running through the data.

"We've got Khalil Amir. Owned the car those dirtbags were driving. As well as being in import-export, he's down as a property developer in the Boston area. Has a lot of industrial and agricultural sites on his books. Handy if you want somewhere with space and privacy."

Lyons grunted something indecipherable. "These guys are starting to get very involved with each other. And they're all into handy businesses. The kind a terrorist cell would find very useful."

"We could go rattle a few cages," Schwarz suggested. "Make them feel a little disturbed."

"I'd substitute rattle for trample those cages down," Lyons said. "I'm getting pissed at these dirtbags bringing their damn religious crap to this country. Time we sent them home, and if it has to be in body bags, that sits right with me."

CHAPTER TWENTY-TWO

"They had to do this by posing as a legitimate customer," Kurtzman said. "You don't walk into an airport with a handful of dollar bills and rent a hangar. Remember this operation has been ongoing for some while, so the renter needed to become familiar with the airport setup. Be known to the everyday staff. Cover themselves for routine checking. Inspections. That's what they did. Employees were all vetted and passed as legitimate. The cover was an agent for a company freighting goods across the country. Small stuff, but enough to give them status. Records go back eight months."

"Done through a dummy company?" Lyons asked.

"Not exactly. The registered company had all the required paperwork and licenses. They hired an office in Boston and ran the business from there. Employed locals. A lot of thought went into this, Carl. Don't forget these people work from long-term plans. No rushing into things. This business actually worked at being normal, using innocent employees to front it."

"I expect a *but* in there somewhere."

"But since 'all roads lead to Rome,' a fact I'm sure you're familiar with, all financial trails will bring us to the folks who actually financed this setup."

"Jabir Rahman?"

"Think further back, my friend," Kurtzman said.

"The Taliban? I know they offer finance—"

"But they're not in the same league as al Qaeda. Think 9/11. How much planning and money that cost."

"This is down to them?"

"They bankrolled it. We worked our way from Khalil Amir to a paymaster in Europe, then a series of electronic transactions until it unwound in Brussels. That's where the money trail started. When a certain name was flagged it showed this guy was a financier for al Qaeda. Took some confirming, but the end result was that this son of a bitch regularly handed out big amounts to terrorist cells on the al Qaeda friendly list. It would appear that Rahman must have convinced them his plan was worthy enough to bag himself one hell of a bankroll."

"And Amir is the Boston arranger?"

"It was this Amir-generated company that made the deal for the hangar rental. His only error, but it led back from there all the way to Brussels."

"Error? That was one big mistake. Sometimes these guys are not so damn smart."

"Amir probably didn't even consider it would be looked at. His company handles all kinds of commercial properties in and around the city. A number are registered under his name. The guy has expanded his business interests. On top of his export enterprise he now operates a real estate company. Specializes in commercial properties in and around the Boston area. Useful to a terrorist cell looking for an out-of-the-way setup."

"Like an isolated place where Rahman's group could hide out while they converted the nuclear rods into a workable dirty bomb."

"I'll get the team to run a search on out-of-town sites Amir's been involved with."

"Dammit, Aaron, when we picked up Lasko's car he was moving in an easterly direction. Turn it around and target areas to the west. The guy was sick. Wanted to get away from his partners. They were set on grabbing him before he was found. He didn't know the area, just got in a car and drove. This could be a total waste of time, but it might point us in the right direction."

"And maybe in a straight line, because he had no idea where he was. Worth a try, Carl."

"Give me something," Lyons said. "Anything."

"Where are you heading now?"

"Time we had a talk with Khalil Amir."

"Pol, with me," Lyons said as they climbed out of the SUV.

"Hey, why don't I go around the back?" Blancanales said tonelessly, a faint smirk on his face.

"That's fine," Lyons said, refusing to bite.

Blancanales vanished without another word, leaving Lyons and Schwarz to approach the front door of the real estate office. The business section they were in had closed up for the night. The street was quiet, with only security lighting showing in office and store windows.

"Maybe Amir has gone home, too," Schwarz suggested.

"And maybe not," Lyons said, indicating a lit window on the upper floor. The shadow of a figure moved across the glass.

"Cleaner?" Schwarz volunteered. "Security guard?"

"You want to be somewhere else?"

"And miss all the excitement? Not me."

Lyons's cell vibrated. He took it out. "What?"

"I'm in," Blancanales said. "No need to be rude 'cause I beat you."

"Any interference?"

"Not unless you count a hostile guy with a large SMG who tried to stop me."

"We're on our way," Lyons said. "Let's go. Pol found a way in."

They jogged along the side of the building. There was a parking area at the rear, holding three vehicles. Blancanales was standing at an open fire door, an impatient expression on his face.

"It's like waiting for a pair of geriatrics."

Inside the door a big man lay on the floor. He was unconscious, a heavy bruise forming above his right eye. Blancanales had bound his hands with the man's own belt and gagged him with the tie he had been wearing.

Blancanales held up an MP-5 SMG. "Maybe they have some dissatisfied clients looking for Amir."

Schwarz closed the door, then followed his partners along the corridor that opened up on the main showroom. A door at the side revealed stairs leading to the upper floor.

"Seeing as you have the biggest gun," Schwarz said to Blancanales, "maybe you should go first."

Lyons was already on his way up, his Colt Python in his hand. At the top of the stairs he turned right, pointing the way to one of the offices. "That's the one we could see from the street."

As they approached the door the sound of raised voices could be heard.

"Someone isn't having any fun," Blancanales murmured. "It isn't in English, but it's tetchy."

"We'll just have to change that," Lyons snapped.

Reaching the door, he raised his right foot and crashed it against the panel just below the handle. The door swung wide, slamming against the inner wall. Before it hit, Lyons was in the room, stepping to the right, his Magnum revolver sweeping the interior. Blancanales and Schwarz backed him, clearing the door and spreading.

There were four men in the room, one seated behind a

large desk, a second in a chair facing him. The remaining pair were on their feet. All four turned to the newcomers, registering shock at the sudden intrusion.

"Hands where I can see them," Lyons barked, the thunder of his voice filling the office.

One of the standing men uttered a shrill mix of words as he went for the autopistol holstered under his jacket. He managed to touch the butt before Lyons hit him with a pair of Magnum slugs from his Python. The guy spun around and slammed facefirst into the wall, his body ravaged by the .357 slugs at close range. Both went through him, chunking into the plaster wall before the guy performed his about-face. Tattered holes gaped in his back.

As Lyons fired, the guy facing the desk hauled out a squat handgun and twisted in his chair. His weapon was still rising when Blancanales triggered the MP-5 and riddled him with a burst of 9 mm slugs. The target went sideways, taking the chair with him, and crashed to the office floor, his weapon bouncing from his hand.

Schwarz thrust his own Beretta at the other men. They both flung their hands into the air, faces showing shock and fear at the violent demise of their companions. Moving forward, Schwarz expertly frisked them, producing two more handguns and a sheathed knife. He flung the weapons into the far corner of the office.

"You," Lyons said to the standing guy. "Get over to the other side of the desk. Do it now. I've got four more shots left." When the two were facing him, Lyons said, "Khalil Amir. It had better be one of you because I haven't the time or patience to play games."

"I am Khalil Amir," the seated man said. "Who are you? What is the meaning of this slaughter?"

Blancanales saw the fury that gleamed in Lyons's eyes. Before anyone could react, Lyons leaned across the desk and slammed the Python against Amir's left cheek. The blow was brutal, the sound ugly as it struck. Amir almost fell out of his seat. He managed to steady himself, pushing upright. There was a ragged gash in his cheek, blood pouring from it.

"You'd know about slaughter, Amir, seeing you were in on the airport explosion. You were behind the hangar rental."

Amir's eyes stared into Lyons's. His thin face, sallow and lined, set in a fixed mask. "I know nothing about it."

"You want me to list all the dead? Or the ones missing arms and legs? Innocent Americans killed by your dirtbag friends."

"There is no such thing as an *innocent* American. You are all evil followers of Satan. Corrupt defilers and killers of Allah's children. The world will rejoice when America and its filthy allies lie dead at our feet."

Blancanales shook his head as he listened to the ranting man. "Somebody switch him off. Do these guys sit in a room and prerecord these speeches? I'd want to kill myself if I was forced to listen to that crap every day."

"Only there won't be any glorious suicide for you, Amir," Lyons said. "We got you on enough counts to make sure you spend the rest of your life in a federal pen. Solitary confinement. A concrete cell for twenty-three hours each day. One hour to walk outside in a concrete yard. Even you can't call that paradise."

"If Allah wills it then so it must be."

"Even *I* don't believe that," Schwarz said.

By the expression in Amir's eyes Lyons could tell the man was considering what he had just been told. The prospect of life locked away in a small cell, with no contact, *might* appeal to Amir. It was a powerful commitment.

Though not something any would relish, even taking in the man's religious beliefs.

The possibility of Amir offering some kind of compromise in exchange for a lesser degree of imprisonment?

Whatever Lyons might have been thinking, even he was taken aback by the man's decision to take matters into his own hands.

Amir rose from his seat, his head shaking slowly from side to side.

"Allahu Akbar," he shouted, his voice full and loud.

Lyons put out his left hand. "No, you son of a bitch."

He was too slow.

Amir kicked his chair aside, turned and hurled himself across the room. Arms thrust in front of him, hands closed into fists, he hit the closest window, overlooking the street. His solid bulk propelled him through the glass. Glittering pieces erupted around him as he cleared the sill and vanished from sight. When Lyons reached the window it was over and Khalil Amir was a crumpled, broken heap on the sidewalk. Blood was already spreading out from beneath his shattered skull, where bone and brain matter marked the concrete.

"You want to join him?" Lyons asked the surviving man.

"No."

"Convince me," Lyons said. "There are more windows handy."

"Why would you do this to me?" the man asked.

"Playing stupid isn't helping your case," Lyons said. "You and your dumb-ass buddies are planning a nuclear explosion somewhere in this city. And you still ask me why I'm mad?"

"Nuclear what? Look, I don't know what you're talking about. All I signed on for was to provide protection for Amir. That's it."

"Just throw him out the damn window," Schwarz said. "One less radical nut job to worry about."

"He makes a pretty good case," Blancanales said. "I don't have any objection."

Lyons slid his Colt back in its holster and advanced on the man. The Pakistani was lean, close to being skinny, and his physical strength was no match for Lyons, who caught hold of his clothing and lifted him off the floor, swinging him around to the broken window.

"Good to go?" Lyons asked. "Made your peace with Allah? You figure he's booked your place in paradise?" He gripped the man's jacket as he tilted him across the windowsill.

Sweat popped out on the Pakistani's face as he stared into Lyons's eyes. There was no sign of pity there. Just the blazing intensity of a man who was reaching the end of his patience. Lyons's lips peeled back, exposing teeth set in an angry grimace.

"Please, no. Tell me what you want to know...."

Lyons didn't respond. He held the man where he was until tears formed in the guy's eyes. "I will give you what you want."

"So help me," Lyons said. "If you try to fool us I will toss you out myself."

He yanked the man away from the window and threw him bodily into the room.

"Make this the best speech you've ever given," Schwarz said as he escorted the shivering Pakistani to a chair.

Blancanales was studying maps showing the area around Boston, location maps for Amir's real estate business. He checked them out before turning to stare at the Pakistani.

"So which is the one we're looking for?" he asked. "And remember, you don't get a second shot at this."

CHAPTER TWENTY-THREE

"Still no reply from anyone," Qazi said. "I am starting to become worried." He paced across the floor, hands clasped behind his back. Outside the streaked window of the farmhouse the late evening darkness hid the falling rain.

Syed Alam watched him for a moment. "Umer, sit down. Surely if there had been a significant breakdown the American authorities would be swarming all over the area by now."

"We have lost people," Qazi said. "Lasko broke away. The men you sent to bring him back? Where are they? For all we know they could be in the hands of the police. Or the FBI. Telling all they know. If Lasko is found to be suffering from radiation poisoning the Americans will realize what is happening. Whatever else they may be, they are not stupid."

"So what do we do, Umer Qazi?" Alam asked. "Call the authorities and confess? Tell them where we are so they can come and arrest us? Give up everything we have planned, everything that Colonel Rahman has worked on for the past years?"

"We cannot surrender," Talib Ahmed said. "Now that we are so close. Pirzada has almost completed his work. The device is near to completion. When we hear from the colonel that the device back home is also ready we can complete our mission."

Qazi stopped his pacing and turned to face the two men. There was a bleakness in his eyes when he shook his head.

"There will be no call from Rahman to tell you that," he said. "I have already been informed, by the colonel himself, that the Barracuda UAV was destroyed during an armed attack on the launch base. The defending force was killed and the uranium rods were taken. According to Rahman they were placed on board an American helicopter and flown over the border into Afghanistan. The intended attack on the U.S. military base will not happen."

The stunned silence might have been comical under different circumstances. Ahmed and Alam were suitably frozen as the revelation hit them.

"I do not believe you," Alam said eventually.

"Oh? Why not?" Qazi asked. "Are you thinking what I said is nothing more than a joke? That I made it up just so I could see the expressions on your faces?"

"But how did this happen?" Ahmed asked. "Rahman had men to defend the launch base. His own security. The local Taliban. That so-called warlord, Hajik. What happened to them?"

"The Americans sent a covert team into Pakistan. They defeated Rahman's forces and regained control of the nuclear rods."

"All that planning. The gathering of personnel. The finance from al Qaeda." Amal threw his arms into the air. "Wasted. Lost." He turned to face Qazi. "What does Rahman say?"

"That we carry on here. Go ahead as soon as we're ready. No waiting for the original date. Just set off the device."

"Hah," Ahmed said. "So easy to say. Rahman is not here. If matters have become this critical does he believe we can carry out the attack so easily? There are things to organize, people to place. We were going to deliver the device to the center of the city. The route has been worked out, checked for access. Will it still be usable now? If the Americans believe a strike is imminent, won't they close off the core? Search vehicles?"

"Perhaps so," Qazi said. "If that happens and we find ourselves challenged before we reach the detonation point, the solution is in our hands. We activate the nuclear device and allow it to detonate where we are. We will still achieve a victory. The explosion will still spread radiation and the effect will be the same. Panic. The Americans will be shocked at what has happened. There will be dismay. Fear. And do not forget the deaths that will occur at the time, plus the lingering effects of the uranium poisoning. However it happens, we will have achieved what we set out to do."

"He is right," Alam said. "Talib, our success is guaranteed. Even if we only reach the outskirts of the city the damage will still be substantial. Brother, we *must* do this. Though Rahman's intentions in Pakistan have been prevented, we still have our part do carry out."

Ahmed was not entirely convinced. He found it hard to accept that all the planning, the effort, the dedication, was being eroded. Up until this moment everything had seemed set in stone. Qazi's revelation that Rahman had lost his battle hit Ahmed hard. He struggled to come to terms with it all.

Grudgingly, he came to the conclusion that Alam was right. They had to make the Boston strike work. America needed to feel the pain, had to suffer for its intrusion and betrayal of the Islamic way of life. The arrogant U.S.A., with its blatant disregard for Allah, had to pay the price.

"Get the device ready," he said. "Show me what has to be done. I will drive the vehicle. I will take it into the city."

Alam stepped forward, grasping Ahmed's arms. "Are you sure of this?"

"Yes. I am prepared. There must be no more mistakes. Our mission here is clear. Americans must taste Allah's rage. They live in a corrupt society that defiles us all. This strike will help to cleanse the decay." He turned to leave the room. "I will go and prepare myself. Remain in my room and pray. Call me only when the device is ready."

"An unexpected development," Qazi said after Ahmed had left them.

"One we must honor," Alam said. "Umer, when will Pirzada have the device ready?"

"He is making final adjustments to the detonator. Because of the way he has constructed the explosive it will have to be activated by hand. He was having problems with the autotimer. We spoke earlier and agreed the device will have a better chance of working by using this method."

"So it will not take as much time to complete?"

"No. Only a few more hours. Before morning."

"Then we must do it as soon as the device is ready. Try to get into position for the morning rush hour. There will be more people around. The streets and roads will be busy."

"Good. And here we will be well outside the blast zone and the radiation spread. Syed, we can do this."

"No, Umer, *we* must do it. *You* must leave now. Take your car and go. Drive to New York. Book yourself a flight to London or Paris."

"I do not understand."

"Once the device is detonated and the Americans see the devastation, Boston will be sealed off. And the surrounding countryside. It is possible we will be discovered. Captured and jailed. Even killed."

"That has always been a possibility, Syed. Something we all accept."

"As warriors for Allah, we expect such things. But you are not the same. Umer, you are a teacher of our philosophy. A recruiter. Your talent lies in being able to persuade others to join our cause. As you have done here. As you must continue to do. Our fight, whatever happens here, will go on. The jihad stretches into the future. It does not end in Boston. It is an eternal struggle against our enemy. Your death must not be part of this. Go, my brother. Draw more believers into the war so that we can hold out against the Great Satan." Alam embraced Qazi. "Go. Take whatever you need. Leave this place, and we will complete our mission knowing that Umer Qazi will continue his work under the guiding hand of Allah. Now go."

Qazi withdrew and went through the house to the small room he had occupied while staying at the farm. He checked his watch, calculating how long it would take him to reach New York. Then he used his cell and contacted flight bookings. He managed to get a seat on a flight leaving LaGuardia at eleven o'clock the following morning. He packed his small holdall, checked his documents and passport.

Making his way out of the house, he went to the parking area and remote keyed the rental car. He placed his bag inside, slid behind the wheel and drove slowly away from the farm, reaching the highway at the end of the long approach road. He settled in his seat as he tapped in the route on the built-in sat-nav unit. An easy drive of four to five hours. Qazi followed the computer instructions, in no hurry. He stopped at the first gas station he saw and filled the tank. Inside, he bought bottled water and energy bars, paid for his purchases and returned to his car. Buckling up, he eased back onto the rain-slick road, smiling to himself as a Massachusetts Highway Patrol cruiser pulled in at the gas station. If only they knew, he thought. He set the radio to a Boston news station, adjusting the volume so he could listen to the reports.

SYED ALAM WATCHED Qazi's car vanish along the farm road, its taillights finally fading in the darkness. With Qazi on his way Alam felt some relief. Whatever happened here, at least Qazi would be safe to continue his vital work.

Alam picked up the comm set and spoke to the outside guards. They were patrolling the grounds around the house, and especially the large barn, which stood some distance away. Inside the barn Pirzada was at work constructing the bomb. He had made precise calculations for the amount of explosive needed to fracture the protective container and the rods, exposing the inner core that would be spread by the blast. His calculations had been meticulous, repeatedly scrutinized until he was satisfied. Using a state-of-the-art computer, he'd designed simulations that presented him with detailed schematics of how and where to position the plastic compound for maximum effect. At this final phase he was working on the manual detonator. The moment he announced his work was complete, the device would be placed inside one of the waiting vehicles and transported to Boston.

Alam recalled Qazi's concern over the lack of communication with their people in the city. They'd heard nothing from Khalil Amir or Khalib Mustaph. Alam was unable to work out why their cell phones were dead or why they had not made contact for a while. True, at this stage of the operation nothing was expected from them. Their contributions were complete, and neither man would call simply to pass the time of day.

Qazi's concern may have been from overinflated worry

following the Lasko incident. Even Alam remained unsure why no contact had been forthcoming from the retrieval team who had gone after Lasko. They had been told to capture him and take him somewhere well away from the farm before disposing of his body. There could be valid reasons why they had not returned or gotten in touch. Alam understood the reluctance of some of the brothers to be around the nuclear device. Despite being assured there was no problem, some were still fearful. Which was why there had been the insistence concerning Lasko's presence at the farm. Sevisko, the other man from the plane, had suffered from exposure, as had Lasko himself. And the irradiated rods were still close by.

The retrieval team had been supplied with haz-mat suits for handling Lasko. It had been explained that as long as they wore them, contamination would not occur. Alam, watching them closely before they drove away, had had to convince himself they would carry out their mission. On the other hand, human nature being what it was, he accepted they might err on the side of caution and do the opposite. If they had decided not to pursue Lasko, they might very well be miles away by now. Another reason why there was no contact. Blind religious faith might not be enough to make them stay the course. If that was the case, there was nothing Alam could do about it.

He did wonder if they had been apprehended by the police, along with Lasko, and were being interrogated at that very moment. If so, he hoped they would refuse to reveal any information. He doubted that had happened. If the farm's location had been passed to the American authorities it would be overrun by now.

Enough time had elapsed for Alam to radio another check to the guards. His first three calls elicited confirmation that all was well. When Alam made his fourth call he was greeted with silence. No electronic buzz from the comm set. He tried again. Nothing. He forced himself to stay calm, asking one of the others to go check out the silent radio.

Now he was starting to become concerned.

Moments later that concern became alarm as the faint but unmistakable rattle of automatic gunfire reached his ears.

"YOU THINKING WHAT I'm thinking?" Blancanales asked.

"If I knew what you were thinking," Schwarz said, "I'd be able to tell what—"

"That ends right now," Lyons barked. "If I want Abbott and Costello I can watch them on television."

"Okay, boss man," Schwarz said, sneaking a grin at Blancanales.

Clad in combat black, Able Team was gearing up for the assault on the farm Khalil Amir had provided through his real estate business.

Carl Lyons's threat to drop the survivor from Amir's office window had brought a flood of detail from the guy, a local hired to provide protection for Khalil Amir. He'd been recruited at the tail end of the scheme, without being told too much information regarding the extent of the operation. It had been an eye-opener for the man when it had been explained fully what was being planned. At first he had refused to accept that such a thing could happen. It was difficult for him to grasp the vision of a nuclear attack on Boston. As far as he was aware the farm was being used as a stopover location for Islamic refugees wanting to settle in America.

"You figure that's why we got such a reception when we showed up?" Schwarz had said.

"Just because of a few Muslims wanting to shack up for a while?" Blancanales added.

"I thought you were ICE," the guy had said. "Those guys are hard. They play rough sometimes. Look, I didn't plan on people being shot. What do you think I am, a terrorist?"

Lyons had pushed himself into the man's face. "You're working for terrorists. Taking their money. Or are you doing this for Allah?"

"Hey, I'm a Muslim, I don't deny it, but I draw the line at bombing people."

"Let me put you straight," Lyons had said. "These bastards are planning to set off a dirty bomb. It *will* kill people. It will blow a cloud of radiation poison across a big piece of Boston and it will make a lot of people sick. A lot of them will die. You could be one of them."

"How do you square that with your benevolent God?" Schwarz said.

"This is crazy. You *are* telling the truth?"

"Why would we be making it up?" Blancanales said. "Think about it, pal. Just take it on board."

The Pakistani saw the look in their eyes and recognized a truth that couldn't be denied.

"I know where they are," he said. "I'll show you on the map...."

TWENTY-FIVE MILES OUT OF the city and five miles from its closest neighbor was an empty property surrounded by acres of rural terrain. The family farm had become vacant due to death and taxes. No one seemed interested in purchasing it, given the current economic climate. Khalil Amir had it on his books, and its location had seemed ideal for his purpose, so he'd turned it over to his extremist brothers for their upcoming operation.

"Give me the wisdom of your thinking," Lyons said.

"Just a notion," Blancanales replied. "The moment we hit this place won't the guy with his finger on the trigger just blow this bomb, taking us and the rest of this ragtag crew with him?"

Lyons looked up from loading his Daewoo USAS-12 shotgun. He considered what Blancanales had said. "It's a chance we have to take," he said. "Way I see it that would be a waste. These bozos want to make a statement. Blowing their bomb out here in the middle of nowhere isn't going to make that much of a dent. Apart from leaving a radioactive glow for a while."

"Such understatement," Schwarz said.

Lyons snapped in a 20-round drum of 12-gauge shells. "We hit them hard and fast enough, maybe we can persuade them to quit."

Able Team wore combat vests that held extra ammunition for the weapons they carried. While Lyons had additional magazines holding 12-gauge shells, and .357 speed loaders for his Python, Blancanales and Schwarz were loaded with more magazines for their Beretta handguns and M-4 A-1 autorifles. Each man wore a lightweight radio comm set so he could maintain voice contact if the team became separated. They carried sheathed knives and fragmentation grenades for extra defense.

"These guys get no easy ride," Lyons snapped. "I'm not interested in prisoners."

"We understand," Blancanales said. "Hell, I can't see them quitting."

"So don't give them the chance," Lyons said. "Pol, how many outside guards did we spot?"

"At least four circling the barn."

"That's our main target. Has to be where they're dealing with the device."

"Those first?" Schwarz suggested.

"Let's do this," Lyons said. "Silent kills."

They checked the comm sets. At Lyons's command they moved out, cloaked by the shadows beyond the light spilling from the barn.

Around the barn items of farm machinery aided Able Team's initial approach. Falling rain helped conceal them, too.

Schwarz encountered the closest guard. The guy had an H&K MP-5 slung across his right shoulder. He was hunched over, the collar of his waterproof jacket turned up, and the ball cap he wore was dragged low across his forehead. As Schwarz came up behind him he turned abruptly, either from a giveaway sound or pure instinct. He looked Schwarz directly in the face, his eyes widening in alarm. There was a split-second difference in the two men's response.

The Pakistani began a shout of alarm, his hands snatching for the SMG on his shoulder. The shout failed to materialize. The SMG remained on the guard's shoulder.

Hermann Schwarz flexed his right arm, the blade of the Cold Steel tanto knife catching a faint sliver of light as it slashed up and across. A heavy spurt of blood erupted from the guard's throat as the keen tanto blade cut wide and deep. The guard felt a strange coldness where the knife had cut, not realizing yet what had happened. By the time he did, Schwarz had moved on, leaving the stricken man to drop to his knees, frantically clutching at his bleeding throat. He felt the hot flush of his own blood, started to choke on it, and went down without a sound.

At the far end of the barn Lyons intercepted the guard patrolling that area. Despite his size and weight, Lyons moved with surprising grace and speed. He tackled the guard without a break in his stride, one big hand cupping his face, fingers holding the mouth closed, while his right buried the tanto blade into the base of the man's skull, working it back and forth so that the upper spine was severed quickly. The guard went into a severe yet brief spasm as his limbs collapsed and he fell facedown in the mud. His left hand, fingers splayed, was the last part of him to shut down.

Lyons sheathed the knife and spoke into his comm set. "One down, east corner."

"West section clear," Schwarz added.

BLANCANALES HAD HIS FIRST MAN spotted as the guard tramped through a heavily waterlogged patch. He was carrying his SMG in his hands, eyes scanning the area.

"Listen up," Blancanales said softly. "I've got the one guy who really loves his job. He's like a mobile radar unit. I move another inch, he'll make me."

"Stay put," Lyons said. "We're cutting around to the barn door. I'll go in. Hermann can hit the last guard, then you take your man. And forget the silent approach now. Soon as you drop him, follow us inside."

WITH SCHWARZ CLOSE ON his heels, Lyons moved in on the big main doors. They stood ajar, the occupants depending on the roving guards to maintain security. That had worked until the appearance of Able Team. Light spilled out from the gap in the doors, and as he flattened against them, Lyons could hear the murmur of voices from inside.

"I'm in position," he said into his comm set.

"Ready here," Schwarz replied.

"Go," Lyons said.

He yanked open the barn doors and plunged inside, his USAS up and ready.

CHAPTER TWENTY-FOUR

Schwarz saw the guard ahead of him turn at the sound of Lyons's voice. His SMG swung in response. Schwarz already had his M-4 on line and he fired, his triple burst catching the target chest high. The guy stumbled under the impact but stayed on his feet, triggering his own weapon, the slugs going wide. Schwarz hit him again, taking a moment to settle his aim, and this time the guard went backward, slamming to the ground, his MP-5 flying from his hands.

Behind Schwarz, the sound of Lyons's shotgun added its own distinctive sound. Schwarz turned and ran for the barn and the open doors.

BLANCANALES SAW THE guard's head turn fractionally at the sound of gunfire. He took it as his cue, raised his autorifle and put a pair of triple bursts into the guy. Immediately after he fired, Blancanales spun and sprinted in the direction of the barn.

The barn interior was lit by powerful lamps staged around the side walls. Off center was a twenty-foot-square isolation chamber, and a couple of haz-mat-suited figures could be seen inside through the thick viewing panes. They were standing over a unit of some kind, making adjustments.

The armed figures standing around the chamber had already been alerted by the gunfire, and as Lyons rushed into the barn they turned in his direction. Knowing that total surprise had already gone out the window, Lyons did what he knew best and opened fire, triggering the Daewoo as he dropped to his knees, reducing his target mass. The boom of the 12-gauge filled the barn, the spreading shot hitting men and anything else in its path. Above the sound of the shotgun Lyons heard the crackle of autofire and felt the impact of slugs striking objects around him. He felt something tug at his left arm, but his combat nerves were hot-wired now, and Carl Lyons was committed. He saw his first target go down, the impact of the charge shredding the guy's left side in a welter of bloody gore. Pulling the shotgun around, Lyons fired at a moving figure, saw the ripping effect as the guy took the full burst through the head, and half his skull vanished in an eruption of blood. The guy remained on his feet for seconds, even as Lyons spun around and kept firing.

Schwarz barreled through the doors, all caution swept aside as he took in the scene. Two men were already down and Lyons was triggering his shotgun without pause, hitting everything in sight. The M-4 spit out triple bursts, dropping another terrorist in his tracks as he swung his MP-5 at the Stony Man warrior. The guy fell hard, clutching at his shattered hip, cursing wildly in Pashto until Schwarz put another burst into his skull.

Blancanales added his weapon to the fray, his controlled bursts finding targets every time. He spotted a pair of MP-5-wielding men working their way around a stack of metal drums, and turned his rifle on them, the 5.56 mm slugs piercing flesh and metal alike. The two men staggered under the impact of autofire, bodies riddled and starting to bleed. Blancanales laid more bursts into them, stopping all movement.

With a metal workbench between them and Able Team,

three of the terrorists made their intentions clear. They were defending the isolation chamber, attempting to protect whoever was inside.

Over the comm sets Schwarz and Blancanales heard Lyons.

"That thing has to have some kind of power supply. We need to cut it. Pol, work your way around it. See if you can spot it."

Blancanales turned aside and used the clutter of machinery and barrels as cover. He heard the slap of slugs striking, the whine of ricochets. He stayed low and kept moving, leaving the opposition to Lyons and Schwarz.

He was just reaching the side of the chamber when a dark shape caught his peripheral vision. Blancanales was given the impression of someone flying before he realized it was a man in a long black coat launching himself in a dive from the top of a metal drum. Blancanales started to turn, but the dark shape was on him, thudding against his back and shoulders. The solid impact threw him forward and he went down on his knees. An arm snaked around his neck, gripping him tightly.

Blancanales jerked his head around and saw his attacker's other hand. It was in the air, swinging the shining blade of a knife toward his body. For a second Blancanales felt panic. The naked blade of a knife coming in his direction relayed many images to him, including the kind of harm that knife could do. It galvanized him into a defensive reaction, and he let go of his rifle and threw up both hands in an attempt to stop the attack. He partially succeeded, catching the terrorist's wrist, holding it for a second before it continued descending.

Blancanales made a second attempt, getting a firmer grip, but not before the cutting edge of the knife sliced across the top of his shoulder. The slash was deep enough to make him cry out; the edge of the blade ground against bone. With a yell of rage, pain and not a little desperation, he snatched at the wrist with both hands, dropped forward and hauled his attacker over his shoulder. The Pakistani's grip on Blancanales's neck remained until the guy lost his concentration.

Blancanales drew in a gulping breath to fill his lungs, shrugging the guy clear and following through. He bore down on the knife wrist, his own grip solid now, and twisted viciously, turning the blade to one side. Letting go with his right hand, he bunched it into a fist and hammered the terrorist's face. Blancanales felt bone crunch. He kept hitting over and over, reducing the guy's visage to a bloody mask. The nose was reduced to a pulped ruin, the mouth split, teeth driven from the gums. Blancanales's knuckles were torn and split, numb from the impact, but he continued striking until the terrorist stopped moving.

Ignoring the blood coursing from the deep gash in his shoulder, Blancanales snatched up his rifle and ran along the side of the chamber.

He found what he was looking for—a diesel-powered generator, its exhaust vented out through the side of the barn. The pulsing engine pushed electric power into the chamber via a thick cable connected to a junction box. Moving closer, Blancanales found the switch that operated the engine and turned it off. The generator faltered, then died. Blancanales stepped back and leveled his autorifle, pumping a couple of bursts into the control box.

CARL LYONS WAVED for Schwarz to circle the workbench as he took the opposite end. He crouched, extending the shotgun, and opened fire, using up the last rounds in the drum. He aimed low, through the gap between the bench's shelf and legs. The 12-gauge shot hammered at the contents of the shelf, scattering tools. But enough got through, embedding in the exposed limbs of the terrorists.

The screams of pain from the wounded were accompanied by the chatter from Schwarz's M-4 A-1, his 3-round bursts catching the men as they attempted to avoid Lyons's devastating shotgun volley. As one terrorist stood upright, favoring his bloody legs, Schwarz hit him with a burst that cored through his left side, cracking ribs and puncturing a lung. The terrorist fell forward across the bench. Schwarz put another burst into his skull. The crackle of autofire from the surviving pair mingled with the ongoing blasts from the Daewoo USAS until it clicked on empty.

Lyons, pushing forward, dropped the shotgun and yanked out the Colt Python. His two-handed grip steadied the heavy pistol as he tracked in and placed two .357 slugs into the partially exposed skull of one terrorist. The guy flopped back, a large portion of his head torn away. Schwarz used the moment to angle around the bench, seeing the last target, turned in Lyons's direction as he raised his SMG. Schwarz cleared his M-4's magazine as he triggered quick bursts that shattered the terrorist's spine and dropped him facedown on the floor.

When Blancanales moved to the front of the chamber he found bodies on the barn floor. Schwarz was walking to the open door to stand guard, while Lyons reloaded his shotgun with a 10-round magazine.

Blancanales unsealed the outer door of the chamber. Through the window he could see a low-power emergency light illuminating the interior and two suited figures raising SMGs.

"Carl, there could be radiation," Blancanales warned.

"You think I'm going to be in there that long?" Lyons answered tersely.

The muted sound of autofire came from within the

chamber. Slugs shattered the thick Perspex of the inner window.

Lyons was standing to one side. He worked the handle to release the door, ducking low and going in fast.

Autofire was briefly heard before the heavy boom of the 12-gauge, Lyons racking out shot after shot until the weapon locked on empty.

He pulled back, hauling the door shut, stepped out through the exterior door and closed that, as well. There was blood streaking the side of his face, with more in his blond hair. He ignored that when he saw the crimson patch on Blancanales's shoulder. Blood had run down his sleeve and was dripping heavily from his fingers.

"Pol?"

"It's just a graze," Blancanales answered, feigning nonchalance as he leaned against the chamber wall. He felt weak, and the gash was really starting to hurt now.

Schwarz was crossing toward the farmhouse. He had seen movement as at least four armed figures came down off the front porch and turned in the direction of the barn. As he got closer he heard their excited voices calling to each other in Pashto.

"We're clear inside," Lyons said over the comm set. "Pol's taken a bad knife wound."

"I'll handle things out here," Schwarz said.

"I'm calling in backup," Lyons said. "Just watch yourself."

The figures emerging from the house had spotted Schwarz and turned to face him. The Able Team pro had no time for any fancy confrontation; he simply wanted an end to the mission. He took one of his M-67 fragmentation grenades and pulled the pin, holding the sphere in his right hand. He gauged the distance and waited until the shadowy figures, backlit by the farmhouse lights, were closer together. He allowed the lever to spring free, counted, then threw the grenade, crouching quickly.

In the semidark he couldn't see the grenade as it flew, but he did see and hear when it detonated. The flash lit the figures for a split second. The sound of the blast barely hid the shrieks as the grenade spit out its lethal dose of steel splinters. Men were scattered, their bodies torn and bloody. Only one remained upright, hugging his badly wounded arm close to his body as he struggled to bring his MP-5 into play.

Schwarz, back on his feet, moved forward and triggered his own weapon. The M-4 jacked out 5.56 mm slugs as fast as he could work the trigger. The man dropped, Schwarz closing in and delivering a couple termination rounds.

The Able Team warrior checked the men who had taken the grenade hit. One was dead, while two others were moaning in agony from their wounds. Schwarz gave them each double taps to the head. His actions could have been seen as mercy shots to ease the suffering of wounded combatants—but as far as he was concerned he was giving the terrorists exactly what they deserved, considering what they had been trying to do.

No mercy.

No compassion.

No consideration.

He picked up the distant sound of an approaching siren, then more. Lyons must have attracted local law enforcement. Once the word got out, the farm would be overrun with officials. Blancanales hoped there would be an ambulance among the vehicles on their way.

He turned to check out the farmhouse, stepping around the dead and loading a fresh magazine into the M-4. There was no way of telling what he might find in the house, so it was wise to be prepared.

As it was, the place stood empty. The four terrorists Schwarz had brought down were the last. He didn't know it then, but one of them was Syed Alam. Just before he'd stepped out of the farmhouse, alerted by the gunfire, Alam had put out a sat phone call to Jabir Rahman, to tell him the farm was under attack....

EPILOGUE

Nothing about the double-threat affair was released to the general public. The presidents of the U.S.A. and Pakistan clamped down on any speculation both within their own houses and outside. Security agencies were issued with nondisclosure orders. It was decided that it served no purpose to reveal the urgency of the nuclear threat.

Good men had died during the mission.

The deaths of Steve Hutchins and Nasir Hanafi would unnoticed by the public, but would be remembered by the men they had worked with. In London Greg Henning recovered slowly, in the capable care of Sister Jenny. That covered official and unofficial treatment. The visit from Jack Coyle a week later boosted his morale.

"So did we get the buggers, Jack?"

"We did," McCarter said, perched on the edge of Henning's hospital bed.

"Your mates okay?"

"We lost a couple of good allies, but my teams are alive. Some walking wounded."

"What about the main man, Rahman? Did you deal with him?"

McCarter shook his head. "Bastard slipped the net. By the time the Pakistanis pulled their fingers out, he'd gone. Probably squirmed down some dark little rat hole and hid himself away."

"Why is it these greasy buggers seem to get off scot-free?"

"Don't worry your head about Rahman," McCarter said. "I have a feeling, Gregory, that his days are numbered."

"Oh?"

McCarter grinned. "Never mind about Rahman, mate, I want to hear about you and the lovely Sister Jenny. Come on, you sly dog, Uncle Jack wants all the details."

THE PAST FEW WEEKS HAD not gone well for Jabir Rahman. As the machinations of his operation started to filter into the light, Rahman found support dwindling, and many of his former comrades disentangled themselves from his life. No one wanted to be associated with a loser or be arrested for complicity.

He learned that the Pakistani president had been presented with a dossier prepared by the late Nasir Hanafi. The ISI agent's undercover work had logged a great deal of incriminating evidence. The data named names alongside Rahman's crimes, and many of his former associates were arrested once the information had been confirmed.

Rahman fled the country as soon as the dominoes started to fall. He flew out from Pakistan, accompanied by his three personal bodyguards and a large valise full of cash that would keep him comfortable for some time. There were also several bank accounts he could fall back on. As long as there was a plentiful supply of untraceable cash, Rahman knew he could maintain his security.

He rented a villa overlooking the Caribbean on one of the many exclusive islands where the privacy of the client was paramount, and indulged himself while he considered his future.

The status quo lasted only a month.

After that Rahman's world began to crumble. By degrees. First he found that his bank accounts were being stripped. Money was disappearing at a startling rate. When he tried to move funds about he found he was locked out. Someone had broken through his online protection and was freezing his finances.

One of his bodyguards vanished a few days later. His body was never found. Security for the villa estates was unable to offer any explanation. When a second man disappeared Rahman began to panic. He tried to work out who could be doing this to him.

Was it coming from Pakistan? An elimination squad sent by the president as retribution? The covert team of Americans who had destroyed his operation? He didn't know, and that was the worst part. Not knowing who was doing this to him.

The day his last bodyguard vanished Rahman decided enough was enough. He packed his luggage, picked up his valise of money and went across the jetty to the moored sixty-foot motor cruiser he had rented when he'd first arrived on the island. Previously, he had enjoyed his leisurely trips around the islands. Now he saw the cruiser as his last hope for getting away.

He took his luggage on board, started the powerful engines and went to cast off the bow and stern lines. Back behind the wheel, he increased power and eased the gleaming white-and-blue craft away from the jetty. It was a serene day, with blue sky and sea. A gentle breeze carried the scents of flowers and ripening fruit. For a moment Rahman's problems vanished as he steered the boat across the wide and empty ocean. Out here there was nothing. Simply himself.

Until a quiet, yet familiar voice broke through his thoughts.

"Jabir, you haven't called. I could be hurt by that."

Rahman swung around and came face-to-face with Umer Qazi. His longtime friend, dressed in a white suit and shirt, was leaning against the brass handrail.

"Umer? Where did you come from? Have you come to help me?"

"You sound upset, Jabir. Why would that be?"

The question threw Rahman. If anyone would know why it should be Umer. He had been fully aware of everything that had happened, from the inception of the operation to its—Rahman had to admit it—to its failure.

"I don't understand. After all that has happened, you ask me why?"

Qazi moved away from the rail, his hands thrust into the pockets of his suit jacket. He slowly looked up at Rahman. For once the reserved, almost benign expression was gone from his eyes, and to Rahman it was like staring into the face of a stranger. He barely recognized Umer Qazi, the teacher, the recruiter.

Qazi took an object from his pocket and held it up. It was a digital microrecorder.

"Do you remember this, Jabir Rahman?"

Qazi pressed the start button.

"If I call again, Jabir Rahman, you should hope it will be to congratulate you on a successful mission in America. Pray to Allah this is how it will be. If you fail to put things right, God will not be able to save you. He may be merciful. We are not."

Rahman looked from the recorder to Qazi. Slow realization was dawning.

"You? It was you, Umer? How...?"

"Technology is a wonderful thing. It can slightly alter a voice. Or divert funds from bank accounts. Of course, it cannot recover all the money we gave you, Jabir, because you have spent it on the operation that you failed to carry through. Now we will have to start over. Create another plan."

"You work for al Qaeda? All this time and I thought you were my friend."

"No one *works* for al Qaeda, Jabir. It is a commitment to bring our belief to fruition. We strive to defeat our enemies. As for friendship, you promised much but failed. I tolerated you, Colonel, because you were considered useful. Now you are an embarrassment. An expensive embarrassment. Al Qaeda has no more use for you."

Rahman stared around him. He wanted to flee, but there was no escape.

Movement caught his eye. He turned his head and saw a second, then third, silent figure standing no more a couple feet away. One of them made a swift motion with his hand. Rahman felt a sharp, stinging sensation in the side of his neck. He looked again at Qazi as a warm feeling enveloped his body. The old, benevolent expression was back, and as Rahman slipped into a deep coma the last thing he saw was Qazi and the blue Caribbean sea and sky.

IN THE *Daily Telegraph* newspaper a two-column article caught Greg Henning's attention. He read the item, a smile creasing his lips as he was informed of the death of former Pakistani Colonel Jabir Rahman. The man, who had been missing for a couple months following a rebellious incident in his country, had been discovered on board a rented motor cruiser in the Caribbean. Rahman's decapitated body had been found in the main cabin. He had been brutally slaughtered, his blood almost drained from his severely mutilated body. According to the report, no one else had been found on the cruiser, and there were no fingerprints or forensic evidence of any kind.

Jack Coyle had been correct when he had said Rahman's

days were numbered. The man's past, and obviously his former associates, had caught up with him.

"You were right there, mate," Henning said to his empty hospital room. "When they let me out of here I'll have a drink to that."

* * * * *